Sins
of the
Father

Books by Stephen Weeks

The Countess of Prague Mysteries
The Countess of Prague
Sins of the Father

Awakening Avalon
Daniela
Sword of the Valiant—the Legend of
Sir Gawain and the Green Knight
Decaying Splendours—Reflections in an Indian Mirror

Sins
of the
Father

A Countess of Prague Mystery

Stephen Weeks

Poisoned Pen Press

Poisoned Pen Press

First Edition 2018

10 9 8 7 6 5 4 3 2 1

Library of Congress Control Number: 2017954433

ISBN: 9781464209949   Hardcover
        9781464209963   Trade Paperback

Poisoned Pen Press
4014 N. Goldwater Boulevard, #201
Scottsdale, Arizona 85251
www.poisonedpenpress.com
info@poisonedpenpress.com

Printed in the United States of America

To
SNĚŽANA SMITHOVÁ
who walked the course with me.
With thanks for those years.

This book was written at
8 Maltézské náměsti, Prague 1 — Malá Strana
The Café Louvre, Prague 1
&
Gabi's kitchen table, Prague 8

Prologue

At five o'clock it was already nearly dark, and the electric globes of the Rozhledna Tower on Petřín Hill were still blazing, giving the tower the appearance of a huge, inverted chandelier. After fourteen years it was already a well-loved fixture of the city. Built as a part of the Prague Jubilee Exhibition of 1891, it was only a modest tribute to Paris, being a virtual miniature of the great Eiffel Tower, but its position on the hill opposite the Castle gave it an extraordinary prominence.

The snow blanketing the parks and orchards that cloaked Petřín Hill was strangely luminescent in the last minutes of twilight. The funicular's final journey of the day was descending the hill to its lower station, just a few steps from Újezd Street. Originally, the inclined railway had been planned to take tourists to the Rozhledna, or lookout tower, but over the years it had become a useful shortcut for those living in Strahov to get down to the river and the city proper.

The clerk was putting up the shutters of the pretty fretted-wood chalet that comprised the lower ticket-office with its sign that read: 12 kreutzers up, 6 kreutzers down, return ticket: 15 kreutzers. The car rumbled to a halt there. At the same time, the 'up' car would be arriving at the top, counterweighted by the 'down' car's full tank of water. There was only one down passenger, but he must have hurried away as soon as the car had stopped since he was no longer to be seen. The conductor, having locked the control handle, began walking back up the steep steps in order to give the car his usual cursory inspection. With its four sections, each rising higher than the one in front, it resembled a thin slice of some ancient Roman stadium or of the medical school's anatomical theatre.

He was nonchalantly waving the beam of his lantern over the floor of the first section — some people did manage to drop small change — when his eye caught a shape in the shadows of the second tier. His first thought was that it was that lone passenger: drunk, asleep, or perhaps taken ill — an extremely rare occurrence as the whole journey only lasted six minutes. The lantern lit up the shape as he approached it.

For a moment he thought his eyes were deceiving him, that it was a trick of the near-darkness. Then suddenly his whole body seized with terror. Sitting upright in the middle of the second row was the body of a man. A headless man — the stump of his neck still glistening with uncoagulated gore.

The conductor, a family fellow — a grandfather nearing the age of retirement from the West Bohemia Railways, who had taken this job because it was calm, safe, easy, and near to home — could approach no further. He halted, paralysed by the grisly spectre, until the ticket clerk came striding up the steps to join him. The conductor turned his terror-stricken eyes to the clerk, finding himself rendered speechless.

"Jesus Maria!" the clerk said. "I'll go across the road and call the police." Then he added ruefully, "I don't think he needs a doctor."

Chapter One

An Unlucky Number

I was just thinking of something Mamma told me only a week ago, soon after my Irish grandmother had left to return home. The conversation in the drawing-room of Morštejn, my parents' castle in Bohemia, had been about so-called mixed marriages. In due course we ended up turning to that of Archduke Franz-Ferdinand, who had married — against his uncle, the Emperor's, wishes — a woman who was socially beneath him, although she was born of perfectly respectable Bohemian aristocracy: the Countess Chotek von Chotkowa und Wognin… or Sophie, as we knew her. A 'mere' Countess ranked well below a Royal Duke.

Grandmamma, that canny, and quite adorable, old lady — whose own marriage was a mongrel mixture of native Irish and the English imperial aristocracy — put the cap on the discussion, according to Mamma, by declaring: "After all, all marriages are between men and women, and you can't get much more mixed than that."

I sat musing on this because beside me was an empty seat. Trying to get Karel, my husband, ever to attend anything with me was virtually impossible. I was severely questioning our compatibility. All Prague had been clamouring to get seats for this gala evening at the German Opera, and I felt guilty now owning a vacant one — especially as we had 16, 17, and 18, in the second row of the *Grand Balkon*. Fortunately, Mamma was with me, sitting on my other side, as otherwise I could not have come unescorted. In my evening bag was Karel's wretched telegram. I hadn't even bothered to read what his excuse was this time, just that he was

UNAVOIDABLY DETAINED STOP

I wondered if I should leave it on the seat as my excuse. And his shame. Stop.

There was nothing for it but to distance myself from the gaping emptiness of unoccupied plush and gilt by my side and look about me. The auditorium with its tiers of boxes was still lit by a giant gasolier, not yet electrified. Down in the stalls, men were leaning over their seats to chat, and the hum and buzz of their conversation rose to fill the great space with its satisfying wealth of stucco ornamentation. A mix of *parfums* streamed from hair and clothing, mingling with the more mundane odour of the illuminating gas. A confusion of sounds rose from the pit as the orchestra tuned up — a noise guaranteed to stir in anyone's breast the fierce excitement of anticipation.

Society ladies were fanning their bosoms in our *balkon*. Indeed, it was hot, and how much I was enjoying this simple, basic, pleasure…a whole sublime evening of it stretching ahead almost to infinity. Thanks to the sale of the Fenix Theatre, I had money to spend on installing central heating in our rented palace — it was to have been completed before winter, but was now well on its way to being ready next month, in March, when temperatures would begin to rise again. I thanked Providence that I had not worn the dress I have trimmed with chinchilla. Even so, I was beginning to perspire a little, so unused had I become to such warmth. The late Empress Sissy had firmly believed that perspiration brought on freckles. She had also said that wrinkles begin at thirty. That was more troubling; only a year to go before I would have to start straining my eyes in the mirror every morning.

With a subtle twitch of my fan, I acknowledged the nod of Mr Pinkerstein, who appeared to have a whole box in one of the better positions close to the proscenium. I always thought of him as a charming rogue, and always counted my fingers after shaking hands with him. Yet, I was certain he could count those same fingers in front of me and convince me there were eleven!

Thanks to him, I had done well out of the Fenix Theatre affair. Being Jewish, he had taken all the criticism for closing the place. The district committee of local worthies had then strengthened its resolve to complete its own theatre, to be called The Royal Vinohrady, on Purkyňovo Square, and to be much more splendid than the Fenix ever was. Karel's view on the matter was that Jews only take decisions that make financial sense; that they have no shred of romance or sentiment. Pinkerstein had explained to me, at our last interview, that if a 'romantic' enterprise is allowed to fail financially, then 'one loses a hundred percent of the money *and* all the damned romance or sentiment wasted in it — so where's the good in that?' There was some sense in this view.

From time to time, Mamma sneaked glances across to my bosom, itself a study in artistic *décolletage*, on which was pinned the emerald and diamond brooch that had arrived last June by special messenger from London. I had never encountered a King's messenger before. He was a dapper Englishman with a good suit and bowler hat, yet a hard, strongly lined face, a Mr Henderson. On unwrapping the package, a handwritten card had fallen out:

> *Trixie:*
> *with grateful thanks for saving our life*
> *and that of our nephew.*
> *Albert Edward.*

How delightfully understated for a monarch!

Mamma was basking in the regal glory of the brooch, although I suspected that nobody here actually knew its provenance. Not that I hadn't received some discreet recognition by those in the highest places who had been put in the know, though — of course — none of those events of last year ever reached the newspapers. The controlled smiles of recognition I received across the theatre were answered not only by my gentlest of acknowledgements but also by Mamma's rather broader (and am I permitted to say *coarser?*) movement with her own fan. Thus we both answered in our own ways old Eleonora von Ehrenberg, who always dressed in dark purple silk, and also the Viennese lady whose name I had quite forgotten and who was sitting with Princess Lobkowicz, here with her husband Prince Ferdinand just in front of us, in the first row. The Princess herself turned, as if adjusting her stole, and awarded me a faint smile.

The orchestra at last was quiet, ready to begin the overture. I glanced down at my programme and caught the names of Eugen Wiesner and Rudolf Kafka before the lights dimmed and the gas jets finally popped all into darkness. Following a rousing and thrilling piece which I did not recognise, the great curtain finally began to draw upwards, revealing the stage which was bright with new electric arc lighting, although buzzing quite audibly. The great Kafka entered an empty village scene in a splendid musketeer costume and there was a cannonade of applause. The actor, before uttering so much as a line or a note, stormed triumphantly from the back stage to the footlights as the ladies' satin bodices creaked at the seams as they leaned forward in adulation. Such is fame.

It was just at this moment that there was a commotion in the *balkon*. A gentleman was trying to find his seat, causing ladies and their menfolk to rise while he squeezed past. I had been under the impression that admittance was not allowed once the orchestra had started the overture — that latecomers had to wait until the first interval. I glanced at Mamma, first catching merely the whites of her eyes in the darkness, hoping as hard as I could that it wasn't Karel creating such an unfortunate stir. Then she languidly arched a single eyebrow — something I had unsuccessfully practised mimicking for years before my marriage, but alas! I was not cut out for the sardonic.

In the confusion of my neighbours having to rise, and a dress getting caught as the seat cushion tipped, I hardly noticed that a figure did indeed slump awkwardly into Karel's empty seat. I was so angry I could not even bear to look at him. Ours was certainly a mixed marriage.

"Countess, I am sorry to disturb you…" — I heard a loud whisper. It was a voice I knew and it wasn't Karel's. I turned.

It was Inspector Schneider's.

☙

A few moments later, having extricated ourselves with even more commotion from the *balkon*, I found myself with the young inspector in the first-floor foyer. It was not fully illuminated and was deserted except for waiters setting out drinks glasses for the interval. All he had told me was that there had been a gruesome murder and the body was on the Abt's Rack — the Prague name for the Petřín Hill funicular railway, derived from that of the Swiss engineer who had designed it.

I was of course flattered that the Police Department should deem me someone to consult. I admit I was at rather a loose end after the excitement of those heady days of last year. Only a small matter had been brought for my attention in the interim, but then very few people actually knew of what had happened at Marienbad and around the Fenix Theatre. This was evidently an important enough affair to drag me from the opera.

"You see, Countess, we think you may be involved in this in some way," he announced. "Or at least you may know the victim."

"Oh." So I wasn't being involved as a result of my talent for solving criminal mysteries. I felt a little deflated. "Oh, really?"

"There was nothing to identify the victim."

"But what did he look like?"

"We don't know. He's been decapitated."

Oh, dear! This was indeed a frightful and serious business. "How ghastly," I found myself exclaiming, but I could have no idea of just how ghastly it might be.

"This is what's so unusual. His pockets had been emptied, although oddly his watch and chain had not been taken. The only thing we found on him was tucked into the corner of his waistcoat pocket: this tiny slip of paper." And here Schneider produced the torn corner of a page.

"And written on it, Countess, is your telephone number."

I examined it. The paper was the exact shade of green used for the Telephone Directory, and indeed, on the other side of it was part of a printed page number — ending in a 6. Yes, it was my telephone number scrawled there in pencil. I didn't like the fact.

"My dear Inspector… yes, I own it is my telephone number. But then there are plenty of other four-figure numbers the deceased may have had cause to keep: a lucky lottery number, a laundry number, a… er… share certificate…" I was quickly drying up. He was right, of course. What else could it be? Unless… "And was he from Prague?"

"We have no idea." He could see what I was about to say: "Also, I cannot tell you if the telephone books in Vienna or Berlin are the same shade of green, either, if that's what you're thinking."

I noticed that Schneider was turning his hat in his hands — a sign I had recognised of old. Not a good one, either.

"And was the murder committed on the Abt?" I asked, trying to broaden the scope of the discussion.

"We don't see how it can have been."

"And the body now?"

"Still there. Until we have finished formalities and photographs have been taken."

I could see from the window that snow was gently falling onto Angelova Street. It hadn't been when I'd arrived at the theatre. New snow — which could so permanently cover vital evidence… it was even covering a bill-poster as he sloshed paste from his pail onto a wall of previous advertisements, well situated to catch theatregoers as they left. Impudent fellow, I thought. May the snow melt down the neck of his rough tunic. I could clearly read the text of his advertisement since it was set in bold block letters. Doesn't he understand, I was thinking, that those patronising the opera would hardly be likely to want to see The Great Orsini — Master Illusionist?

"Don't you think I should view the body?" I could at least ascertain whether or not the victim could possibly have been someone I might know — if only from the quality of his shoes or his suit or gloves. In any event, his general build might be familiar. For the moment I discounted the fact that the very sight might be utterly repugnant. Perhaps I wouldn't be able to look at all.

"I was hoping you would come, Countess. I have a fiacre wait-ing outside."

❧

Downstairs, Schneider helped me with my cloak. I was mildly furious that my new black chiffon opera gown would now not be admired coming down for the intervals. Naturally, I could not wear it again — *someone* might have seen it! Unfortunately, Karel was still paying for my wardrobe. Generous as kings were with jewels and thanks, they did not understand the realities of everyday survival. And, as yet, Karel hadn't thought to balance my wifely expenses against the income derived from the Fenix Theatre sale.

Along the way, except for a short delay while I called in at home to get out of my dress and change my shoes, I tried to find out from Schneider all that was known about the murder. Three men had boarded the up car, which had crossed with the down one, and three men had left at the Petřín Hill Station. One of these men had been, apparently, drunk — or so the ticket clerk thought — and was supported on either side by his companions. The down conductor was certain that only one man had boarded at the top, but he was unable to give any further details of him. In fact, he thought he had been a slight man, which certainly the corpse was not. The poor conductor was suffering from shock.

Only one event had been remarkable on the short ride: the down conductor had not only slowed at the passing place of the two cars, but had momentarily stopped, causing both cars to do so, as a figure had darted in front of the train, crossing the line a few metres in front of the car.

Müller had been most concerned for my welfare as I left Jindřišská Street, so much so that I hadn't dared ask for a lantern. I had wondered if a rope would be necessary, but requesting either would have sent him into paroxysms of worry. At least I hardly ever had to explain myself to Karel: oh! ever-absent Karel. That was some relief — even explaining oneself to a servant was hardly something I should be deigning to do, although strangely I was. Dear solid, reliable Müller; perhaps I should have asked him to come along.

When I came out of the palace in my warm fur-lined cape, hands in mittens and almost sensibly shod, Schneider was standing there running a finger round his collar. Another nervous gesture of his I remembered. I looked at him for a long moment, in fact waiting for him to open the fiacre's door. My withering glance had the desired effect. I think he flushed red right up to the roots of his fair hair… unless it was just the poor light. He still had that *gauche* look of youth about him, but I knew he was more experienced than he seemed — and quite used to handling a deadly weapon, if not a woman.

"The telephone number…" he began. I felt he was about to repeat himself. How tiresome of him.

"I agree it is the number of an instrument here," I said, hurrying to the point. "But have you thought it could also be the combination of some safe containing fabulous stolen jewels, or the passcode of a bank account where misappropriated funds have been deposited?"

He smiled.

"For example…" I added, my fortitude weakening slightly.

He finally held the door open for me. "But for your limitless imagination, we would never have cracked last year's mystery…"

"*We?*" I questioned. Hmm. How stories embroider themselves in less than twelve short months.

❧

The lower station of the Abt was a hive of activity and ablaze with light. Kerosene lamps had been brought in to supplement the few electric globes there and to add to the dim glimmer of the gas-lamps along Újezd Street. Schneider paid off the fiacre and turned to me.

"Are you quite sure you wish to view the corpse? It's a fearful sight."

I nodded my assent.

The photographer was just setting up his apparatus. The doctor who had been examining the ghastly remains came running across to the inspector: "There's something else," he declared. "The corpse is also missing his right hand."

"And where were these amputations done?" Schneider asked.

"Not on the Abt. After death, but only about an hour or even less, I should think, before the body was moved here."

There was a bright flash as the first of the pictures was taken.

I didn't need to get any closer to see the thing. I had been trying my best to be brave, but that was fast failing me.

"So, now then, Countess," said Schneider, changing his tone, suddenly coldly official, "you still say you have absolutely no connection with this man?"

Oh, now I understood. His amateur psychology was that I should see both the full horror and enormity of the crime, and then admit that I did know the man in some way.

"Officer," I replied straightly, "had I the slightest knowledge of him, I should have told you so at the outset." I did not add "and what do you take me for?" — or slap him in the face! Taking umbrage would get us all nowhere. Better to be practical. "So what about the men who left the body, Inspector?"

"They were well away by the time we were called..."

"But their tracks?"

"Since the Abt isn't able to run at present, I have arranged other transport to the top station to investigate, although the snow..."

It was true, but the flakes were falling only lazily through the night air. There was a chance that tracks made three or four hours ago would still be visible. With Schneider and his men walking around, those footprints at the top would be quickly obliterated. It was the accomplice who ran across the line halfway up who interested me... the diversion.

"Well, if you are sure there's nothing you can add, then I shall get a fiacre for you..."

"That won't be necessary," I said as huffily as I could manage in four words and turned on my heels. Luckily, a consignment of uniformed men arrived, presumably those detailed to search for footprints at the top station. If the Nebozízek Tavern decided to open its doors for them up there, it could probably do very well serving them hot grog on a night like this, and this might preserve the footprints a while longer. But, no. I would stick to the diversion, halfway up.

In the ensuing hustle and bustle I was able to slip away unnoticed. A man from the Abt company was filling more kerosene lanterns. I simply approached him and picked up one which was already alight. Being absolutely brazen is often the subtlest way of achieving one's aims.

There was a path of sorts following the line of the funicular up the hill. The climb was steep and taxing, and soon the lights and activity of the bottom station almost disappeared. Petřín Hill — or the Laurenziberg, as it was known in German, after St Lawrence's Church whose domes and spires had formerly been the crown of the hill before the great iron tower was erected — well, the hill was strangely silent. I had never been there at night, and certainly never unaccompanied. The blanket of snow was weirdly iridescent even in the darkness. The branches of the park's trees were now weighted down with snow, which was dusting the thick steel cable that pulled the cars up the funicular's steep incline. Eventually, I reached the passing place, where the track widened to allow for the two cars, side-by-side.

I paused to catch my breath, looking out over the city with its lights twinkling — the furthest horizon being the slopes of Vinohrady, dominated in daylight by the spiky twin spires of the modern St Ludmila's church. After this moment's respite I turned to business. It was not difficult to find a set of footprints crossing the track and to find how this person had approached from the direction of the Castle District — those prints now almost lost under the snow which had subsequently fallen — and how he had waited near a tree, stamping his feet, so I presumed, against the cold. I searched this area intensely in the hope he might have dropped a cigarette end or knocked a pipe out on the tree, but no. Then there was the dash across the Abt's tracks, alarming the down car's driver, followed by the man's doubling-back. The footprints returned roughly in the direction he had come.

There seemed to be no other footprints in the vicinity of the passing place, or marks which would have indicated a body being dragged along. All I could do now was follow in the tracks of the mystery man who had momentarily stopped the Abt.

I wasn't able to tell if he'd followed a normal pathway or not, as such features were already buried under much earlier snow. Here and there I was able to discern the footprints in precise detail. Bending over with the lamp, I could make out that the imprint of the left foot was less clear than the right. Perhaps this meant that the man walked with a slight limp, his left leg being a little lame? And the more I examined that less-distinct print, the more I thought the left shoe to be slightly turned-in to the right. I was surprised that I could learn so much from a footprint when I had assumed the task to be mostly of matching footwear. From the soles of the man's shoes there was nothing to learn, except that the sharpness of the heel's outline, especially with the right shoe, suggested they were either new or recently re-cobbled.

Over the next half hour I followed this man's path past the ghostly snow-clad orchards which were planted above the formal gardens of the Lobkowicz and other noble palaces. The trees looked like those of some petrified forest from a children's fairy story. The journey, the sights, and the task were fascinating rather than frightening as I was sure my quarry was trying to distance himself from the scene of the crime, rather than to tarry.

I had visions of the scene at the top station where the three sets of incriminating footprints would by now be lost under the clumsy boots of the Prague Police Department. My would-be ace detective, poor Schneider, must by now be — I sincerely hoped — regretting how he had given his countess the brush-off. Fancy him implying I had some incriminating knowledge of the victim! Phooey!

Even in the night's blackness I thought I could make out the dark shapes which would describe the geography of the bowl in the hill I was passing through. Behind me would be the tall — and now unlit — form of the Rozhledna Tower, close to the cluster of shapes which would mark St Lawrence's. Over to the left would be the dark bulk of the Strahov Monastery. Still moving my mostly imagined gaze in a clockwise direction, I should have caught the huge dark rectangular form of the Czernin Palace, now a barracks, and, further round, beyond a few more palaces, the spires of St Vitus' Cathedral crowning the castle. Indeed, I could just make out the far-off glimmer of lights from some of the castle's many windows.

My way took me almost in a line towards the old Czernin Palace. It must have been a full hour since I left Schneider at the lower station. Snow had long since decided to squeeze itself into my ankle boots, and my arms ached from carrying the lamp before me. Ice had formed a delicate lace in that part of my hair open under the hood of my cape. Although I was feeling quite exhausted by the time my way took me through one of the park gates and out onto Úvoz Street, I felt a renewed sense of energy as my feet slid on the reassuring cobbles of a city thoroughfare.

A flight of steps leading between two buildings connected Úvoz Street with the much higher Loretánstká Street. Halfway up was a landing and the entrance to a tavern, of the kind used by the grooms and stable-lads from the nearby grand houses. The footprints headed for the door of this place and then, as if changing his mind before entering, my invisible target had headed back down the steps again and hurried (I could see this by the greater length of stride) once more down Úvoz Street.

Here and there the prints were lost, but I would soon pick them up again. However, at the junction with the broad way to the castle, I encountered a mass of foot and hoof prints and I lost him. Dejected, and not for want of effort to see if I could make out my slightly lame man with newly heeled shoes, I made my way down Nerudova Street to try to get a fiacre at Radeckého Square. On the corner of the street was painted its old German name, Sparrengasse, a name that derives from the steep climb to the castle — so steep that one had to spur on even the strongest of mounts.

There were usually two or three fiacres lurking beneath the rather grand, larger-than-life statue of General Radetsky, standing on a shield borne by his soldiers, and on the crook of whose warlike arm, or in the bronze folds of the flag that he held aloft, beleaguered pigeons sheltered from the icy wind. They had my deepest sympathy; I was frozen.

Finally, I attracted the attention of a common cabman, who doubtless first assumed that I was some lady of easy virtue (the presence of the dowsed kerosene lantern I held was probably responsible for his change of opinion) when, leading out of the mass of snow and sludge churned-up by horses and wheels, I noticed the familiar footprints pressed into the firmer snow covering the pavement. They were unmistakably the same as those which had led me from Petřín Hill. I asked the cabby simply to follow me. In his estimation, I passed from erstwhile dubious lady to certifiable lunatic.

The footprints led through a small street into Maltézské Square, so beloved of the poet Rilke in his recent lyric verse, passing by the statue of St John at the centre and leading directly to St Mary's-below-the-Chain, the church of the Maltese Knights. The street passing the church's gothic portal had many foottracks through the snow and for a moment I lost him again, but luckily, St Mary's has a peculiar history. At some stage the nave of the church of the Hospitallers of St John of Malta became ruined. Beyond the gothic west façade, set between two truncated towers that would have looked more at home in Normandy than Bohemia, the old nave was now open to the sky. What had once been the chancel was now the whole church, with its own large baroque doorway. I was stopped from going further by the iron gates closing the old nave from the street, but beyond I could see the footprints leading across the stone flags… good, clear prints as the ancient walls sheltered the space from the wind — then turning left and into a stout door which led directly into the palace of the Knights of St John adjoining the church. The snow was no longer falling and the ancient gothic arches, which once had echoed to the vespertine plainsong of monks, were bathed in a pale shroud of moonlight. In other circumstances it would have been romantic.

There was nothing I could do at this time, it being far too late to rouse a gatekeeper or guardian of the palace, so I vowed to come back in the morning. I had some result, at least, from my labours of the evening. I climbed into the fiacre which sped over the night-dark Charles Bridge, past its statuary gallery of saints and martyrs forever frozen still in baroque animation, and across the cobbled expanse of the deserted Old Town Square to get me home.

Exhausted as I was, I asked Müller, who seemed as relieved at my safe return as if I had come back from remotest Africa or had escaped white slavery in the Balkans, to get me the telephone book from what we called Karel's Business Room—although, *au contraire* to my husband's version of the situation, I counted this room nowadays as my own.

In my boudoir I rustled through the telephone book's green tinted pages. I was turning to each of those whose numbers ended in 6. And there it was. The corner of page 56 was missing, torn off exactly as the scrap of paper Inspector Schneider had shown me. I would have no need to ask Schneider to see that wretched morsel again — it was clearly taken from my book. I felt sickened and I just wished I could think of an explanation.

Chapter Two

A Strange Cabinet

Next morning I awoke to the sounds of hammering and miscellaneous bangings and raspings. The plumbers were hard at work again on the palace's nascent central heating system before it was even light. I had never understood why, just because K&K (King & Emperor) Franz-Josef habitually rose at five each day to attend to the pressing affairs of Empire, his routine had been inflicted on all the labouring classes in his domains. Far be it from me, a humble countess, and of Bohemia no less, to raise a revolt of the indolent classes on this matter. However, I could not countenance the idea of sleeping with ear-plugs and, besides, each blow of the hammer and twist of the wrench brought the prospect of satisfying warmth ever nearer.

Fortunately, this early start saw me full of resolve and ideas. Firstly, I called Müller to me as soon as Sabine had finished dressing me — delayed somewhat by her wish to show me a new style of drawers that had little apertures round the legs to allow modern stocking suspenders to thread through and lay more comfortably against the silk, rather than irritating the skin — which had been my overriding objection to the things. So I would have to get attuned finally to the twentieth century and also contribute, if only by a few hellers, to the growing fortune of Mr Pinkerstein, one of whose enterprises manufactured these items. Worse still was that these new drawers were to be purchased only from U Nováků — Prague's very first department store, opened only last year. Whatever next?

That Müller came with the breakfast tray I had forgotten to ask for the night before, was a pleasant surprise. Part of his job, of course, was to read my mind. I hated eating alone even in our smaller, marginally less cold, family dining room. Eating at a table should be a social occasion, rather than sitting there in solo splendour listening to the gloomy ticking of the long-case clock and waiting in aching silence for the next deft serving of items I'd rather fiddle with myself on my favourite tray. Müller had not forgotten the patent device he had acquired to neatly decapitate the tops of boiled eggs. As I contemplated the notion of decapitation, I found myself shuddering and vowed to peel my egg manually when Müller was safely out of the room, rather than watch him behead the thing.

"Now, Müller, have there been any callers recently of whom I've not been informed…?"

"I always present any callers' cards, as Milady knows." He seemed put out by such an insinuation.

"Any callers, for example, to my office? In connection, say, with my *travail?*" I had for the moment adopted the French *travail* for my work. *Travails* there would certainly be, as I was probably just about to find out.

"Well, come to think of it, there was one. It was when Your Ladyship was at Morštejn last week. A gentleman called at the Business Room entrance and was a little agitated that Your Ladyship was not in residence…"

"Agitated?"

"Yes, so much so that he suggested he sit down a moment while I fetched him a glass of water."

"And had he asked for my telephone number?"

Müller looked surprised, his normally cocked eyebrow now more elevated than ever. "Why, yes, Milady. But naturally that is something I would never give out. I suggested he should call back in a day or two or write a letter."

I was about to ask him why he had not told me about this when he added, "I am so sorry it slipped my mind. If it had been a matter of consequence, then of course he would have returned or sent the letter. There are a number of such callers every week … salesmen, commercial travellers, and the like."

"And what impression did he give?"

"A man who was past his best and in clothing which had once also seen better days. His spats badly needed brushing, as well. I suppose that is why I assumed he and whatever matter he wished to discuss were of no consequence."

I could have told him that the man was foully murdered, but relationships with servants should be kept on as even a keel as possible, and thus I merely said the usual, "That will be all" and he glided out of my boudoir.

I could easily reconstruct what had occurred. My letter rack with fresh stationery was located quite near to the corner of my desk on which sat the telephone book. (I, of course, was not in the public directory). The caller could stand looking at my letterpaper, while jotting down my telephone number on the corner of a page of the book. At least he hadn't simply stolen a sheet of my paper, which said something for the man's character.

As for Müller, I would have to explain to him on another occasion that in my new *travail* any callers, of whatever status, could be significant. We would have to abandon the social norms.

So one part of the mystery of the headless man had been resolved, only to present a greater one: Why had he wanted so much to see me? Rather than answering this question, the day's first delivery of mail would make the mystery even deeper.

❧

In the meantime, at eight-fifteen in the morning I arrived too late at St Mary's-below-the-Chain. A stout woman with a round, rosy face and rounder, redder elbows was already brushing the snow from the flagstones that paved the old nave, open to the winter sky. I began to doubt that the footprints did indeed belong to the unknown gentleman I had been following. They had got lost in the churned-up snow on the pavement outside, so perhaps it had been too easy for me to believe that these were also his inside the precincts of the Order of St John. Worse still, I could see — vanishing before my eyes — another solo set of footprints heading out of the palace door and across to the portal of that part of the old church building actually in use. I rattled the iron gate and was about to call out when the old fussock noticed me. Before coming to me she neatly completed the last strokes of her brush — with the finesse of some artist perfecting a masterpiece — and obliterated the final traces of my quarry.

She unlocked the gate and stood in that defiant stance of the annoyed, hands on her broad hips and her ample bosom thrust forward like one of the private boxes at the opera. Under her bright kerchief, tied to her head in the peasant manner, those narrow eyes in a moon-shaped Slavic head betrayed her origins from further east in Europe.

"Have there been visitors to the church already?" I asked. Obviously not, but it might get a telling response.

"No, madam. Father Antoine said mass alone. Is that all you wanted to know? I noticed you staring in here last night."

I looked at her for a brief moment, I was a little nonplussed by her night-time vigilance.

"I was, my dear woman, trying to find out if Father Antoine was in residence..." (The use of the name that she had herself given me felt immediately convincing.)

"He comes and goes. Prior Braunstein will be back next week. Then things will be back to normal. I hope."

I took my change purse from my handbag: "Is there a poor box in the church... would you be so kind?"

Coins tumbled into my gloved hand. She nodded, and the brightness of a few kreutzers immediately made her more talkative.

"To tell you the truth," she said, "I don't get on with this Frenchman. The sooner the prior is back, the better."

I sorted the larger coins from the smaller.

"He's been to the Holy Land. Very ill after swallowing the water of that River Jordan. St John must have had a stronger stomach, is all I can say."

And he was not the only one, I was thinking. Wasn't it Archduke Karl Ludwig, our Emperor's brother, who had died of typhoid after a good immersion in the Jordan just a few years back? What had promised to be a second baptism had turned into his first, and last, rites. I wondered if that was yet another example of the

"Curse of the Habsburgs." They certainly were a most unlucky family. Hopes now rested on Franz Ferdinand, the terminally baptised archduke's son.

For the moment I thought I was done here. I pressed the coins into the work-hardened palm of the woman while she did her best for a curtsey, and I walked the short distance to where my carriage was waiting in the square. I hadn't been able to ascertain that the mystery man of the night before was this Father Antoine — or indeed if my mystery man had entered the palace at all. And I had just discovered, I felt, the true meaning of 'in the cold light of day.' It had hardly been a very satisfactory interview, but then it must have resembled dozens, if not hundreds, of such encounters that a person in Inspector Schneider's position must endure. Until the truth finally emerged.

As my carriage drew away I suddenly realised that I had quite forgotten to ask the golden question, that which would have settled the matter... did this Father Antoine walk with a limp? I cursed at my stupidity. I could hardly return now and ask; it would most surely put the creature on the defensive or arouse suspicion in my subject, if he were to be told of such a pointed enquiry. No, it would have to wait.

During the brief ride I pondered whether the notion of being a detective really was something I should engage myself in. I had doubts about the salubriousness of the various tasks it always involved, as well as my own abilities to carry them out. As usual, events took over such introspection. Once back at Jindřišská, Müller presented me with two envelopes which had arrived by the first post and another, larger one, which had just been delivered by messenger. This last I immediately opened. I had only sent a message round to Schneider by pneumatic as I was eating breakfast. This, indeed, was rapid service.

It was a police report, typewritten, and mine looked to be a third carbon. A hand-written note from Schneider apologised for his behaviour the night before, stated that he would be truly grateful of any help I might be able to give, and enclosed the overnight report on the headless body that I had requested. He also admitted that his quest for interesting footprints had revealed nothing conclusive. Too many police boot-marks, I felt sure! Criminals would be well-advised to wear such footwear.

I quickly ran through the sheets of flimsy typing paper. The first page was devoted to what I assumed was the usual police protocol, and the second page contained the information on the discovery and location of the body. The third page was more interesting:

> Age - late 50s or early 60s; Cause of Death - heart stoppage, as could have been caused by a sudden blow (to the head?); Amputations - head and right hand cut off after death (perhaps consistent with using a wire?); Marks on the body - no signs of struggle, but bruises on the fronts of both thighs 7 cms above the knees. Small puncture mark (1mm x 1mm) of some kind just below left breast. Another curious feature was that the body hair on his left forearm was noticeably coarser than that on his right.

The next page dealt with the man's clothing:

> Dark jacket (frayed cuffs) which did not match the waistcoat and matching trousers which were shabby too and were from a dinner suit (right back pocket had vestiges of powdered chalk in and around it); flannel shirt with perhaps 5 or 6 days' wearing, cuffs fresh, collar missing. The shirt and waistcoat had been pierced corresponding to the wound on the body. Plated cuff links, no stud. Underwear — worn cotton vest and woollen briefs (soiled by evacuation at time of death), wool calf-length socks without suspenders, twice darned. Worn black patent boots (well-stitched, bespoke), one noticeably more faded in colour than the other. The leather around the lacing seems unusually worn and stretched. One shoelace missing, the other knotted. Muddied dark grey spats.

The next page dealt with the paltry contents of his pockets — namely the scrap of paper with my telephone number — and his watch and chain. The watch was of reasonable quality, in a silver case, made in Germany like tens of thousands of others. The chain, also of silver, was unremarkable and had no fob. The watch had been pawned more than once, judging from the several tiny pawnbroker's marks scratched inside the lid. The rest of the document was devoted to a technical discussion on how long it had been after death that the body had been decapitated.

The page after dealt with cause of death. Clearly the decapitation had taken place after death. The writer speculated as to whether the small puncture wound, near to the heart, had been the cause. Various tests were to be made on blood samples.

The only real question was: Who was he?

One thing was certain — from the clothes and the boots, this man had been down on his uppers, as they say. The boots, I realised, could provide a clue. I would suggest to Schneider that he make enquiries at shoemakers who are having a closing-down sale. It could be too late, since such sales are usually short-lived, and these boots were already quite worn — in fact, it was a ridiculous suggestion. But those boots — one faded — certainly did tell a story.

I have an uncle on my father's side, Alfons, who is as mean as they come. In the window of a bespoke bootmaker's shop in the New Town he spied a brown brogue shoe he particularly liked. Enquiring within he found the pair to be more costly than the sum he wanted to pay. The single brown shoe remained in the window for some years until one day a grand sale was announced, as the bootmaker was retiring. My uncle finally bought the pair at a price he was very pleased with. But when he got them back home, and put them on, the right shoe which had been in the window for so long was extremely faded when compared with the left. It didn't stop him from wearing them — nor other members of my family from laughing at him!

I hardly even looked at the first of the other envelopes I had received as I tore it open. The hand which had written my address was barely literate and looked penned by a woman. I assumed it to be a servant enquiring if I had a position.

But inside was a small folded piece of paper. It appeared to be a receipt of some kind, bearing an impression of a rubber stamp. I rang for Müller and asked him if he could assist me. After closely examining it, he concluded the stamp was that of the Zemská Bank, but for what he couldn't say. I tore open the third envelope, noticing it was in a different hand — a man's, most probably, and not from this part of Europe. In this was a smaller receipt which he recognised almost immediately. "A pawnbroker's establishment in Josefov," he announced. "I could even take Your Ladyship to it..."

I was concerned that he should know the intimacies of such establishments or that he might have got mixed up with such people. He was watching my reaction with growing horror.

"What is it, Müller?"

"Well, Milady, I do hope Your Ladyship doesn't think that I would frequent such a place on my own account."

My look in response did not reassure him. I knew that Karel never paid top wages. Had poor Müller been driven to such an extreme... and indeed, had the items pawned been *his*?

"If you remember, Milady, we had a young footman here last year that His Lordship had occasion to dismiss? I was walking in Dlouhá Street at that time and I noticed something familiar in the window of a certain shop. I didn't want this errant boy to get into any more trouble."

"Are you saying you bought something back... something from here?"

"Redeemed, Milady. Only a small sum had been secured on the article. It was a rather distinctive cigarette case."

"From your own wages?"

Müller reddened and nodded.

"Well," I said. I would get Karel to investigate and to reimburse Müller. It was Karel's duty to deal with the male servants. "I am sure His Lordship will make it up to you."

I handed Müller the "ticket," as I believe these slips of paper are called, and asked if he might find out what on earth the item was and, more importantly, who had pawned it. Why the thing had been sent to me would be my task to fathom. Instinctively, I felt that these papers were connected in some way to my unsatisfied caller, and that the man had been the one who had had his final ride on the funicular railway. Or should that have been *in Abt?* Quite why I had this feeling, I couldn't say... only that of the little I had learned in the last year, certainly one thing was certain: trouble comes in ranks, marching in brisk step together.

❧

I was prevented from immediately ordering my carriage to visit the bank by the fact that my mother was due to come down for breakfast at nine-thirty. She insisted on having it laid in the dining room, and even though I made sure the temperature in the room was only marginally above freezing, it failed to put her off. I was hoping to get there before her, for although I had long since breakfasted, I wanted to clear away my little cards which I had already begun to lay out on the table for this affair.

Only a few were facts, and many consisted of elements of wild speculation with which I was hoping to find some connecting thread — so far without success. However, I was greeted by my mother impatiently awaiting her coffee, toast, and single boiled egg. As usual, there would be four eggs prepared, each to a slightly different timing, so that the kitchen could be spared her wrath for the egg being not hard or soft enough. They were numbered in pencil on their shells; "Four" was the hardest boiled at six and a half minutes.

There was something up; I knew it. "I'm afraid I've had to send Müller out on an errand, Mamma," I said, "but he promised me everything is in order and the kitchen maid can serve."

Just as I noticed that my cards were no longer on the table, she launched into "Beatrice, my dear, I saw you had those silly cards again. I gathered them up and told Müller to dispose of them in the stove." And she smiled in that curiously venomous way of hers.

I suppressed my immediate anger, trying to remember what little was of actual value on those cut-up pieces of old *At Home* cards from grander days. My system had certainly been useful in the Marienbad affair, and I was blowed if I would abandon it now. My mother's "again" was referring to the time when my brother and I, as children once and long ago, had conducted "séances" with our little cousins and had written down what the "spirits" had said to us on just such cards — or at least that's what we had told them. Mamma had accused us, quite wrongly, of being no better than gypsy fortune-tellers.

Instead, I decided not to tell her about the headless man, nor the sudden idea which had come to mind on the recollection of those childish ventures into occult spiritism that Max and I had tried. We would seat a group of our relatives, all children of about our own age, around the oval table in the nursery at Morštejn, palms flat on the tabletop in front of them. The curtains would be pulled and a candle lit. Leaving a window casement ajar ensured the flame guttered with the full drama of the occasion, especially as a secret cord was attached to the curtain and controlled by Max's foot. Summoning the spirits of Napoleon or Julius Caesar (Max's choices) or of widowed Queen Kunhuta or the beautiful Nefertiti of Egypt (mine, but seemingly chosen by the spirits themselves from names neatly pencilled on the little cards we had prepared), our awestruck audience would first feel the rising and falling of the table, then, as the candle flame seemed to glow brighter, there would be the mysterious raps of the dead trying to communicate with us: one knock for yes, two for no in answer to our questions. How bruised afterwards were our legs from lifting and rocking that heavy table! This had given me the idea.

In a few minutes Müller returned looking a little flustered from his errand. I made an excuse to leave the table and spoke to him in the corridor.

"The object pawned at the establishment of one Moses Reach, Milady, is a large wardrobe. I was not permitted to examine it, as it is in a store behind the shop premises. They have promised to have it available for inspection next Monday, if I would care to return. They seem very anxious to have the pledge returned…"

"But my dear Müller, is there anything else troubling you? I agree a wardrobe is perhaps somewhat unexpected in these circumstances, but surely nothing to discompose one?"

"Well, Milady, it is…"

"Yes?" I was now impatient for the fellow to tell me.

"Oh, it can be nothing. Just a fancy, I suppose…"

Well, really! "Yes?" I repeated, at greater volume, a command he could hardly ignore.

"I fancied I was being followed, that's all. It is ridiculous, I know. Those badly dressed men in tight suits — and brown shoes, would Your Ladyship believe — don't only work for the police, do they? But they do stick out like sore thumbs."

"You are right. Just a cruel fancy. Think no more of it, please. Now tell me, were the rolls fresh?"

"I shall enquire," he replied, gratefully relaxing back into normal butler mode, and he padded off. However, I knew that his suspicion was far from a mere fancy. So Inspector Schneider was keeping my home watched. I didn't like the feeling one bit. It was, apart from anything else, quite insulting.

❧

The premises of the Zemská Bank on Na Příkopě had been constructed in the last few years in the style of an Italian *palazzo*. Until last year it had been known as the Landsbank, its Austrian name. But now with the revival of Czech nationalism, and with the monument to Jan Hus under construction in the Old Town Square, the bank directors must have realised that patriotism was good business!

Inside, as I now discovered, the sumptuous marble-lined hall in the renaissance manner on the first floor was adorned not with statues of Dante or the Medicis, but those of common peasants and labourers elevated in style to reflect the nobility of honest labour. Perhaps these reflected a rather fanciful notion that the poor should save — and make up for the losses and follies — of the rich. On presentation of my *carte de visite*, I was immediately shown into the office of the directors. Mr Veselý, the co-director, was very courteous, and after a brief explanation of the circumstances, I handed over the deposit slip.

In a short while a large and well-filled envelope was brought in. "This is what was deposited," Mr Veselý stated, "with instructions for it to be delivered up to the bearer of the receipt."

"And does anyone recollect who actually brought the item in?"

The clerk who had taken it in was summoned: "Mr Orsini... The Great Orsini himself."

Having established that The Great Orsini was wearing the trousers of a dress suit, noticed by the observant Mr Veselý, I was satisfied that he had been the dead man. My intuition about the séances and the bruised knees had been correct. On returning home, I learned that Karel had finally arrived from Vienna. I hurried to my boudoir to open the mysterious envelope.

I pulled out three large blueprints. Each was stamped by the patent authority in Paris. However, I couldn't make head nor tail of the drawings themselves. Time to see Karel. I was planning to keep him waiting in fearful anticipation of the storm over his missing the Gala Evening, but I would have to forget about that. Husbands, of course, do have their uses. Anything technical is in their domain, for instance, such as instructing a servant to replace a light-globe.

Karel's Business Room had returned to its order — if that was the applicable word — prior to my working on the Marienbad affair. I said nothing about this, knowing that this new matter would soon require me to take it over again.

After some very cursory social remarks, we got down to the business in hand. The plans were unfolded onto the table. They depicted a mass of wires or cables of some kind supporting some kind of vehicle, I supposed. Karel looked puzzled too.

"There's a new kind of bridge just constructed in France, I believe," he said. "Or was it in England? I saw a photograph. The foot passengers and carts travel across the river on a sort of cradle like this," and here he pointed towards the centre of the main drawing, "suspended over the water. I would say it's a bridge. These cables," and here he pointed again, "must be quite massive. And there is a note here to say that to support the load they must all be employed in equal tension. Hmm. Very ingenious. A bridge for the twentieth century."

Having agreed that we would dine together, I carried the blue-prints away. A bridge? Was a magician likely to be a part-time civil-engineer?

As I was folding the drawings again, I noticed, on the back, the legend "Device for the Improvement of Stage Illusions." Perhaps such a patent was obtusely labelled so to deter copycats? I would have to cut-up more of those old *At Home* cards, and move the furniture around downstairs again.

လ

Müller had managed to get the address where the pawn pledge had been registered, and although it was in Orsini's name, the transaction itself had been carried out by a young woman.

The house at the address in Žižkov was in a narrow *cul-de-sac* which backed onto the railway before it entered the Vitkov Hill tunnel. I waited in my carriage while Müller made the initial enquiries and soon we were being shown to a ground-floor set of rooms at the rear by a landlady who appeared none-too-scrupulous. She *believed* that the old magician and the young woman, who went by the name of Hélène, were married — and Hélène wasn't a Czech or Austrian name; that would have been Helena.

As soon as the door was shut behind us, I thought to ask Müller what reason he had given for our visit. "I said we were interested in taking on the apartment, having heard about it from a friend of Orsini's," he replied. Luckily the headless body hadn't been named by the newspapers as the magician… yet. I hoped that the woman hadn't mistaken Müller and me as another couple! Or maybe it was better she did. I would have to swallow my pride. Had I known, I could have dressed more appropriately.

It was odd to think of Müller having a wife: his whole being was that of a man married only to his work. It had never occurred to me he might have needed "consolations."

The rooms contained minimal furniture, no personal possessions of any kind and, according to the landlady, had already been swept and cleaned for a new tenant — the last having departed only the day before. The furthermost room was large and with a glass roof, standing in what must have passed as the garden of this apartment house. The glass had been painted over in cream so no-one could look down into the room which at one time could have been a billiard-room or even a conservatory. A weak light permeated from outside. This would have been the ideal place for Orsini to have his workshop, supposing that working on plans such as I had or devising his illusions needed such a space. The terrazzo floor had been swept absolutely clean. Nothing whatsoever remained of any previous use.

I examined the top of what must have been used as a dressing-table in the bedroom and found not a trace of anything. I began to scan the parquet floor there… and something caught my eye. It looked like a single blond hair, caught between the wood blocks.

Since it was the only clue to former occupation, I decided to take it. I had already brought a pair of tweezers and an envelope as suggested to me in an American publication, *The Modern Detective*.

But it was no strand of hair. Instead, it was a tiny piece of metal wire, as fine as silk thread. That was the sum total of my findings. Back in the hallway, and now pestered by the landlady, a small anaemic woman in her late forties, I noticed, protruding from the lowest of the mailboxes, a large manila envelope. "Madam," I said, "Miss Hélène has asked me to collect any mail which may have arrived for her or at least to give you twenty krone for forwarding anything which might arrive. If there's anything here now, I should be delighted to give you the money in any event…"

That settled the matter, and in a moment the envelope was in my hands. "It wasn't delivered by the post," the woman said. "A man handed it in this morning."

"Oh… and who was he, do you know?"

"I didn't recognise him, and he turned away before I could get a good look at him."

In the carriage on the short ride home, I tore open the envelope. Despite its size, it contained only one single photograph.

On this mission it was quite inappropriate for Müller to sit on the box with the coachman. He was sitting opposite me. "Milady," he said with concern furrowing his brow, "has turned quite pale. Is Your Ladyship all right?"

The photograph was of a young woman in a fashionable copy of an English sport dress in wool. She had gloves and a hat, and — unless I was very much mistaken — she was sitting on the funicular railway. Her head was back, laughing. Sitting behind her, but with one hand on her shoulder, was a man, but because of the woman being the centre of the picture, the man's head was cut off by the edge of the frame. His waistcoat did not quite match the dark jacket, and it bore a silver watch-chain… none of these details unusual in themselves, but they did match what we knew of Orsini's corpse, for it was, without doubt his. The man's other arm also reached out of the frame… or, in other words, his right hand was cut off. A dreadful chill at seeing this image swept through me.

"I shall want you to telephone Inspector Schneider for me as soon as we are back," I said, trying to regain my composure.

Monday — the day when the wardrobe could be inspected — came all too soon.

"We think the photograph was taken on a Voightlaender Reise Kamera," Inspector Schneider was saying as we were being taken round to Moses Reach the pawnbroker in his hired fiacre. "Not many photographers have these travel cameras yet or can develop the film. We have men visiting all photographers' studios. You were right, Countess, it is a most significant picture. What a shame it did not include his face…"

"The whole point, I should think."

We had arrived before I could expand on this idea.

Dlouhá Street, in the old Josefov Ghetto, was alive with activity. The doors of the arcaded shops were hung with their wares which also spilt out into the street — baskets of vegetables were piled on the pavement among bales of cloth and stacks of shiny new buckets. Pots and pans were strung across doorways. Hawkers of every description sat by the gutters with their more meagre offerings, leaving little room for the beggars or for those hoping to convince the passer-by that they could actually play the violin they scratched so inexpertly whilst deftly proffering the donation tin. Urchins pushing handcarts or simply running errands choked the already busy thoroughfare.

The noise, as each seller barked his incredible goods at unbelievable prices, filled the air. This was a world, so close to my own, I seldom visited.

A sign above the door to Reach's premises read:

```
MONEY LENT UPON EVERY DESCRIPTION OF
         VALUABLE PROPERTY
```

Mr Moses Reach himself greeted us at the door of the shop, bedecked as it was with every conceivable article from false legs to silver salvers. He was what one would expect of a Jewish merchant.

"Entertainers!" He shrugged. "Always problems with entertainers!"

"It seems to me you gave a very good price for this wardrobe," Schneider remarked.

"Look — these people live from show to show. If they have to come to me for a little advance and they leave their most precious things… the things needed for their performances, then it's not much of a gamble. They always come back, except…"

"Except when they can't," Schneider added grimly.

We were led through the darkness of the shop — brushing by silver candelabra, tin trays, empty birdcages, a ghastly stuffed bear covered in cobwebs — to an open yard. Beyond this was a further store which, through its open door, seemed to be similarly stuffed to capacity, but with gloomy, neglected pieces of furniture.

In the centre of the yard which had just been brushed clear of its snow stood a tall wardrobe-like cabinet distinguished by its plainness. It stood alone, and for a second I fancied it as a gallows in some painting I had once seen, except there were no circling crows. The cabinet's corners were battered by frequent transportation and it was painted purple, relieved by none-too-artful stars and crescent moons in gold.

"I'll be glad to see the back of the thing… that's if you're here to take it," Reach said.

I made no reply, but I did notice that the proprietor of this empire of mustiness was quietly wringing his hands behind his back.

"Something you don't like about it, then?"

Old Reach didn't respond to Schneider's question but I knew the answer immediately. There was a faint but perceivably obnoxious odour coming from around the thing. As one approached, it seemed to focus sharply.

I let Schneider get nearest and watched him also react to the smell, although he said nothing. He reached forward and pulled open the door. It was empty inside; no doubt about that. He stepped back quickly, hoping for relief from the malodour — but it is a characteristic of smell that you can't simply look away, as you can with some frightful sight.

"As I said, nothing," said Reach. "It's quite empty. Useful for a number of things…"

"Did you say?" Schneider queried rather petulantly.

I was taking out my handkerchief when I noticed something. It seemed to be a smear of something, floating in mid-air. Was it blood?

With the handkerchief held to my face I pointed out this rogue smear to Schneider. He leant forward and reached out his hand to it. Suddenly his fingers engaged something unexpected and in a second the entire cabinet had transformed. Only now was it clear that a mirror ran across the middle of the interior, and at Schneider's touch this swung open. By its clever positioning it had given the impression that the whole interior was empty. Now it revealed it in two halves — the second half there to conceal The Great Orsini in his famous disappearing act. But there was no magician there, only the terrible sight of a severed head. Its eyes were still wide open, white and quite horrid. Even in this moment of utter revulsion, I found myself coolly wondering if the two- or three-day growth of beard, mainly of white stubble, had been continuing after death.

And as the head rolled forward, propelled by the momentum of the false wall, there was, behind it and just as gruesome, a severed hand. Now we knew what had been cut off by the photographer's inadvertent shutter.

"The Great Orsini's last trick," Schneider said flatly.

I found myself gasping. I needed to sit down. Old Moses Reach, realising his loss and no doubt aware of all the complications this event would bring on him, solemnly led me back through the shop to a sofa, above which ran a wall of long-silenced cuckoo-clocks, each hung with a price-tag of much-faded ink.

"Please, a glass of water. And perhaps you would be so good as to find me a fiacre."

Chapter Three

An Irresistible Invitation

It took several days to recover from this horror. I thought I was made of tough stuff — not one of those *Red Book* heroines who constantly suffers from "the vapours." But the lurid, fixed stare of that severed, incongruous head kept me from sound sleep. A body without a head had simply seemed a forensic curiosity. This was an entirely different proposition: those white, dead eyes gave the whole thing an awful reality. That… that object was once the animate part of a living person who had — at the very last minute, it seemed — sought my assistance in some way. It made the whole situation even more tragic. And who was this Hélène with the foreign name? Where on Earth was she? I dreaded another revelation.

After three days of her supervising my feeding with a thin *boeuf bouillon* (for I stayed in my room confined to my bed for much-needed sleep and refusing proper food), Mamma departed for Morštejn. Last year I had suggested that she take my boys — my four urchin assistants, my little detectives — with her, where the bracing springtime air and open vistas of the countryside might invigorate them. Only now did she choose to take me up on this invitation. That there was plenty of snow on Morštejn

Castle's countless battlements and parapets to clear was merely a coincidence, according to her. I hadn't intended "bracing" to mean "freezing."

On the fourth day, Sabine knocked and came in bearing a card. I could hear Müller in the corridor behind her, giving one of his discreet coughs. I gave the card a cursory inspection.

"Please tell this Mr Palmer, whoever he may be, that I am indisposed, due to illness," and turned back to the novel I was trying none-too-successfully to read. The day before, I had been dipping into the poems of Heine, trying to keep myself suitably gloomy.

In a few moments Sabine returned with a small and very neatly penned note. 'It is extremely important I see Your Ladyship on urgent K&K business. I shall stay in Prague overnight and will call again tomorrow.'

Hmm. King and Kaiser... Imperial business.

How tiresome of him to be so insistent, I thought. Mr Palmer's card had given simply his name and home address in a smart part of Vienna. In fact, the smartest part, right by the Hofburg. Could this be the same Mr Palmer who was chairman of some important bank? I rang for Sabine.

"Is he a rather small man? — rather dapper? His shoes look as if they have been made by fairies, so small and beautifully stitched they are?"

"Madame, he is, yes, small and as you say. I did not look especially at the shoes, but I assume they were also proportionate and... what was Your Ladyship's word? Crapper?"

"Dapper, Sabine."

I remembered being introduced to the man at a soirée at the Archbishop's Palace, here in Prague. No, it can't have been there, surely? The Palmers were, very discreetly, Jewish. The old Archbishop would never had allowed a Jew, however assimilated, over his threshold. The argument that Lord Jesus Himself was a Jew went for nothing with him. Somewhere, undoubtedly with Karel, we had met. Maybe shooting…

By the next morning I had cast aside the feelings of the last days and was up, dressed, coiffed, and breakfasted by nine. At nine-thirty Müller knocked, this time bearing Mr Palmer's card on his salver. And this time my caller had chosen his business card, grandly embossed as befitting the head of one of the most prestigious banks in the Empire:

Mr Edward Palmer
Director General
Royal and Imperial Dominion Bank
Vienna

After the normal pleasantries — and my caller did look quite as small and dapper as I remembered, beautifully turned-out and with his moustache waxed — Mr Edward Palmer got straight down to business.

"His Majesty requires to see Your Ladyship," he began. "It is imperative we get the morning train to Vienna."

He waited a moment for my reaction; I gave none. "Just for a few hours, you understand, and without creating any undue attention. Naturally, your husband can accompany us if you wish."

"No, that won't be necessary," I replied with unseemly haste. "I presume this is not a social invitation?"

"I am afraid it is not really an invitation, as such…"

"You mean it is an invitation which I cannot refuse?"

"Once Your Ladyship puts it in those words, then I can only concur."

"I shall prepare myself at once. Are you in a position to give me any idea what this is about?"

"I am not in possession of any further facts. I am merely His Majesty's most humble and obedient servant."

I hastened to my rooms where Sabine prepared an outfit for me. How inconvenient! Given more notice, I could have bought a new dress; I even knew exactly which one I'd have had made, too. I made arrangements with Sabine to join me in Vienna with a small trunk in the event I chose to — or had to — stay. I left a note for Karel, who was sleeping late. I sent a telegram to Mamma, who would otherwise kill me for not being promptly informed of such an event. Lastly, I instructed Müller to telegram Mr Palmer directly if there were any new developments in the case of Orsini, or — as the sensational press was now calling it — The Case of the Headless Magician.

"Oh, and Müller," I called back to him as he had almost left the room, "when you send the telegram, can you also please send my apologies to the Ladies' Toxophily Association? I should go there tomorrow evening." I was going to add "with my bow," but he might have understood that as "with my beau." I'm sure all the servants would have been intrigued if I'd had a lover.

"Of course, Milady. And besides the archery, doesn't Your Lady-ship have a fencing lesson on Wednesday?"

"Yes, yes. How distracted I am. That is to be cancelled too…"

✺

Once on the train, as it sped first towards Brunn and thence to Vienna, Herr Bankdirektor's conversation seemed social enough, although I was able to detect in his chatter about various princely and court families a not-so-subtle enquiry about whether I knew any of them well or not. I was able to say, in all honesty, that I did not, with one exception. But my mother knew them all. She was proud of the social connections she maintained, fighting like a cat for an invitation each year to the Hofburg Ball.

As he sat opposite me, facing the engine so there would not be the least chance of my receiving any soot, I realised how close he came to my first impression of him: that for all the world he resembled a rococo statuette, but without the elaborate peruke. I found my gaze wandering down to his tiny patent-leather shoes and idly speculating as to why the Emperor himself should have sent someone so perfect (and renowned) to fetch me! However, he would give nothing away.

We arrived in Vienna in mid-afternoon and were received by a man I discerned at first glance to be an imperial lackey in plain clothes. Escorting us to an unnumbered fiacre, we went to a nondescript little hotel so that I could freshen up a bit. I was allowed thirty minutes for this before proceeding to the great courtyards of the Hofburg Palace, a wing of which we entered by a little side entrance. Dapper Mr Palmer, after taking me round innumerable corners and down what seemed interminable corridors far removed from the splendid salons I had been fool-ishly anticipating, piloted me into a plain, office-like room. As I entered, a tall, distinguished-looking man rose from behind a desk. He introduced himself as Prince Rudolf von Liechtenstein.

"Do sit down, Countess. Now, there are one or two points of protocol to go through first."

This was all so serious. I listened intently.

"His Majesty will speak first. Your Ladyship should not ask His Majesty a question, nor speak on any topic…"

"I… I understand." By now I felt thoroughly intimidated. Almost in a daze I stood then passed through a door the prince had opened. I quickly awakened to the reality that I was in the Emperor's study.

A bent figure which was familiar to me from countless engravings and photographs in the press was seated behind a desk. It was in front of, but at right angles to, a large window. Directly before the desk was a big oval-framed portrait of the late Empress Sissy on an easel, as if permanently gazing at the Emperor at his burdensome work.

I made my deepest genuflection.

Kaiser Franz Josef the First looked up slowly. He had sharp blue eyes almost hidden by a face full of whiskers, but otherwise he seemed tired, so terribly tired. Even his voice conveyed an impression of utter weariness. Perhaps this was from the burden of all the sorrows of a whole empire that weighed upon his shoulders.

"Sit down, Countess," he said, motioning a set of comfortable chairs two or three metres from the plain upright caned desk chair on which he sat. Prince Rudolf von Liechtenstein had also told me that the Emperor always conducted his meetings standing up; it made them go more quickly… unless they were important. I felt more nervous than flattered.

"We have heard well of your handling of that affair in Marienbad last year. Quite the detective!" he said, although not looking in my direction. He seemed distracted.

He was wearing the blue tunic and red trousers of his uniform as Supreme Commander, with three medals on his chest. But who was there above him to award him medals — the Pope? God? Or perhaps other rulers simply swapped them like schoolboys do stamps.

Then he turned to me and sat with his hands on his knees, looking at me with an intensity which was disarming. "We need your assistance in another matter, equally confidential."

I simply nodded; by the rules I couldn't ask him anything and he seemed to be struggling with himself to go on. Eventually, after an endless-seeming few seconds, he continued:

"In 1889 we suffered a terrible loss. You understand, Countess?"

The suicide at Mayerling of his only son, the Crown Prince Rudolf. The biggest scandal ever to have rocked the royal house of Habsburg. It could only be this…

"The year before, we were hunting with our son. There was an accident. We were very nearly shot."

He let this sink in. I had no idea what he was getting to — after all, these events were over sixteen years ago. He struggled again to speak out, hardly looking at me:

"What we want you to find out is quite simple. It is a task we believe you might be able to accomplish with absolute discretion." He looked directly at me, still perhaps trying to ascertain if I was indeed up to whatever challenge he was about to set. He cleared his throat first, and fortified himself with a deep breath before speaking these words: "Did our son mean to kill us?"

I felt myself go numb with fear. How on Earth could I find an answer to such a question? My brain flooded with questions — which I was not permitted to ask.

"We are sure you understand that this is for our person alone — a private, family matter."

My throat felt try. I was being entrusted with what was evidently a matter of great importance. The Emperor had millions of subjects. Why me to do this?

I began to open my mouth to ask a very pertinent question, but shut it again immediately, remembering the strict etiquette of which I had been reminded earlier. The old man with the heavy heart sensed my frustration:

"You will doubtless be wondering what assistance is available to you in this task. We are not able to offer any. You shall be on your own. We think it is the best way. Herr Palmer can answer any other questions."

The Emperor extended his hand and I knew the audience was ended. I rose, stepped forward, dropped on my knees and kissed his hand. Then I felt his royal hand patting me gently on the shoulder and heard the door behind me opening.

As I rose to leave, I thought I saw a tear glistening in one of his eyes. I couldn't let my Kaiser down, of course, although I somehow felt I was being offered an impossible task.

Back in the outer office, Mr Palmer sat me down at a desk. I didn't know if this had been a test of some kind. Prince Liechtenstein disappeared into the Emperor's office. We were alone.

"How much will your fee be, Countess?" he asked without ceremony. After such an emotional scene, I was taken aback by his adroitness. I now knew why he had been sent to collect me.

"Herr Bankdirektor," I replied almost curtly, "it is my duty to serve His Majesty. There is no question of any fee."

"Well, that is very noble of you — but there will undoubtedly be expenses. Please simply come to my bank and withdraw whatever you need. The Chief Cashier will have your name listed and clear instructions to attend to your wants."

"And do you know when His Majesty is expecting me to...?" Here I suddenly realised that I was already under the obligation of secrecy, "... to report back?"

"Within three months, I understand. Now, do you have any further questions, Countess?"

I was almost in a state of shock and at that second couldn't think of any at all; at the same time I knew I would probably regret this almost immediately. "None," I said.

Mr Palmer rose and proffered his hand: "I am so glad we've been able to resolve the fiscal arrangements so effortlessly. The matter, so I am given to understand, is of considerable importance to His Majesty."

Unfortunately, I understood that only too well.

୧

Since I was anxious to demonstrate that I was a capable and independent operative, I had refused to be accompanied back to Prague, or even to the station. Indeed, with this sudden new development, I probably would need to consider my next move here in Vienna. Just as I was about to leave the palace by the main Michaelerplatz gate, a young man from Prince Liechtenstein's office came running up to me with a telegram. Who on Earth could have known I was here?

Mother.

How embarrassing. I was supposed to have told no one of the meeting. The telegram read:

```
AM COMING TO VIENNA TONIGHT STOP MEET ME
AT THE IMPERIAL AT SIX-THIRTY STOP MAMMA
```

Having bought some chocolates at Demel's and looked at some hats — and, quite frankly, not having the foggiest idea of how to start immediately on my Imperial task, I decided to take the short walk to the Imperial Hotel on the Ringstrasse. I soon found myself promenading the great thoroughfare girding the old city of Vienna where only thirty or forty years before had stood its fortifications. Prague's version of this was a more muted affair. The smart *equipages* of the rich with their high-stepping horses swept by. On the wide gravelled walk moved a cross-section of the diverse peoples of the Dual Monarchy which stretched from the High Tatras to the Dolomites, from Turkey to Transylvania: a Muslim from the Balkan province of Bosnia, in crimson fez and pointed white slippers, hawking ornate teakettles and inlaid snuffboxes; Orthodox priests, with mitres and Old Testament beards, violet waistbands girding their long dark cassocks, trooped beside Silesian Jews in black silk caftans and large-brimmed beaver hats. I noticed a Carpathian peasant taking off his white fur cap and holding it to his chest before crossing this wonderful street — a form of Slavic humbleness before the grandeur of it all.

Why Mamma had to waste money on this hotel would have to be the subject of enquiry: didn't she know we were all trying to economise? The Ladies' Writing Room on the hotel's ground floor would at least provide shelter for me until Mamma's arrival. Her fiacre from the station came laden with luggage. What on Earth was she doing here, anyway?

"I just had to come to find out how you got on," she explained over aperitifs. "I'm so proud of you… an audience with the Emperor!"

"Mamma, it could just be that it was on highly confidential business…"

"Exactly. So now you can tell me all about it."

Mamma could actually help, that was the truth of it. Having extracted her promise of secrecy, I told her all that had transpired.

My mother's air of half-amused, aloof disdain for the events of the world around her suddenly changed. This was a serious business, and no mistake. "Mamma," I eventually confessed, "if this is going to involve trying to gauge whether guns were pointing this way or that, whether bullets or pellets or whatever were of this type or that — that kind of thing, then I am out of my depth. For that, the Emperor needs a normal police detective, surely? Why me, for Heavens' sakes?"

"There is obviously more to it, Beatrice. It can't be that simple and it clearly involves something which can only be exhumed with extreme delicacy. However, have you thought what you have to do?"

"What do you mean?"

"Regardless of the facts, or even the truth, surely you have to deliver to His Majesty the answer he wants to hear. It's as simple as that."

That was all well and good — but what answer did he want?

"Mamma, do you think he wants it to be confirmed that the Crown Prince had been rotten all along — a dangerous madman who had even attempted to kill his own father? Or that he was a poor misunderstood creature, driven to suicide?"

"You're dealing with some very difficult people, Beatrice. You remember we were discussing mixed marriages with my mother when she was over? Well Rudolf was the result of one of the most mixed marriages ever."

"But Sissy was the first cousin of a King... Ludwig of Bavaria..."

"Mad Ludwig, you mean? He was as nutty as a fruitcake..."

"A fruitcake, Mamma?"

"A nutcase. You should remember your English slang, my dear — you never know when you might need it. Sissy was nothing short of an inherently unstable libertine, and a female Narcissus to boot. Most unsuitable for an empress. She was a real handful, to put it mildly."

I wouldn't ask her what she thought of Franz-Josef. Not much, I supposed, but we'd have been talking all day, or — rather — I'd have been doing the listening.

Yet nothing could take my mind off the fact that the so-called "double suicide" of Prince Rudolf and his terribly young mistress, Countess Vetsera, had actually been first the murder of the young woman by Rudolf — albeit with her willing complicity — before Rudolf then turned the gun on himself. I could see myself trapped in an impossible conundrum. Best to go back to the basic question.

"Mamma — what do you know of this hunting accident in 1888?"

"It must have taken place during the visit of the Prince of Wales to Hungary. Everybody who had English connections was summoned to make up the numbers. Countess Czernin was there, of course, but I've forgotten her English family name. We stayed in Budapest and went on to the shoot at Gödöllo, which was a very grand affair. Something happened there... I thought so at the time. That was before Prince Edward, as Wales then was, went on a bear hunt to Transylvania alone with Crown Prince Rudolf. One could clearly see then that father and son weren't getting on…"

"But what actually happened?"

"At twelve that particular day, the party was to make its way to the railway station where a light lunch was to be served for everyone in the Emperor's dining car. It was a case of first come, first served and when we got there, the Emperor himself was not yet present — but the rule was one could start anyhow. About twenty minutes after our arrival, the Emperor, accompanied by Prince Rudolf, appeared with about half a dozen others. The Emperor had swapped his customary uniform for his lederhosen and wore his hat decorated with that *Gamsbart,* that damned tuft of chamois hair, looking exactly like an ordinary citizen. Forgive my use of such a blunt word."

I nodded my forgiveness. I would have used an even stronger word. I hated those hats; Karel always wore one.

"The Crown Prince, I noticed, was as white as a sheet and looked agitated. The Emperor led his son into the carriage and I remember him saying 'A bite of lunch will be just the thing for you… what's left anyway?' — and the Emperor enquired from somebody standing nearby. 'Just a few sandwiches, Your Majesty,' was the reply. 'What, no caviar canapés left?' 'Sorry, Your Majesty, all gone.' Then the Emperor marched without a moment's hesitation to his own little table, which no one else could touch, and returned with some of that simple cured smoked pork with sauerkraut and dumplings, the stuff he liked, with a small glass of wine, on a platter. '*Guten appetit*,' he said, handing it to his son."

Mother stopped. "Is that it, Mamma? That sounds the very reverse of what is at issue."

"No, you don't understand. It was the way he said 'Guten appetit' which struck me. His manner was actually as cold as ice, and there was a certain look in his eye."

"But surely it should have been the Emperor as white as a sheet and upset — in the…circumstances?"

"No, not if some attempt had been made, had — shall we say? — misfired, and thus the intention had been made transparently clear. Don't you think?"

I knew immediately that this task of mine was not going to be easy, especially if all the evidence I would be able to dig up was as vague as Mamma's. The one person who could help was the Emperor himself, and for whatever reason he was going to give no clues… to say nothing. How infuriating! My mother looked across at me, sensing my mood, and cocked an eyebrow in sympathy.

"Look," she said, "by a stroke of luck, one of the chief protagonists in the whole Rudolf affair is in Vienna this week. You are probably too young to remember Countess Larisch, aren't you? The Larisches had an estate near Pardubitz. Marie Larisch was a niece of Empress Sissy and… well, Sissy made *provision* for her, if you get my meaning. Count Larisch was a harmless enough fellow, but with a roving eye. They were married off. After the Rudolf tragedy, it came out that she was also heavily involved in making the clandestine arrangements for Rudolf's meetings with that foolish child, Mary Vetsera. Not only that, but that Rudolf paid her handsomely for it. It is one thing to abandon one's moral scruples, and quite another to do it for money! After the tragedy, neither the Emperor nor Empress would even see Marie Larisch again. She was banished from Society and went back to her parents in Bavaria. Since then she has been the subject of a divorce from her husband — that was the last time she was in the news, I suppose, about ten years ago."

"So she is allowed back now?"

"It was a surprise for us to learn this. Her current husband is the famous Munich singer Otto Bruchs. He is giving a performance of *Die Meistersinger* tonight, and his wife has been allowed to come with him. However, the rumour is that she was about to publish her memoirs, including everything about the private affairs of the late Empress, and that the Emperor has purchased the manuscript to prevent it all coming out. This visit — kept to a minimum number of days — is really to conclude the matter, and the opera to mask its real purpose."

"So how do I get to meet this Countess Larisch?"

"Princess Salm has invited me over to listen to the concert this evening. Originally, I had said I would be in Bohemia. I shall telephone and have you invited, too. She's an old friend. I understand Marie Larisch will appear."

"But Mamma, I can't possibly. I have nothing to wear... and Sabine..."

"... will be here in a few minutes. I had her sent for as soon as I learned your plans. Summoned by the Emperor, indeed! You need to be prepared for any eventuality!"

ℂ

In the first floor drawing-room of the Salm Palace on Salesian-ergasse I found myself seated around a very large round table with the elderly Princess Salm and fourteen other guests. The Electrophone apparatus was set up on the table-top and each of us held one of its octopus-like tentacles. Somewhat similar to a speaking tube, held to the ear we were able to hear the proceedings almost as if we were in the front row of the Imperial Opera itself. Certainly Otto Bruchs, singing the role of Hans Sachs, had a fine voice... all by the miracle of the telephone wires.

Luckily, Sabine had brought my turquoise silk gown and had managed in the very short time allowed her at the hotel to iron out the worst creases. It was rather refreshing, if not a little intimidating, to be in the company of dazzling shirt fronts and satin-framed busts and diamonds. By comparison to Vienna, Prague was... well, a little... provincial. Too many women at any social event there displayed tousled hair and slipshod petticoats. I would obviously have to get accustomed to the sight of satins and silks, gorgeous trains and sparkling jewels.

The Princess of Salm, our hostess, was a very gracious lady. During the first interval in *Die Meistersinger*, Mamma chose to comment on her:

"She's nearer sixty than forty, and look at her! White satin and pearls. Isn't it touching!"

"Ssshh, Mamma... for heaven's sake. Anyway, *she* can carry it off." Fortunately the performance resumed and we all took up our tubes again.

Eventually, the final applause died away and the Electrophone relay broadcast ended, leaving me wondering if I had had an evening at the opera or been merely here in this house, as if listening to gramophone records. As some refreshments were served to us, Princess Salm announced that Mr Bruchs would be making his way over from the opera house as soon as he could.

"And his wife?" my mother asked, ever the *provocateuse*.

"Marie Larisch was to have been my little surprise," answered the Princess, raising her lorgnette and giving my mother a rather icy stare through its lenses.

At the very mention of Countess Larisch's name, several of the guests stood up and made apologies to leave. Once an outcast, always an outcast.

We were down to seven or eight of us by the time the Bruchs arrived. I had a feeling that those who remained were more curious about Marie Larisch than sympathetic, my mother included.

Otto Bruchs was a rotund man of lesser height, somewhat belying the image one might have had for him from hearing his mellifluous voice. He wore a pointed moustache and with his puffed-out chest resembled more a stationmaster or a provincial mayor than the famous Courtsinger of Bavaria. His wife, the former Countess Larisch, was not quite what I expected. Somehow I assumed she would be dressed in a costume from those heady days of the 1880s — with those balloon-like expansions on either side of the *corsage* which fashion then called sleeves, but instead she wore a quite becoming black velvet dress, cut *en-coeur*. Her hair was fresh from the touch-up of peroxide and a judicious wave of curling irons. Her small eyes were carefully darkened, but her equally small mouth betrayed those long years of disappointment, having a permanent downturn which straightened only reluctantly when she managed to force a smile.

Princess Salm warmly embraced her guest, but after only a few minutes it was clear that Otto Bruchs, and not his wife, was the centre of attention and I noticed Marie Larisch slipping out onto the upper hall of the staircase. No one noticed me as I followed her.

It was a rather gloomy space. The Salms had not installed enough electric globes. Marie Larisch was standing looking down the staircase, one hand on the marble-capped balustrade. What light there was caught the flanges of the gilded stucco ornamentations that bedecked the upper tiers of the hall. She sensed my presence behind her and turned.

"It was here," she said, "where it all started."

"Oh?" I replied, not knowing quite what she was referring to.

"You're too young to remember, I should think. Did you know this house belonged to the Vetseras then? The Baroness had to sell it after... after the tragedy. That was it for them. It was here that I passed Prince Rudolf's first note to Mary Vetsera. She was barely seventeen. That was the start... and the beginning of the end."

"Countess..."

"*Former* Countess, they call me now..."

"Countess, I would very much like to learn more of the *cause célèbre*. As you say, I was too young."

"Well, why don't you come to me at The Grand tomorrow, say at eleven? We are leaving the following day. My only other appointment is to visit the Crypt of the Capuchins. I have never had the opportunity to see Aunt Sissy's sarcophagus. We'll have coffee together and I can tell you a thing or two."

"That will be easy. My mother and I are staying opposite, at The Imperial."

৩৯

When the Princess of Salm's coach dropped us off at the hotel later that evening I thought I saw a figure in a long coat step-ping back into the shadows across the street. For a split-second I thought it might have been one of Schneider's men... but no, evidently not; not here in Vienna. Close behind our carriage was a fiacre delivering the Bruchs. So that was it! The old emperor was keeping Marie Larisch (as she once was) watched. No wonder he always says "We know everything." Yet I was aware now there was at least one thing he didn't know.

The next morning, as Mamma and I were breakfasting in her suite, a telegram was brought in. It was from Müller:

```
SCHNEIDER HAS SOLVED THE CASE STOP
MULLER PRAGUE
```

"Mamma," I said, handing her the telegram, "as soon as I have finished with Marie Larisch, I shall be returning to Prague."

"What is this 'case,' dear girl?"

Of course. I hadn't told her of the headless corpse, of the bloody severed head at the pawnbroker's… it was all too ghastly to think about, even now. "Oh, nothing," I heard myself saying rather unconvincingly.

I had to cross the street to The Grand. It was aptly named. The Imperial had a quiet dignity, whilst The Grand did indeed immodestly think it was just that. The Bruchs' suite was on the first floor. Whatever their financial state, they had been obliged to make a show. Or perhaps the Imperial Opera or the Emperor himself had dug into their pockets.

After the usual pleasantries which I tried to keep to generalities of the most banal feminine sort (I didn't want to excite her regret at not being in Vienna more, nor to mention anyone who was actively giving her the cold-shoulder as some kind of pariah), we got down to business.

"He was such a fine young man," she began. Obviously this was the Crown Prince. "You know the palace accused me of being paid to help him in that affair of the heart, when in reality I was passing his money to the Vetseras so they could keep up. They had to rent two villas on the Riviera…"

I knew she was trying to justify herself and it didn't make any sense: the Vetseras were Lebanese and had pots of money. I let her ramble on.

"And afterwards they were all looking for the famous steel box, said to contain Rudolf's most precious papers." Here she looked at me in a curious way. Was it some kind of test? Did she think I'd been engaged to find this steel box — of which I'd never even heard until that moment?

"But eventually, of course, they found it. I was told it was the Emperor himself who opened it, saying that 'it never hurts to know a few secrets, especially of someone destined to be Emperor,' but it contained virtually nothing!"

So if it had been found, then there was no query here. "But the circumstances of their deaths — that poor young girl and the Prince: is what we know of the facts actually *true*?"

"That's the question! All the papers — the police reports, the findings of the Special Commission — all these files were entrusted to old Prime-Minister Taaffe. I understand they are kept at their seat at Ellischau Castle. I think in the Emperor's place I would simply have burnt the lot, but that is not his way. He probably even keeps detailed records of when precisely his royal and august toenails are cut!"

"And the year before it happened... 1888: was there any inkling of what was to come? For example, between father and son — what were their relations like?"

"Cold, of course. The Emperor is a man who finds it impossible to show emotion... if he has any, that is." Marie Larisch really didn't mind speaking in this prohibited manner, as she was now Bavarian.

"They went hunting together, didn't they — that summer?"

"I can see what you're getting at, Countess. There were always rumours that Rudolf had shot at his father. I've often tried to remember. That was such a time, such a flurry of social events — and..."

Perhaps this would be the first revelation in the case. I was hopeful. Somehow I would never consider anything my mother told me as serious fact. Or, on the other hand, Marie Larisch might confirm her theory.

"...and I think it must have taken place at Laxenburg Castle... or was it in the forests behind Bad Ischl? I know they hunted there that year... or was it in '87?"

I was in despair of ever getting anything of value from her and I began to run the conversation down — back to generalities again — when she crossed the room and opened a small travel valise. Out of it she produced a double leather photograph frame, which she handed to me. It was rather worn and it contained the portrait photographs of Crown Prince Rudolf and his young mistress, Baroness Mary Vetsera. There can't have been another such pair of photographs left in the whole of Austria-Hungary — apart, that is, from in those sensational German books, speculations about what *really* happened at Mayerling that appear with monotonous regularity every year. I looked closer: Heavens! How young she looked... and he...

"Hasn't he the saddest eyes?" Marie Larisch beat me to it.

It was true. They showed intense pinpoints of brilliance which had been suddenly dulled... thwarted. The Emperor's eyes were sad, in their way — a self-satisfied way, weary of everyone else, but Rudolf's were the eyes of desperate disappointment in life itself, a disappointment that perhaps could only be satisfied by death.

"They sent her mother out of the country as soon as the news broke, and poor Mary Vetsera's body was left for two days naked in the wood-shed while They wondered what to do with it. It... no, *she*...left Mayerling propped up between her uncles in a carriage and was hastily buried at Heiligenkreuz Abbey. Her mother wasn't even allowed to see her. That's what you're dealing with..."

Her eyes met mine. She knew I had some involvement in this, evidently. I had to stay mum.

Then, as I was taking my leave, she suddenly caught me by the sleeve. There was something else, apparently, that was on her mind.

"Those years," she began, "those years before the Mayerling tragedy, they were the best. There was a sense of optimism then, that the new generation would sort out the problems of the Empire... and so it was all right to splash the champagne and waltz until dawn. The death of Rudolf was a ghastly dose of reality. I am glad I became separated from it all."

She led me to the door of her suite. "And if you find yourself coming to Munich, do look us up." She kissed me on both cheeks. There was something about her, however, which probably would cause me to avoid Munich, if possible.

Soon I was waiting in the hotel lobby for Mamma to come down to see me off. I didn't need this attention and it was only making me late. At least I'd been able to relieve Mamma of some of her anxiety at having booked into The Imperial. She just couldn't see herself staying anywhere else! Since I felt I was already learning something which might help me understand the tragedy of 1889, I could charge most of the hotel expense to Herr Palmer's bank. Mamma was going to stay on in Vienna for a few days more, but that would have to be on her own account.

Sabine, who had arrived from Prague the evening before, had had the task of repacking all she had brought and she stood with the two large portmanteaus she had managed to bring on the train, the contents of which had been specified down to last lace-edged handkerchief by my mother.

In between cursing Mamma, who only had to put on a wrap in order to wave me good-bye and was managing to take ten minutes to do so, my eyes wandered to the hotel barber's in the short arcade before the main exit to the Ringstrasse. The barber was sharpening his old-fashioned razor on a hanging leather strap and then, in a move he must do dozens of times a day, he turned back to his customer shrouded in white in the barber's chair and tested the keenness of his sharpened blade on his forearm. Satisfied, he set to work. I couldn't at first work out why this particular act so attracted my attention.

At this moment Mamma appeared and Sabine announced that our fiacre was loaded. As I turned in my seat to acknowledge Mamma's gloved and waving arm, I also thought I caught sight of one of those obviously invisible plain-clothes men, abruptly turning away from my gaze.

Not long after I was on the train back to Prague. I felt a lot of what Larisch said or might say could be discounted as unreliable, except her remarks about the unhappy pair and the Vetseras had an undeniable ring of truth.

ços

Müller at once telephoned Inspector Schneider, who came straight round. I was still in my travelling clothes and we met in the office on the ground floor.

"It's absolutely conclusive. This Hélène Johanson was carrying on with Orsini. Her husband was away at the time… has been away for some time, in fact — or so it seems. He had started out as a butcher's assistant in his native Sweden before moving to Prague, then been hired by Lippert's — where he was in charge of their smoked meats and cheese counters. Last year he left and went to work in a restaurant in Berlin."

Schneider was quite red-faced with excitement. I simply nodded, not to interrupt him.

"This man Johanson obviously found out what's been going on, and had his wife and her lover followed and photographed. He then commits the terrible murder, sending his wife the gruesome pictures which show the deceased as he was when with her, the picture cutting off the head and a hand."

"So that was intended as a warning — or retribution in itself?"

"I think the man's mad. Who knows what he might go on to do?"

"Hmm," I said. I needed a moment to digest the theory. Certainly it fitted the notion of sending the pictures. Schneider must have thought I wasn't too convinced.

"You see it was the cheese counter which made it all work." Schneider was beaming, the master detective. "The man is Swedish. And you know what they use there to cut cheese? — a cheese wire — the perfect instrument for cleanly decapitating a corpse. It fits perfectly."

"And what about the means of killing Orsini in the first place?"

"Also solved. The puncture wound in the breast. It appears to have been made with something like a shoemaker's awl…"

"The way Empress Sissy was murdered?"

"Except this was quicker. Less blood flowed. The heart was stopped almost instantly as the awl must have been coated in a deadly poison."

"Do you know the chemical?"

"The laboratory has said that they have only come across something similar once before, and that substance came from Mexico."

"So, as you say, Inspector, you have solved the case. Have you any evidence that this man Johanson has come back to Prague recently, or that he was actually still violently in love with his wife?"

"When we find him, I am sure we will discover he's been back to Prague recently — or may very well still be here. I understand such murderers like their own notoriety; he'll have been studying the newspapers here, I am sure."

"Your theory is all well and good, Inspector — but what do you know, for example, about Orsini, other than he was a well-known magician?"

Schneider was a bit caught out.

"I'll think you will find that he started out in life as a barber, for instance. That might be relevant, when the whole picture is unveiled, surely? Every detail could be important."

"And how on Earth could you know that?"

"By the hairs on his left forearm. You should read the post-mortem report again. And there's something else, too." I bravely ploughed on: "I think you might find that he purchased his boots in a Closing Down Sale — but since that was probably last year or even the year before that, then it might not have been in Prague!"

"Countess, you astonish me."

"Good."

Chapter Four

Abracadabra

After Schneider had left, the more I thought over his theory, the more I didn't believe in it. In a way it was too perfect, as if all the evidence had been set up just so that we would come to this conclusion. The only tangible oddity I had was that single thread of wire. If there was a lot of wire involved, say, in one of Orsini's tricks, then why had it all been so carefully swept up — leaving just one tiny scrap trapped between the parquet blocks?

Schneider's theory of a lone, jealous and obsessed maniac was simply not supported by the facts. As I saw it, there had to be four men involved. Two men had virtually carried the corpse of Orsini onto the Abt at the bottom station. It was said that one of these appeared to be drunk, slumped between his two companions. A third man boarded at the top station. As the cars were about to cross, the fourth man leapt across the track and the two cars halted alongside each other. At that moment, man three helped the first pair to haul the body into the down car and then joined his accomplices on the rest of the journey up. I presume this was meant to remain some kind of insoluble mystery — but they hadn't reckoned on me, obviously! The intention was for someone like Schneider to come to the conclusion of the jealous rage killing. Clearly, there was another reason for the murder, one which was worth engaging these accomplices. It was still hard to imagine, however, a lame French priest as having any involvement.

And having been very smug with the inspector about his lack of knowledge of The Great Orsini, I realised I knew practically nothing about him, either. Those drawings — for example — didn't they show a great deal of wires? Karel had thought they were stout cables, capable of supporting a bridge — but what if they were very thin wires, as my small thread-like sample? I rang for Müller.

"Do you know any magicians, Müller?"

"That all depends on which kind, Milady. Black or white are two choices I could bring to mind..."

"Oh, any race will do." Here Müller, with delightful *sang froid* and a stone face, and doubtless employing his usual tact, ignored my gaff, which I instantly understood, and I went on: "I was thinking of children's magicians. When I was a child, every year on Princess Lobkowicz's birthday we went to a party at their house where there was an excellent magician. I believe he was German..."

"Then that must have been Wilajalba Frikell, Master of Magic. Now, I would presume, an elderly gentleman."

"Yes, yes. That's him. How could I have forgotten?"

"At my late employer's he was still entertaining the children up to five or six years ago. I could enquire of Count Czernin's current butler if he has an address, if Milady wishes."

"Yes... yes, please do." Wilajalba Frikell: how that name brought back memories!

✎

The express to Dresden stopped at the border shortly after the industrial city of Tetschen, and then continued to follow the more rural but nevertheless dramatic scenery of the Elbe until the capital of Saxony was reached. At the central station I would catch a local train and retrace my steps somewhat to get to the small village halt, where I was assured I would find a fiacre to take me to Frikell's house.

From the correspondence we had already exchanged — mine by telegram and his reply by more sedate letter — the old man had seemed flattered that anyone still remembered him. Indeed, these past five years he had been in retirement. In his heyday his name had been the byword for elaborately staged trickery, the stuff at children's parties was merely for the handsome fees that noblemen were prepared to shell out. Of course my parents never permitted us to go to the theatre to see his famous Disappearing Cabinet. I supposed it must have been the same trick as Orsini's ghastly wardrobe.

The fiacre brought me to a neat villa on the edge of a small village. Its style appeared to be that of thirty or forty years ago — perhaps Frikell had had it built for himself — and as it was some way from the next house in the village, and was the last, it was surrounded by neat orchards. The path to the front door was bounded by well-clipped hedges. My assumption that Frikell had built the house was reinforced by the frieze I now saw in the stucco over the upper floors: the motifs were rabbits, top hats, and magicians' wands.

My ring at the bell was answered by a woman in a smart dark dress and in a flood of tears. She was in such a condition that she was hardly able either to lead me into the house or even welcome me. I was somewhat at a loss to know what to do. After some hesitation she beckoned towards what I presumed would be the parlour and I stepped through its open door.

Laid out on the table were many mementos of the old magician's career. Some of the photographs appeared to be in new frames. His medals, including one bearing the head of Emperor Franz-Josef and another bearing that of the first German Kaiser, had been freshly polished. Beyond the table was another, on which rested a serving tray all set with the best china coffee cups, silver spoons and lace-edged tea napkins, and beyond that, on a big, worn chair, sat — or I should say slumped — a figure which could only be Wilajalba Frikell, erstwhile Master of Magic… clearly dead.

The old man was dressed in his gala outfit with silk facings, his moustache waxed and hair neatly trimmed. His wife had now come up behind me, excusing the fact that Frikell's face was still wet from the cologne she had used in a futile attempt to revive him. However, what was simply frightful was the terrible look frozen on his face: one of sheer, unutterable terror.

"He suddenly started out of his chair," Mrs Frikell kept repeating, "just as if he had seen something out of the window, then fell back. There was nothing I could do." This had happened less than an hour before.

A moment later the maid returned with the doctor, who had had to come from the nearby town of Pirna. For the moment I found myself redundant to the proceedings, realising the futility of suggesting to the medical man that Frikell's death might have been anything other than a normal heart seizure.

Nobody therefore noticed my absence while I went outside and found the window closest to Frikell's chair. Directly in front of the window was a rose-bed. Clearly visible on the earth were some footprints, leading from the lawn. There were quite a few of them, and the sight of the left shoe print I had followed over

Petřín Hill in the snow suddenly filled me with a horror so intense that I had to run back indoors. I waited in the hallway a moment to compose myself and for my sheer panic to subside. Luckily, the maid had had the sense to start serving the coffee.

On the table with the medals lay various albums and a portfolio of intricate design drawings. Yes, here was a cabinet like the one in Prague, and a plan view showed the exact angle the mirror had to be set to create the illusion. Further on there were drawings with the wires familiar to me from the blueprints consigned to me by Orsini.

"The Holy Grail of the magician's trade," I heard Mrs Frikell's voice from over my shoulder. She had come up behind me while I had been absorbed in the drawings, perhaps glad of some distraction; the undertaker had just arrived. "The supreme triumph: the act of levitation. A maiden simply floats up off the stage. My husband found the way. He and Orsini were working on it lately — the ultimate illusion. Orsini had finally perfected my husband's idea, you see."

Suddenly I could, indeed, see. So much for Karel's suggestion that Orsini's designs had been for a new kind of bridge! It was an elaborate cradle, bearing up a single body lying horizontally while elaborate counterbalances — high above — adjusted and lowered themselves.

"Orsini's idea was to make the wires even finer," Mrs Frikell went on, "but there would have to be even more of them — hundreds of wires only as thick as fine silk thread... invisible from the audience. Each had to support its tiny part of the weight. For years I had to keep my own weight at 50 kilograms exactly! I was the first 'priestess' to be levitated! Look..." and here she proffered a loose photograph, labelled *Princess Thea levitates*, showing a figure in Eygptian robes seemingly floating but as if on a stiff board. Frikell, also in robes, stood behind holding a hoop around the floating form.

"He would pass the hoop right over me," she went on, "that convinced everyone that I must, indeed, be floating on nothing but air. At least that's what it appeared."

My eyes wandered back to the drawings and thence to one of the framed photographs, being drawn to one face in particular which seemed familiar. The image depicted a group in a garden, perhaps in the garden of this house. There was old Frikell, some years younger; Mrs Frikell; another gentleman in a sharp suit, embroidered waistcoat, and spiky waxed moustache; and a young woman in a summer dress. She was without doubt the woman in the funicular photograph: the mysterious Hélène Johanson.

Mrs Frikell had noticed my shift of gaze. "That's the famous hypnotist and magician, Ira Devine." The one in the sharp suit.

"Russian or American?" The brash waistcoat was the giveaway, well suited to either nationality.

As she answered "American," I believed the name did have a familiar ring to it.

"He visited here?"

"Yes. Several times. I knew he wanted more than anything to find out about the secret of levitation, but we were in partnership with Orsini. Magic is a very competitive business."

"I am sure it is. And the girl, Mrs Frikell? I hope you don't mind me asking these questions at such a time…"

"That was our Hélène. An orphan we took in. She helped around the house. She was just sixteen when Devine... when Devine employed her."

"Employed?" I could feel we were on sensitive ground.

"Well, I suppose he just took her away... as his assistant. She was all starry-eyed of course, but my husband... my late husband, God rest his soul, thought it was unhealthy that they had to share a railway sleeping compartment on tour — and he being such an accomplished hypnotist."

"When did she go off with Devine?"

"It was nine years ago."

"And more recently?"

"Nothing. After she went, that was the last we saw or heard of her — and of Devine."

"Tell me, did Devine ever discover the secret of levitation?"

"No. Orsini is due to open with our spectacle in Prague..."

Clearly Mrs Frikell had not heard the news. This was not the moment to tell her of another death.

❧

I felt it was my duty to stay with the so recently bereaved widow for some while longer. The doctor and undertaker's men had long gone. The maid stayed in her quarters. Old Frikell lay in his coffin in the chilly dining room, which had been cleared for the purpose. Later the protestant pastor would call; they were not Catholics.

It was near nine in the evening before I felt I could leave. Haste would have been unseemly. The fiacre was still waiting, the driver having told the maid he would be found in the inn some fifty metres or so from the house. The railway station — if this halt could be so described — had its gas-lamps illuminated but was deserted. The fiacre sped away as I mounted the platform steps and consulted the timetable board for the next train to Dresden. I was surprised to find the last train had already departed. I was not expecting to have spent so long at the Frikells. To add insult to injury, I could stand on this platform and wave at the night train to Hamburg making its way directly to Dresden from Prague.

There was one late train from Pirna into Dresden — and if I reached Dresden and there was no very late train back to Prague, I could at least stay in a hotel. Pirna, however, was a good hour's walk away — that's if there had been a direct road. As I had observed in coming, this side of the River Elbe, nestling between tall cliffs, was reserved for the railway; the roadway was on the far side. Perhaps, I thought, there was a towpath, directly alongside the water? I found a steep path leading down to the river, and with difficulty and probably making another pair of shoes casualties, made my way down. All was dark and silent, save for the constant ripple of the wide river. Indeed, there was a well-made towpath, and thus I resolved to make my march to Pirna.

Only the faintest distinction in the black-grey hues of the night distinguished the path. No sight was needed of the great river, as I could clearly hear its soft thrashing through the gorge just metres away. For the moment, the situation was merely an inconvenience, that is until I realised that whoever had startled poor old Frikell out of his wits — in effect killing him, as surely as if done with a dagger or poison, for that is what I felt had happened — might still be lingering in the district. They might even be making me the new target of their murderous attentions. From that moment on, my steps were dogged by terrible fear.

However much I tried, I could not believe I wasn't being followed. Stopping suddenly I would discover the noise behind me had been only as normal as some dried leaves blowing brittlely across the gravel, although — somewhat eerily — the leaves would seem to stop their movement as I did mine. I tried to walk as unobtrusively as possible past the camp of some bargees; their cooking fire was still glowing. Had they been awake and seen me, then what a sight would have met their gaze! A lady of quality dressed to pay a call... but they would have assumed a distinct lack of quality about anyone walking abroad at this hour.

As a diversion I tried thinking of the task set me by the Emperor, but all the while the more gruesome events of the last fortnight or so overpowered my desire to keep them at bay: the murder of Orsini, how simple the resolution had appeared to Inspector Schneider — and yet the girl, Hélène Johanson, whose lover— the old magician himself — supposedly was some form of collaborator with this new name, Ira Devine, a man desperate for Orsini's great secrets. Those were the secrets entrusted to me. Would they attempt to wrest them from me, too?

And who precisely were *they*? An old, lame priest, for one. And the others? What on Earth could have driven them to such a terrible crime? What power had this man Devine over them? He would have to be a new card. That's if ever I got back to my writing desk in one piece. I had been a fool to venture forth like this on my own; I could have easily instructed Müller to have accompanied me. But then life is too full of regrets for what might have been. Now I had to rise to the challenge of conquering my fear and stepping on into the darkness — until at last the station lights of Pirna came into view.

❧

There was over an hour to wait for the last train to Dresden Main. The Ladies' Waiting Room still had a warm stove and its gaslights were still illuminated. I pulled down the window blinds. In order to take my mind off the fearful and depressing events surrounding these far-from-magical magicians, I concentrated my thoughts on my problem. Hadn't Marie Larische actually marked my card? She said that all the reports of the Secret Police and the Special Commission on Rudolf's death had been given to old Prime-Minister Taaffe for safekeeping. That, in Habsburg terms, meant quietly burying something. Did the Emperor mean for me to exhume these... or would I now be going beyond my limits, even though no limits had actually been set? But without doubt "the incident" of 1888 and Rudolf's suicide the following January had to be connected.

The old Graf von Taaffe had died a few years ago. Was it possible that the papers were still in the family's castle at Ellischau, down in South Bohemia? We'd had a cook at Morštejn once who had come from the place—Nalžovy, as the Czechs call it. I'd met the old Graf's son, Heinrich, at a shooting party. Perhaps Karel could wangle me an invitation... or Mamma. I was beginning to realise that mothers do, in fact, have their uses!

❧

She replied by return post the day after I was back in Prague. She had also written to Maria, Heinrich's — the current Graf's — wife. She wrote:

When you are there, would you be so good as to enquire about the black pearl earrings that had been given to my distant cousin Lotty when she'd married Heinrich's uncle Otto? You know, my dear, Lotty — who died after only four months of marriage. I'd have thought it would have been almost impossible to get so bored even with Otto after only eighteen weeks — but that was Lotty for you, such a gay young thing she had been! They said it was convulsions, merely because the medical profession has yet to invent a scientific name for bored to death.

My dear mother… ever hopeful that somehow the Taaffes would conclude that four months hardly constituted a proper marriage, so the Morštejns could have the pearls back! But the notion did give me a very useful idea. I rang for Sabine and instructed her to pack for a short journey. I was too busy to open the envelopes which Müller was proffering on his silver salver. However, I did notice a blue one from Munich. That's Marie Larisch, I thought, by the slightly old-fashioned court hand. No doubt she was thanking me for taking an interest in her. I could deal with these later.

My invitation from Maria von Taaffe arrived by the last post. I was invited to what was now being called a "Weekend At Home," an English conceit, always referred to in English as well. That would mean few guests, if any others, and generally quite informal. I toyed with the idea of packing a riding habit, but I was sure that wouldn't be necessary. To keep up appearances my mother advised me to say that I was on my way to Vienna to meet Karel. For all I knew, Karel might even be there! If they had any game left in their forests — any small defenceless bird or four-legged creature — then Karel was likely to turn up sooner or later.

Maria von Taaffe was waiting on the steps below a high central pediment surmounted by a complicated coat-of-arms supported by sculptures of a dragon and a horse *rampant.* Too many dogs of different breeds accompanied her and they jumped around the carriage which had been sent to the station to fetch me.

Ellischau was quite grand in a rather severe way, commanding a view of a wide tract of countryside on one side and almost buried in a hillside on the other. Sabine complained to me that her room, which she had to share with a housemaid, looked out only onto an earth bank two metres away. Mine was near the chapel, in the east wing, so at least was blessed with some of the low early morning sun of the season and a wide view of fields and forests.

Maria had a fresh face and was of a similar age to myself. Indeed my mother had written to her, as the excuse for my being foisted on them, that we might just hit it off. Our big difference was that Maria had a seven-year-old boy, Richard. I could deal with dogs, of course, as I had already demonstrated — even cats which jump on your lap with sudden menacing unexpectancy, but young children I had yet to appreciate. My urchins were a different kettle of fish, being a little older and very much worldly-wise, perhaps too much so. I gave a moment's thought for them, still in recreational servitude at Morštejn! Perhaps in another matter I would need my little force of irregulars.

After a light lunch where Heinrich was not in evidence, being occupied on the estate — but at which Richard was too much in evidence, for my liking — Maria was anxious to show me the improvements they had made to the castle. The boy seemed decidedly odd, yet I couldn't pin down what it was. To start with, he possessed a large pocket watch, which he was continually consulting. The thing had a gold chain and a large fob with what looked like a half-carat diamond: a Prime-Minister's watch, if ever I saw one! While we were having coffee the child stood on a chair and moved the hands of a bracket clock forward by half a minute. Maria seemed not to notice.

At length a governess came and Richard went off with her. Thus we began our perambulation of the house. Maria explained that one could write away to an English company in Derby and they would send a catalogue of complete rooms which one could simply order, as one might a new pair of gloves. The combined library and smoking room in very garish red mahogany was shown with its open fire ablaze. So proud was she of Musgrave and Sons Limited's achievements that we ventured beyond the green baize door into the servants' domain to view the new china closet and silver room — all in similar unrestrained reddish stained mahogany, a wood very foreign to Bohemia. The china closet itself was lined with shelves on an upper level enclosed behind glazed doors and which were packed with drinking glasses. The main level was for cupboards containing the various services of crested china. Maria explained they had far too much china, whole services being the constant gift to the old Graf as Imperial Prime-Minister. There was even a Wedgwood dinner service for fifty presented by the British Parliament. A small vestibule, panelled in the same ubiquitous wood, led to the silver safe, visible only as a large steel strong-room door with a capstan-like wheel at its centre and a simple-looking dial with numerals for a combination. A brass plate bore the words, in impressive letters:

Sargent & Greenleaf
Rochester
New York

"Pappy had it installed. It was then the very latest, from the United States. The government paid for it, of course."

"It must have cost a small fortune... but, tell me, what if the wrong kind of servant learns the number?" I asked, at this moment in all innocence.

"Oh, we can change the number at a moment's notice," Maria replied. "Would you care to see the stables? They have also just been fitted out by Musgrave and Sons with new cast-iron stalls and mangers. Or are you still tired from your journey?"

At last an excuse. Back in my room I began to think of ways I might attain my objective. But surely such sensitive papers would not be kept in the silver safe, would they?

Sabine having dressed me for dinner, it was finally time for me to meet Heinrich and the family for drinks in the library. He was a large bear of a man, clearly someone who preferred working energetically in his forests than employing the urbane guile of his father. Indeed, he hadn't dressed himself yet — and was still in his working attire: head to toe in English tweed. "Do forgive me, Beatrice. I have to make the most of the sunlight out there at this time of the year. How was your journey?"

The grave and weighty hand of greatness had clearly not touched Heinrich, but who was nonetheless an affable enough fellow — that damning compliment. I was sure he was a good guardian of the family possessions who probably disliked spending too much time grovelling in Vienna. He was not the courtier type. I just hoped that he wouldn't be too good a guardian of one family possession. I tried to picture a slim file, bound in Morocco leather. Or was it a large packet, in thick manila, still sealed with red wax: K&K?

"Do call me Henry," he was saying, "You know we're spending quite a bit of time these days on our Irish estates? You're lucky to find us at Ellischau." Maybe that also explained all the English fittings in the castle. The Taaffes were unique in Austrian aristocracy in also being Irish viscounts. It was well known that the old Graf had died of disappointment that his democratic reforms had been rejected. Perhaps his family was now finding the British Empire more appealing.

"And we've taken a villa in Switzerland, too," Maria added. I noticed a slight *frisson* between husband and wife suddenly… as if she shouldn't have mentioned it for some reason. "The air is so bracing there, you see," she added.

Henry rather clumsily changed the subject: "But tell me, Countess, your mother is English, is she not?"

After I had replied in the affirmative and without even bothering to mention my Irish grandmother, I felt that I had immediately become someone to be trusted. A like soul, or so they thought. Maybe they would even tell me the reason why they had a villa in Switzerland (surely Bad Ischl, the Royal Spa, so much nearer to Vienna, should have been the place?)… or maybe they would even show me the Rudolf reports of their own free will. Over dinner I broached the subject, but I could not ask directly of course, as otherwise that would put them on their guard if they weren't going to play ball. Somehow the conversation had veered round to "the old days."

"So was your father very upset by the death of the Crown Prince?" I ventured.

"Of course; like everyone else," Heinrich replied. "But it was the aftermath which somehow disillusioned him."

"Oh, yes?"

"Naturally, he never spoke of it. He had learned too much, I suppose. That was what finished him off, I think — just as much as failing to enfranchise the Czechs… I say, isn't it time for the ladies to withdraw? I hope you won't find me rude if I don't join you. I've had rather a tough day…"

Coffee was served in the drawing-room, a salon of fine French furniture and tastefully worn-out Gobelin tapestries.

After the usual rather meaningless conversation with Maria and her sister, who was also staying, about relatives neither of us really knew, I moved on to Lotty and the pearls. To my surprise Maria wasn't the least bit bothered. "Look," she said, "if they are here and they mean so much to your mother, then you can have them... certainly."

"Come," she said. "Let's look for them now, shall we? Then we can get that over with. Let's play cards afterwards, shall we? It gets so dull here. I wish we would spend more time in Vienna — but Henry..." Tactfully she didn't complete her sentence.

To my utter amazement I found myself being led into the library. Maria opened an unlocked bookcase, took a bunch of keys lying openly on a shelf, and advanced to an area behind a disordered desk. "Don't worry about this mess," she said, "Henry sorts it all out once a month. Next week is his dreaded tidying morning. He hates paperwork."

She turned the key in what at first appeared to be a section of another bookcase, but which in fact was a small door onto which were glued the spines of antique books. Inside this cupboard was a safe... the Graf's private safe. In a moment the steel door was open and Maria was fumbling with various jewellers' boxes, eventually bringing one out. "Here we are. These are the ones, I think."

They were attractive dark pearls, maybe of some high value.

"If your mother really feels they belong at Morštejn, then do get her to drop me a line. We can have them sent. They are not much use sitting in this safe, after all..."

I was glad she didn't think to give them to me. Black pearls are an extremely bad omen. If I believed in superstition I would probably then have to touch a hunchback to get my luck back up to zero.

"That's most generous of you," I replied. But how to get a look inside that safe? "Wasn't there a matching hat-pin? My mother said something like that..."

"Yes, yes — it's upstairs. I do use it occasionally, but it does go with the rest of the pearls. I'll fetch it." She left the room.

This was more than I expected. As soon as the door closed on her I poked my nose into the safe, which was only about the size one would expect in a private study. There were papers in it, but nothing which bore the hallmark of secret state documents. The stuff on Rudolf must have been bulky too; my idea about a slim Morocco-bound file was all phooey, surely? And what about the late Prime-Minister's other secret archives? No, this was clearly the wrong safe.

As I turned away, I was confronted — to my dismay — with the face of little Richard pressed against one of the glass panes of the glazed doors to the drawing-room. The child was in his night things and in a flash he was scooped up by a nursery maid who presumably had come down to recover him. What, if anything, had he seen? The little brat could so easily tell... such a strange creature too. I wondered if he was quite well.

By the time Maria returned I had already decided what to say: "Tell me, it is such a conveniently sized safe and Karel has been thinking of one for what he calls his Business Room... was it also supplied with the rest of the furnishings, from England?" With all that damned garish mahogany woodwork, I stopped myself from adding.

That might at least explain my poking my head into it, if that had been seen. Then the thought came that perhaps, after all, the big silver safe was used to store the sensitive archives. Didn't Maria herself say the government had paid for it?

❧

In my room that night I realistically assessed my chances of getting into that veritable strong-room. I hadn't the first idea even how to open a combination lock. Müller dealt with all things involving locks and keys. It looked simple, but there was probably some trick, even to that. Anyway, one would need the number. I might have to consult with Viktor again.

This gentleman was what is known as a safe-cracker. He had "done time" and was an old acquaintance of Inspector Schneider. The two facts were related.

Schneider had put me in touch at my behest. In the lull which followed the Marienbad affair, I had decided to learn the craft of being a detective from the grass roots, so to speak. If it could be taught, of course. Schneider had given me the telephone number of a well-known jeweller, where this Viktor could be found on Thursday mornings at ten or any evening between six and seven. We had talked on the subject of wax impressions of keys, tumblers (but I never really understood what these were), and finally on getting an unyielding safe open. He had mentioned dynamite — "the most effective way."

At that point I had drawn the conversation to a close. It really just isn't the done thing, as a house-guest, to use dynamite — not in the home, at any rate. I could see its uses when robbing a bank, but I didn't think I would have occasion to do that, and any crime involving this sort of behaviour could surely be solved by ordinary detectives — such as Schneider, who was not averse to consorting with the likes of Mr Viktor.

I lay in my bed, the curtains drawn back so that the nearly full moon could be seen through floating clouds, thinking I should consult with Viktor again — but this notion was ridiculous. First I would need the exact code for the model or type of safe — or, better still, the actual number of the combination.

In this, Fate came to my assistance the following morning.

Maria's sister was out, doing something with horses, so I was breakfasting alone with Maria. She explained that the governess and the nursemaid were also both out of the Castle. Little Richard was thus in her charge, and he was now to be seen through the open door of the breakfast parlour — in an adjoining room.

He was on the carpeted floor winding and re-setting a vast array of watches of different types. Maria noticed my looking.

"He loves watches," she said. "He has all the old and spare ones. Once we turned out drawers, it was surprising how many we had," she explained. Then she lowered her voice and drew nearer.

"He's a veritable little professor. Loves numbers, too. He collects them as another boy might collect butterflies…"

"Numbers?"

"To him they have an extraordinary fascination and magic."

"So he will grow up to be a brilliant mathematician, then? I hate numbers, especially on letters from my bank."

"No, he is not destined for a normal life. You see, he is not like other children. There is something different about him."

Yes, I could see he was constantly flicking one of his hands — an odd, obsessive gesture. And odd, too, I hadn't properly been introduced.

"In Zurich there is a specialist… Dr. Bleuler. He has a clinic at Burghölzi. We had been recommended to him by Dr. Freud in Vienna. Dr. Bleuler says there are other children like Richard who share the same peculiarities. They can fail to develop empathy with the other children, or even with their family — it is if they are in another world. Their world is their self, their *autos*, as the doctor puts it. And yet they can be brilliant too." Then her voice lowered almost to a whisper: "The doctor says it is some kind of dementia. Henry cannot bear even to think of it."

At that moment there was a crash from next door. The boy had fallen over trying to reset the longcase clock.

"Richard… Richard."

He came running, somewhat clumsily for his age I noticed, to our table. Maria's face brightened to see the boy smiling.

"Do you want to know how many window panes we have, Mummy?"

Mummy smiled indulgently, and flashed me a look.

"We have two hundred and twenty-six windows in the castle including the stables, but not including the brewery. And two thousand eight hundred and forty panes of glass, counting all the double windows. This excludes the chapel which has stained-glass windows, which have three hundred and forty-nine pieces."

I wondered… I just wondered.

✀

"Sabine, what do you think of child exploitation?"

The dutiful Sabine had just completed supervising the filling of my bath. Here in the country they still didn't have running hot water upstairs, and the maids had to bring it up in brass cans.

My dress was already laid out for dinner, in anticipation of the scrubbed and clean countess who would soon inhabit it.

"What does Madame mean?"

"I mean, is it right to use poor, defenceless children for… for any kind of… well, work at all?"

"It can be good for them, within limits. Threading the needles for a dressmaker, for instance, means they learn without being taught. Like cooking. No French girl needs to be 'taught' the art of good cuisine. They have learned from watching at their mother's elbows, and helping them peel and stir and so on. But it is a shame that Czech girls — and even more so the English — also are encouraged to watch their mothers…"

I had got more than I had bargained for.

"Now, Madame, the water is getting *un peu froid*."

Dinner was over again.

"It's Thursday tomorrow, Trixie." By now we were on very familiar terms. "We have to go over to Budweiss in the morning. Would you like to exercise one of our horses?"

Yes, I should. I could get to a telephone and consult with Viktor. "Of course," I replied.

I now cursed I didn't have a proper riding habit with me, but Sabine improvised. Just after nine I climbed into the saddle in the stable yard. I just wished I could wear jodhpurs and sit astride.

I had been allowed to as a child when I went riding with Max at Morštejn. How lucky men are!

From around a corner of the yard came another mount, on which sat Maria's sister. "I'll join you. Gaston needs a good canter too!"

Damn. I sized them both up: the rider and the ridden. I would have to lose them. They could both shed some kilos.

Last night's frost was still melting, and obstinate patches lingered thick under hedgerows and in shady hollows. Yellow Fever — my mount's unlikely name (it had once won the Pardubitz Steeplechase) — set forth with the brisk determination to lead the field. It was said that Empress Sissy had the skill to have tackled the Pardubitz course riding side-saddle. I wouldn't have described myself as an accomplished horsewoman, and how I managed to cling on as we sped over gates — usually one stops to open them — and down towards the village, I shall never know. I'd only suffered a very bad spill once, when I was seventeen — but my bones were probably more supple then, and after some treatments I was back to normal after only a few weeks. Now, at first I heard the maddening sister calling me, but gradually she became well and truly lost behind me. By the time I reached the railway station, on the far side of the village, it was nearing ten o'clock.

I was permitted to use the instrument in the stationmaster's office. He tactfully left the room. Soon I was hearing the familiar high-pitched, slightly hysterical tone of the Prague numbers, and a moment later I was speaking with Viktor. I could hardly do this from the castle, even if my hosts were out.

"A straightforward three-cam combination shouldn't be too difficult. If you've got the number, of course, first set the dial to zero. First number: try turning the dial to the right, next to the left, and the third back to the right. It's basically three numbers." — I closed my eyes. I simply couldn't deal with this... "If that doesn't work, try to the left to begin with. Now if you don't have the number, then I can do a lock like that in just under three hours, normally. Having a stethoscope helps, of course…"

I awoke from my trance: "And what happens if I have neither three hours nor such an instrument?"

"As I once said to you, dynamite is the best."

"I think it might waken my hosts. I am told they are light sleepers."

"By the way, what make is the thing?"

"Sargent and Greenleaf, from New York…"

"Jeeesus-Maria!"

As I left the station building, none too encouraged and not in the best of moods, the sister was there, still mounted. She had red hair and that insipidly white skin that accompanies it. Worse still she was "all aglow" — that is, sweating. As was Gaston. I am sure, as far as her wretched hair is concerned, she would use that frightful word *auburn*. Damn her; damn auburn — next thing she'll be telling me her favourite colour is *mauve*!

"I saw Yellow Fever outside."

I know, you're fishing. What was I doing? — you want to know. "I was finding out the train times. I must go on to Vienna in the next day or so."

I caught the eye of the stationmaster who was just stepping out into the weak morning sun. I really would make a hopeless criminal — lying is man's work, surely?

ာ

When I had agreed with Maria to look after Richard for two hours between his supper and bedtime, I have to confess I had malign intentions. Not having any children of my own rather helped, I fancy. I mean the wicked witch of fairy stories isn't also a cheery mum during daylight hours, is she?

"Shall we have a little quiz, young man?" I asked him, as sweetly as I could manage.

"What kind of quiz?" he asked sullenly.

"Why, numbers of course!"

His strangely adult — yet also strangely babyish — face brightened.

"I want you to write down on this piece of paper all kinds of numbers — just ordinary numbers. To see how well you remember them."

"And the prize? Mummy always gives me rewards."

"Ten kreuzers if you get them all right."

He smiled. We were off to a good start.

"First one: in Vienna you doubtless have a laundry which collects all your sheets. They will all bear the same number. Do you know what it is?"

"You're wrong. They all have a special embroidered label — 'Taaffe', and a crown. Do I get points for being right, even though you are wrong?"

"I suppose so. Next, how many days old are you?"

"Three thousand and thirteen," he replied before I had time to think. No sense in arguing.

"Good, now number three: how many books are there in your library?"

"Grandpappy's library has six thousand, two hundred and forty-eight. Pappy has another eight hundred and sixty-two in the corridor to the chapel."

Sounded reasonable. "Excellent," I said.

"Lastly… what's the number of the combination of the silver safe — I am sure you don't know that!"

"Of course I don't. It's a secret. That's unfair!"

Damn — and damn again.

The poor boy's arm was moving in that agitated fashion once more. Flapping — that's what it was doing. I should have brought some chocolate, perhaps.

"But if I get it for you later, will it still count… the ten kreuzers, I mean?"

"Yes… yes, of course. But how…?"

"I imagine there are about eight thousand two hundred combinations, but I know a way! If you want, I can show you. But you must promise you won't tell."

"No, *I* won't tell. Not a soul!"

We agreed a secret rendezvous that night at half-past nine, by the door to the servants' passage.

When I was engaged to my husband, and we did a good year of house parties together, I got quite used to corridor-creeping in strange mansions and castles. And there was the time before that... before I was engaged. However, I have to say, it was never for a tryst with a seven-year-old!

Chapter Five

Caught in the Act

The muffled double strike of the half hour could be heard from the passage on the other side of the baize-covered door to the service rooms; otherwise the house was quite silent. I had made my apologies soon after the coffee had been served and retired to my room. I should think the others soon went up too. There is really nothing to do in the country, and I was sure my hosts must by now have exhausted every possible topic of conversation between them. Where was the boy? Hadn't his parents taught him yet that the paramount virtue is punctuality? At least by being deliciously late a woman can excite a man by giving the first signs of not being too virtuous!

I was peeved because I was nervous. It was simply impossible to come up with any plausible excuse if I was caught out... if we were caught out. How could I ever hold my head up in Society after such a scandal — a common thief, using children for one's crimes: the thing was unpardonable.

I heard a tap and looked up. Hidden high up in the plasterwork cornices of the hallway was a tiny window. The grinning face of the boy was visible before it disappeared, presumably to run down some hidden staircase — the kind Morštejn has to allow servants to remove night-soil from the rooms. It still lacked bathrooms in three of its four wings.

Little Richard, clad in starched nightshirt and red velvet bedroom slippers, opened the baize door from the servants' side and soon we were inside the butler's pantry and before our adversary: the steel door of the safe. Without needless talk he drew up a small wooden crate and, standing on it, began at the dial. In his other hand he held a paper which was filled with sequences of numbers. His little fingers were terribly agile and the dial moved rapidly this way and that.

"They call this cracking the number 'by brute force' — that is, trying every combination. I'd read that in a novel I wasn't supposed to read in Daddy's library. In theory, it should take three hundred and sixty hours…"

That long! My God, I thought it would take minutes. "But that's impossible," I began.

"Ssshh," the little fellow whispered, "I'm just picking up the first wheel…"

There was the faintest sound from within the grey steel door.

"One done. Two more to go, but they get harder," he said, but without looking round to me. His nimble fingers quickly resumed their long, if somewhat circuitous, journey of exploration.

After what was probably only a few minutes, but which had seemed like several millennia, he relaxed a second. For the first time he looked up at me. My expression was still wearing the shock of all those impossible hours to come.

"It won't take that long. I've worked out that it can't take longer than 2.78 hours," he said. His piece of paper was filled with pencil calculations. I supposed I was lucky to have found a little genius.

At length, during which time I felt I must have sufficiently aged to look like that unwrapped mummy in the Vienna museum, he drew back. There was now a satisfying — and highly audible — clunk from within the mechanism.

"Good," he said — at last turning round, "that's done it. Do I get my reward now? The number is…"

"But aren't you going to open it?"

"You said you wanted the number," he replied, looking extremely mistrustful.

I had to keep him on my side, otherwise he might spill the beans. "Well, I thought that might just prove it, that's all."

"Then you don't understand. This has the famous time delay lock. That's why it says New York on it. It's from there."

"So we can't open it?"

"Oh, yes, it will open half an hour after the combination is turned."

To be condemned to a further thirty minutes was like a life sentence. "Here you are," I said, rummaging in my skirt pocket for what I had promised him. "Run along now. I shall wait so that when it does open, I can close it properly. I just turn the dial, do I?"

He nodded, giving me what seemed the most suspicious of glances, then ran off.

Left on my own I found that I thought I heard noises. I nearly jumped out of my skin when I felt something touch me, but it was only the kitchen cat brushing against me. I also found myself staring at that steel door much as a cat, like the one now purring in anticipation, stares at its empty bowl believing that by so doing it will magically fill up. I should have brought a book to read… or something, but then I had switched the light out when the boy left. Only a slant of moonlight filtered in from the courtyard window.

Somehow the time did pass. At the appointed moment there was another mechanical noise and the door just opened. Inside an electric lamp had already gone on. My pulse raced. The endeavour was going to be a success, I just knew it.

As the sound of the mechanism died away there was the sound of a single pair of hands clapping. Someone else was in the room, behind me, clapping slowly. I was terrified.

"Well done, Beatrice," said Henry's voice. That boy must have run straight to his father — but in that, at least, I was wrong…

"I don't know how you did it," he went on coldly, "very clever, I'm sure. I must say I thought a Sargent and Greenleaf would be more secure than this, but thank heavens the secret alarm worked. And what are you after, the gold table centrepiece presented by the Hungarian Parliament? Maria tells me you've already asked for jewels…"

"I… I…" I didn't know what to say. And damn Mamma with those blasted jewels!

"I happen to think that centrepiece is the ugliest thing on God's Earth. It's heavily insured in the hope that someone does make off with it — but not a guest of the family."

Now I shouldn't confess this. It does nothing for my reputation as a detective, but I burst into tears. It was all too much to bear, far too much. All I remember, apart from my wailing and trying to mop up a flood with my handkerchief, was his voice saying — perhaps just a little reassuringly — "Come with me."

We were in the study when I came to my senses. I was seated on a small sofa; he was standing over me. He had had to light a lamp as the castle's electricity-generating apparatus was switched off at midnight. I had not said anything to him about my real purpose. But was it better that I should be ostracised by Society — when word got round that I was no better than a common burglar — than that I should betray some secret and arcane wish of the Emperor?

Henry's prompting solved my dilemma. "I can't believe you wanted the family silver," he said calmly, offering me a dry handkerchief, "Your husband probably hasn't got much, from what I know, but I assume Morštejn is groaning with it...."

"Yes, and mostly in the bad taste of the last century," I found myself saying. I was obviously climbing out of total despair.

I went on: "It's a secret. An Imperial secret... I simply cannot divulge why..."

"Why you were breaking into my safe! Come now, Beatrice..."

He was getting a little angry again. I felt those tears rising; they would at least blot out this terrible nightmare. But Henry changed his tack.

"This family's greatness is founded on Imperial secrets. Look..."

He grabbed my wrist somewhat roughly, pulled me to my feet and opened another door in the bookcases — this time a full-size door and not a cupboard. "Look!"

He almost pushed me through it. Like a common criminal being pushed into a prison cell, I imagined.

I found myself in a complete room full of row upon row of file boxes on shelves, each carefully numbered or with a word or two of description. "I suppose you're here about some damn papers. Every so often someone tries it, sent by that damn fool of an Emperor. If he wants to keep secrets, then why doesn't he destroy stuff?"

"Yes. It's about the Crown Prince. I wasn't sent directly by the All Highest, but I must find out what happened in 1889… or, more importantly, why."

I actually liked Henry. He was straightforward. Perhaps that was why on first impression I found him lacking in potential greatness: he wasn't devious, as I'm sure his father must have been. He was right — one imperial secret more or less would be no matter. I simply told him everything. "I hope you don't mind if I have a cigarette," was all he said, as I neared the end of my narrative, and then he was silent.

At length he leaned back against one of the bookcases, as if he needed it to support his weighty burden. "That's a tricky one," he muttered, " — for you especially."

"Yes. Mamma said I was caught between two millstones."

He exhaled some smoke. The Turkish tobacco caught my nostrils. "She knows?"

I blushed, and I detected a wry smile being held back on his lips.

"I know that my father and Chief of Police Baron Kraus, and the one or two other important figures in this case gave a solemn oath to the Emperor never to talk. And, indeed, Father never spoke to any of his family about Rudolf's death, and we knew we were to ask him no questions about it. He died rather unexpectedly, as I'm sure all these papers wouldn't simply be here like this, if he'd had time to plan."

Henry put down his cigarette for a moment, pulled a set of library steps across to a particular shelf and brought down a box file. In it was a single envelope, heavily sealed.

"I do know this: there's one other copy of what's in this envelope. It is presented to each new Prime-Minister on accession, with instructions not to open it. It is said to contain the secrets of the Crown Prince affair."

"Said to?"

"Yes, because I also know that it contains nothing but sheets of old newspaper, as this one does. My father used the racing papers, too! This I remember because I saw him stuffing the envelopes when I was a little boy."

"So there was something to hide, then?"

"It seems so. But, typical of the Habsburg skulduggery, it's something extremely important and at the same time absolutely nothing. On the other hand, we do have in here all the correspondence files." He took down another box. "These are the original papers exchanged between my father and Baron Krauss," and he drew out another longish official envelope. "Take them up to your room, by all means."

Suddenly — and almost painlessly — I had perhaps gained my objective. I looked at him with a mixture of joy and surprise as I took the envelope.

"You are, after all, here on official business," he said as he turned down the wick of the lamp.

૭

I found that Sabine had been in my room. A lamp was burning, but dimly, making a pool of rather comforting warm light onto the bedclothes. She had turned down the quilt and left my nightdress on the pillow for me, so I was soon settled in and had almost forgotten the strong emotions of the evening. Out of the envelope I pulled letters, both originals and duplicate copies, and a collection of twenty or thirty reports on heavy sheets of government paper. On the upper left corner of each was an official dry seal and above it the words *Streng Reservat* — Most Restricted. The address on each of the letters was either Prime Minister to Chief of Police or vice versa, and each began "Your Excellency…"

As I was getting prepared to read the first page of the bundle, a small slip of paper fell out that had been pinned to one of the papers. I smoothed it out and saw it was a telegram sent from Heiligenkreuz, the location of the great Cistercian abbey where Rudolf's young lover had been hastily buried, near to Mayerling. It was addressed to Chief of Police Krauss, 1.2.1889 : 10.39am. It read, simply:

EVERYTHING DISPOSED OF STOP HABRDA

I guessed this was the report of the officer at the scene — poor Mary's body had been "disposed of" — no funeral, no mass, no chance for her family to grieve. It was a heartless beginning to the cold drama that these papers would unfold.

The Report of the Court Commission described the situation during the hours and days after the catastrophe that had taken place at Mayerling, Prince Rudolf's very private hunting lodge in the Vienna woods:

The Crown Prince was in a frightful condition, his brain sprayed forth and clinging partly to the walls. The revolver was found in or next to his hand. In the case of the Baroness Vetsera, her carotid artery had been hit from the side. A coagulated flow of blood extended from her open mouth to her feet.

Then there were the post-mortem examinations describing that Archduke Rudolf had shot himself in the mouth, which explained the shattering of the temple. Mary Vetsera's corpse had been examined at Mayerling. She had been placed in a dark, dusty little storeroom — another of the reports even admitting it was the wood-shed — and there laid naked on a table. Only some while afterwards was she completely covered with her clothes and by her fur coat, then simply left lying there for nearly two days. The result of the correspondence was that both Taaffe and Krauss concurred that "with the girl's consent, the Crown Prince killed her and then himself."

Yet there were several things which jarred. In all the reports, various witnesses heard what turned out to be a pistol shot shortly after 6.10am. There was a second shot, which the Crown Prince's personal servant, his valet Johann Loschek, said he had heard immediately after. In a personal statement pinned to one of the last pages of the file, he said that he had been woken at 6.10 by his master, fully dressed. In his first statement, reported by Count Hoyos, the Crown Prince was wearing his dressing gown, and roused Loschek in his room which adjoined the ante-room to the Prince's bedroom at 6.30. His statements both agreed in that Loschek was ordered to waken his master again at half-past seven, and to order his breakfast. He was also told to go and order his coachman Bratfisch to get his carriage ready for the same time, 7.30. Then, whistling, the Crown Prince had returned to his bedroom. It was while going to find Bratfisch that Loschek said he heard the shots. Yet the hurriedly done post-mortem on Mary Vetsera, carried out by lamplight in the wood-shed, concluded that Countess Mary had been shot several hours before the Crown Prince. The revolver found in the bedroom had had only two shots fired from it.

Whichever way one read the various statements, there were nearly two hours missing from the time when Loschek said the Crown Prince roused him until 8.09, when Count Hoyos had been apprised of the locked bedroom door and the silence, and decided with Prince Coburg to have the door broken down. All the reports compiled from the various witness statements simply chose to gloss over this important detail — to ignore it, in fact. This aroused my curiosity to the extent that long after I had put the papers down and extinguished the lamp, I couldn't get to sleep.

I thought about Dr Widerhofer, the Emperor's physician, who stated that the bullet had entered the temple. Yet it had already been reported that the Crown Prince had shot himself in the mouth. Herr Slatin had been secretary to the Court Commission and I had read his report — what he had seen only hours after the discovery of the body: "Rudolf's face showed hardly any disfigurement, but the crown of his head was blown off. Blood had flowed from the top of the skull and parts of the brain were exposed and scattered."

The crown of the head had been so mutilated that Prince Hohenlohe's plan had been to have a wax model made of the whole head by the well-known sculptor, Tilgner, and to have this attached to a dummy body for the funeral. But Tilgner had needed too long to do this. In the end, the Crown Prince's shattered head was plastered and bandaged — and visible traces of burns on the face were covered in pink wax for when he lay in state in his open coffin.

All the powers that had existed in Austria had conspired to wrap the whole thing up speedily and effectively — yet there were still these mysterious inconsistencies in the basic evidence. I heard the courtyard clock strike half-past three, or perhaps it was four, then I must finally have fallen asleep. It had been a harrowing day.

Sabine dressed me at eight and commented that my *fraicheur* was somewhat lacking. I blinked into the looking glass as she was brushing my hair. What I could make out was certainly a terrifying spectre. "Perhaps that's what I will look like when I'm forty," I commented.

"But Madame, this is today, 'ow you look…"

The French really do not have a sense of irony. *Why I put up with it, I just do not know*, I was thinking, although wisely saying nothing. What on Earth would I do without her?

Over breakfast Maria said nothing, either about my appearance or about the near *fracas* I had had with her husband. That could only mean one thing: Henry had said nothing. For that, he was a saint.

After breakfast I found Henry in the study, and returned the file to him.

"Interesting, isn't it?" He motioned me to sit down.

"Thought-provoking, I should say." I was being cautious.

"Amazing how callous the old boy can be when he wants to be. He could have gone to his son's deathbed — a half-hour by train, an hour and a half by carriage to Mayerling, at the most — but he always avoids being present at the scene of action. He prefers to have everything submitted to him on paper."

"I was shocked by the Emperor's callous disregard for the Crown Prince's companion in death, that ghastly telegram sent by Habrda…"

"Yes, Police Superintendent Habrda's report — you saw that? — the body of Mary Vetsera that had lain in the wood-shed for nearly two days then taken by carriage at night to the church-yard of Heiligenkreuz Abbey, all dressed and propped up with a broomstick, between her two uncles. But by that time our August Presence had shaken off his grief as a dog shakes himself when emerging from water.'"

"There was something I didn't understand," I admitted. "In one of the reports it was claimed that the Emperor said to Prince Hohenlohe, 'My son died like a tailor.'"

"He's said that more than once. I'm told that this refers to one John Libényi — a Hungarian who tried to assassinate him in 1853. He was a tailor's assistant, but I can't say I know exactly how he died."

"And there's the discrepancies about the times of the deaths...?"

Henry looked up at me. "If you believe the shots weren't one after the other, then it means that Rudolf for some hours lacked the courage to kill himself. My father didn't particularly like the Crown Prince, but he didn't think he was a coward."

How terribly complicated it all was. The Emperor only wanted a simple answer, but to get to it, I had to go through all this.

Henry continued, "Don't you think it would be interesting to find out, for example, if he was shot in the temple or in the mouth?"

I didn't answer, other than a querying look.

"I mean," he went on, "if it was covered up that he was shot in the temple — then, why?"

"You mean, it would be unlikely that a third party would shoot him via the mouth?"

"Exactly, Beatrice. You have it!"

He leaned back in the padded leather armchair, almost with a sense of relief. "I suppose it's our British ancestry, yours and mine, but I don't think we should follow the 'official' line, do you? Yes, there are many inconsistencies which cry out for clarification from all reports — but the big question is so big that it is never even alluded to."

His eyes stared into mine, maybe searching for any small flicker which might render me unsafe for his next thoughts....

"The Emperor had all the resources of the State, and a story which was almost under control — and yet the official version ends up with Rudolf being a murderer, then possibly a coward — but then certainly a suicide."

"Yes, I think I'm beginning to see what you mean. In one of those reports there was something about French agents or Russian ones — or were they Prussian?"

"Exactly. How easy it would have been for the official version, for example, to have found that Rudolf — and his young mistress, too — had been murdered by unknown foreign agents."

"Yes, I think…" I began, but there was no stopping Henry now. This was obviously something he had thought a lot about.

"It can mean only one thing…" He gave me another strong look, but this time I was in his confidence. "It can only mean that the truth was even worse…"

"That your father and the others felt relieved that the accepted version they put out was safer, shall we say, than what really had happened?"

"I think we are seeing eye to eye."

Now I was beginning to doubt my effortless flow of logic. "But what could be worse than what was said had happened?"

"Suppose, for instance, that Rudolf was murdered, and that it had been ordered from very high up indeed…."

"You are trying to say—?"

Henry's voice lowered to a grave whisper as if even here there might be spies, yet outside the window it was a very ordinary grey day and in the distance a smudge of smoke from a railway train crawled across the white landscape. His eyes once more raised to mine.

"The All Highest. Yes. Precisely."

Chapter Six

Into the Depths

Two nights later, I was waiting in a fiacre on the far side of the Neuer Markt in Vienna. Directly across the empty market stalls I could see the somewhat austere façade of the Capuchin Church. A lot had transpired since that conversation with Henry. He had persuaded me that I needed to find out exactly how Rudolf had died, and the only way to do that was to open his tomb... over there in the *Kaisergruft* — the Imperial crypt below the Capuchin Church. He had apparently been planning this for himself for some while. He had four strong men from his estate, who were not known in Vienna. He knew one of the Capuchin brothers could be "compliant" — which meant he would accept a bribe. An old Jewish doctor would conduct the examination. He had once been retained by the Vetseras, so he had sufficient motive to assist. Henry himself supervised the lanterns, ropes, crowbars, and also had the forethought to arrange for his estate carpenter to be with us, too, to make good any damage to the late Crown Prince's sarcophagus. Our presence must never be discovered.

I had every confidence this would work smoothly. Henry was not a desk man, like his father, but a man of action and deed. According to Maria, he often used to forgo comfortable nights at home in his bed to spend them in some rough shelter on the hills, stalking a stag. Yet Maria had, at the last minute, become the problem. She had absolutely refused to let Henry go down into the Imperial vault… what if we were caught? It was too much of a risk for a man in his position, she said. It was impossible.

I was somewhat annoyed to see Henry capitulate to his wife, however good her logic, and in a few short minutes he had cried off. He must also have let Maria into the secret, which I wasn't expecting, and didn't care for. He had, however, arranged everything — just left me in the lurch! Now I was waiting for Müller to arrive from Prague. Sabine was waiting for me in a small hotel nearby, a hotel Henry knew of, a hotel that does not want to know who one is, and keeps no proper register. I did not ask him how he knew of such a place. There are, I am told, many such establishments around the Neuer Markt. I could imagine them filled with girls who normally spend the day dressed only in their chemises and black stockings, draped on red plush and gilt sofas. However, usually hunting types don't have — shall we say? — cosmopolitan lives. It is with this hope that hunters' wives console themselves.

I was not frightened in the least at what I might see below the Capuchin Church. I vividly remembered my brother Max leading me down into the family vault below the chapel at Morštejn when I was about twelve. That had certainly been terrifying. Max had led the way through the various elaborate coffins of the Morštejns until we were right at the back of the vault where there was one small plain wooden casket. "It is the only one here who is not one of us," he had explained, putting the candle he held onto a projecting ledge, "Old Doctor Hausenblass was our great-great-grandfather's tutor. He went on to live with the family for the rest of his life as a faithful retainer. He was much liked. That's why he is here."

It appeared the lid had already been opened before. Inside was lying a man in finely stitched leather boots, silk stockings, and a neat black outfit. His skin was like stretched parchment and his hair was still red. His eyes had dried to almost nothing. "These maggots are new," Max had said, "probably because he's been opened before." But there was nothing frightening about the old man; he had, after all, died in his sleep at age eighty-one. It was simply the course of Nature. The crypt had lost its horror.

Punctual as ever, Müller was soon visible striding across the square to where I was waiting. "Good evening, Milady. I have brought your gardening gloves as instructed."

Then as St Stephen's Cathedral nearby boomed out the hour, our small force converged upon the monastery church. We were to go to a side door where a hooded monk awaited us. He unlocked a heavy bronze door and we made our way in silence down the steps. I was slightly alarmed to hear the lock being turned behind us. Müller was, as ever, reassuring. "I assume it is for our own protection," he whispered. "I don't believe such crypts have keyholes on this side. The occupants rarely need to leave."

I supposed the dead didn't need electric light either. The light from the candle lanterns made wild shadows as we passed, making the place, in contrast to Morštejn, exceedingly creepy. The elaborate bronze sarcophagi of the Habsburg Emperors were adorned with all the images which show death as a mockery of Earthly pomp: skulls wearing their elaborate crowns being a favourite motif. And were those fine bronze teeth locked into some kind of grin… some cruel grimace? We filed by the huge double sarcophagus of the Empress Marie Theresa and her husband. The more recent emperors and their wives were interred in a cross vault beyond.

I found myself catching up with the old doctor, who was lingering at an inscription on one of the tombs. "Doctor…?" I asked. "We haven't been introduced."

"Just call me Doctor," he replied. "It is better without names."

Yes, I supposed he was right. He looked slightly sinister, lit from beneath by the lantern he was carrying and which had been directed to the bronze plaque he had been reading. "You know the Emperors were dismembered — their hearts to be kept in silver urns in the Augustinerkirche, and their entrails in the catacombs of the Stephansdom." I presume he offered this in an attempt at casual conversation to make up for his rather curt abandonment of the social rules. Of course, casual conversation is all relative to circumstances. It wouldn't have done at the dinner table.

Finally we were there. On one side was the sarcophagus of the Emperor's wife, Sissy. On the other, his only son, Rudolf. The central space was vacant. This was undoubtedly where Franz-Josef the First would lie, in time.

Müller hurried up to me. "The men ask permission to begin."

I nodded my assent. It took only thirty or so minutes for the lid of the sarcophagus to be lifted and the inner coffin to be opened. Thirty minutes, I might add, that seemed hours and with the constant fear that we would be found out with each muffled tap of the hammers or tortuous, squeaking wrench of the steel crowbars. The bronze celebration of death all around us was getting to me.

Müller held up his lantern for me. Apparently, I was expected to look. There before me was what remained of the great hope of the Habsburgs. The great hope of the Czechs, too. The only impediment to his dreams had been his father.

"We're lucky his head is intact. I understood that the faces of the Habsburg Emperors were stoved in at burial," the doctor said rather matter-of-factly.

"I don't understand. Who could do that?" I was shocked by the idea.

"It was part of the rites — with the heart being extracted and sent to the Augustinerkirche, and the entrails to St Stephen's."

"The entrails?"

"Thought once to be the seat of the emotions. Their faces were disfigured so that they might not appear too vainglorious in front of their Maker. But Rudolf, of course, was never Emperor."

The upper part of Prince Rudolf's head was bandaged, and one side of the lower half had turned quite black.

The doctor peered down at him. "Some chemical has bleached through the cosmetics," he said drily. "Now, if you will excuse me, I must begin my work."

I stood back. Beneath the bandage appeared to be plaster of Paris, as the reports had indicated. As the doctor began lifting a flap of the scalp, I decided to withdraw. "Wadding," I heard him mumble. "The skull is much damaged."

Some of the estate men were now playing a game of cards on Sissy's sarcophagus. They were quiet, I had to admit. As a woman of Society, I was not, of course, invited to join them. Müller came to the rescue with a small flask of spirits. "I took the liberty…" he began. I waved him not to bother to continue. Of course it came from home! And I held out my hand eagerly for the small silver cup.

"I hope you will be joining me," I said. In such circumstances one shouldn't stand on rank.

Over an hour elapsed. I was then aware of the men moving in to close the various lids and make their work invisible. The doctor approached me, packing instruments into his bag.

"Well?" I was impatient, not to mention frozen. However, before he could speak, Müller — who had been keeping watch through the only small grille which covered a ventilation flue — suddenly spun round, with his finger over his lips.

"Hold the work," he whispered.

Everyone froze where they stood and lanterns were either extinguished or their slides drawn. In the eerie silence we could all hear footsteps through the flue, which acted like a speaking tube. After shuffling around for a moment, these footfalls slowly made their way into the distance. Everyone got back to work, and as lanterns were re-lit, I noticed beads of sweat on the doctor's temples. He continued in a quieter whisper:

"He wasn't shot through the mouth, that I can say. Some reports stated he had shot himself that way. Not true. I believe he was shot through the temple. I found traces of the pink wax they used to cover up the burns…"

"Suicide?"

"It is difficult to say precisely. Yes, suicide is possible. But it could have been… otherwise… too. And there's more. There appeared to be so much damage to that side of the head… damage to the skull. I have seen this many times when I worked as a young man attached to the coroner's office. If I had to make a guess, I would say he was bludgeoned first."

"Which would, of course, throw suicide in doubt?"

"Quite so. I am sorry I cannot be more positive in my findings. You appreciate the difficulties."

"Doctor, you have given me and my associate quite enough to think about."

The doctor, whose name I would never know, shuffled uneasily on his feet, as if he could not go.

"And there is something else, Milady," he said, as if after contemplating not telling me.

"Yes — don't hesitate…"

"His whole body bears the telltale marks — a darkening of the skin, amongst other signs — that the Crown Prince had been suffering from the advanced stages of syphilis. It would have been evident in his eyes, I am sure, by the small size of his pupils."

He bowed, turned, and walked away.

My God, that could explain why Mary Vetsera had chosen to die. At seventeen she must have known what she had ahead of her — that she could never have children, or at least that any children she might have could be in all likelihood weak, sickly, and die early — no gift to a husband.

❧

The cold night air of the Neuer Markt quite revived my spirit. I had got away with a most audacious act — or so I thought. On the other side of the square I noticed a very plain four-wheeler, so plain that it immediately aroused my suspicion. As the rest of my party emerged from the vault, I saw the carriage drive away. It was nothing — said one voice within me… but was it? — said another.

Müller had a nondescript Vienna fiacre waiting in a side street. Soon I found myself at my discreet hotel not five minutes away. I told Müller to meet me tomorrow at the station. To his raised eyebrow my shocked expression reminded him not to judge by appearances, but he did not move.

"Yes, Müller?"

"Milady. I still have the unopened letters you asked me to bring. Does Milady require them?"

I had forgotten. "Just that blue envelope, if you please. I can deal with the rest at home."

"And there's something else, Milady, which I'd quite forgotten to tell. If I may…?"

I nodded. Müller was such a stickler for form. If a ship were to sink he'd be asking permission to cling onto a floating door or some such.

"The priest in Prague — of the Church of the Maltese Knights — he has now left the city, and they say he has gone back to Paris. I believe Your Ladyship wished to be informed…"

"Yes, yes," I replied somewhat irritably. It wasn't his fault, but I hated being reminded of all the things I should have been doing rather than fooling around on the whim of a damned old Emperor spooked by too many bad memories. I'd almost forgotten. He of the game leg. "Anyway, that will be all for tonight."

Müller turned to go on his way. Then I thought to call after him. "And you did wonderfully tonight. Without you, I don't know…"

But he was already gone into the night.

The old crone receptionist gave me a cold stare. "Good evening, *Fraulein*," she said, "the gentleman is waiting in your room."

If I had been the hitting sort of person, I would have been sorely tempted to give in to my weakness. My handbag was quite heavy enough to deal a very satisfactory blow. But this insult to a patently obviously married woman, I would have to suffer. This "hotel" was, I supposed, nothing more than *une maison de passe*. No one could suspect my presence here, at least.

As I ascended the narrow staircase to the first floor, noting the dust and the shabby linen runner on a windowsill, I wondered if Maria knew of Henry's familiarity with such places — how awful for her, if she did. And then there was Karel; did my husband have some mistress tucked away in Vienna after all? And did they have to use a place like this?

"Good evening, Henry," I said on entering my room. "We did it."

He looked relieved — and impatient: "And?"

"Like everything in this saga, nothing wholly conclusive."

I explained the night's findings as I slit open the Munich envelope and read its contents. My eyes ran over Marie Larisch's handwriting, as I had suspected — but far from being a little social note following our meeting, it was something much more intriguing:

> *Dear Beatrice,*
>
> *I wasn't very candid with you. The matter is quite simple. There were two identical steel boxes. Crown Prince Rudolf gave me one of them and told me, if anything happened to him, to pass it to Archduke Johann Salvator. This I did. I hope this might be of some use to you…*

I showed it to Henry.

"Who knows what this famous steel box contains? What secret could endanger the Imperial power? On the other hand, finding it would be like coming across the Holy Grail."

"Maybe this is why I have been engaged by the All Highest — perhaps just to prove that the secret, if it exists, is harmless. But clearly something's bothering him…."

"These days the Archduchess — Johann's sister — is in Paris. I can find out when she is expected to visit Bohemia next."

But I was also thinking of that old priest. The lame priest.

"Paris, then," I said.

Chapter Seven

Entente Hardly Cordiale

It seemed strange to find myself in Paris again without any thought of strolling by the shops on the Place Vendôme, looking in the windows of the great jewellers, Cartier and Boucheron, or trying out the latest perfumes at Guerlain. Last year's visit had been so brief as not to count. This time I didn't want to attract attention to myself so I stayed at a smaller hotel on the Left Bank, near to the Odeon.

I had been lucky in my journey as I had transferred to a French train at Strasbourg. Sabine was delighted, of course. There was nothing so thorough as the service of a truly first-class train in France. Toilet articles had been put in their proper places, night-clothes laid-out, the light adjusted, the bed turned down, the slippers in place — and there were farewell gifts for each one of his departing guests with the card of the carriage superintendent when we arrived at the Gare de l'Est.

Late into the night I had been reading a book about occultism. The Paris occultists seemed to be particularly strong, and "spirit reading" seemed much more common than the occasional party trick, as it was in Prague... and yet I had been curiously plagued by things I had remembered from all those official reports of the Mayerling Affair — particularly from that of the castle warder, Zwerger. There was Rudolf's last telegram, lying on the bedside table, ready to send and addressed to the Pope, begging permission to be given a Catholic burial in spite of being a suicide. And Mary Vetsera's final note, which ended in the pathetic "Bratfisch played the pipes wonderfully." Yes, Rudolf's coachman had played his bagpipes for them on that last, fateful evening. How long ago all this now seemed, and Johann Salvator was today almost forgotten. Johann and Rudolf had been the two swaggering royal princes of the Austrian empire, young men of intelligence and vigour. Between them it must have seemed then that they held the world in the palms of their hands. Today, no one really knew for certain if Johann Salvator was even dead — and Rudolf, as only I knew, was black in his tomb. It was said that even Salvator's sister — his mother having now passed on — didn't really know.

I had an introduction to a friend of my brother Max. Philip Seymour, who did something at the Paris Bourse, mixed well with kings and queens — especially those in exile in the city, with Italian noblemen and with French countesses. In fact, said Max, Philip collected them. His mantelpiece, so I had been told, was a virtual forest of social invitations, although all those white cards might have looked more like a graveyard! Max had felt sure he would know the Archduchess, and that there would be some social event or other at which it could be engineered that I would meet her. Philip had arranged to meet me at the Les Deux Magots, one of the great *brasseries* of the Left Bank.

No sooner had I begun walking with Sabine down the broad Boulevard Saint Michel with its pavement cafés and wide roadway jammed with traffic, than my eyes were drawn to one of the circular kiosks entirely devoted to advertising, which are a feature of the French capital.

What I saw on the kiosk nearly made my heart stop. I was approaching at an angle and could only see a part of the main advertisement. Wasn't it exactly the same as I had seen framed on the wall at the late Wilajalba Frikell's? I hastened forward… yes, it was the same. I remembered the little fairy characters, and the Egyptian princess rising like a wraith out of her sarcophagus. Looking closely I could see that the lithographic colour printing had left various boxes which could be filled later with ordinary black type. Maybe these posters had been acquired somehow from poor old Frikell's widow, and now they announced:

IRA DEVINE'S WORLD OF SPIRITS SHOW…
ILLUSION! SPIRIT READING! MESMERISM!
THE FIRST EVER VIEWING OF THE LEVITATION OF
PRINCESS AYA!

I staggered back a moment. Devine — surely the murderer, or the man behind the murder, of Orsini, and somehow of causing the death of old Frikell. I felt quite ill.

"Is Madame all right?" I heard Sabine say.

I looked round. Due to the inclement weather the chairs of the pavement tables had all been tipped forward, like so many slumped bodies… and Sabine was steering me towards one of them. For the moment I resisted, but she pushed the chair upright and I felt her arm firmly guide me into it.

"I shall have a glass of water fetched, shall I?"

I didn't answer, but my eyes returned to the poster.

"The magic show, Madame? It starts in two hours, so it says. The first performance in Paris…"

Resolve now gripped me as the first drops of rain began to fall, and I stood up. Almost in an instant the whole of the Boulevard St Michel was transformed into a sea of umbrellas.

"Then we go to it," I said.

❧

I think we managed to get the last two seats available. We found ourselves in the stalls, and yet even in the very low light (I assume to make the magic trickery harder to detect) I could discern the glitter of expensive jewellery on matronly bosoms and pinprick glints from tiny diamond studs on starched shirt fronts. Devine had attracted no ordinary audience. There was hushed excitement as the curtains opened and onto a bare, dark stage — bathed only in a spotlight's glare — strode Ira Devine himself.

He seemed a short man, dark hair well waxed, and by his gaudy silk waistcoat was without doubt an American... either a show-man or a charlatan, or both!

Through a trapdoor in the stage rose a small green baize table on which was an egg, a lemon, and an orange.

"Is there a lady in the house who will lend me her handkerchief?" Devine asked in a rather sharp voice, heavily accented.

I felt Sabine stirring beside me, but motioned her to keep still. There were several offers of handkerchiefs and one was passed forward to him. Devine rolled the handkerchief into a small bundle and placed it beside the other items on the table. Then he picked it up again and rubbed it between his hands — get-ting smaller and smaller all the while — until it disappeared completely.

"Mesdames, messieurs… the handkerchief has now passed into the egg."

Next he picked up the egg and rolled that in his hands until it vanished too. "The egg is now within the lemon," he announced, allowing himself a little smile.

He repeated the process with the lemon. "It is now inside the orange."

Taking now the orange into his hands, he rolled it between his palms until it appeared to be getting smaller and smaller until he literally crushed it into dust. A silver bowl now appeared on the table, and Devine sprinkled the dust into it, and ignited it with a woosh of blue flame. A gong sounded.

Two assistants, dressed as ancient Egyptian priests, now brought onto the stage a wooden box decorated with hieroglyphs from which sprouted a small orange tree, about half a metre across. This was placed on the table over the flames still licking round the silver bowl.

The audience gasped as the leaves of the tree, presumably by some mechanical contrivance, were spreading, twisting, and then falling to reveal white blossoms. Devine passed his hands over the tree in a priestly way and the blossoms fell and its orange fruit began to be visible between the leaves until they grew before our eyes into full-sized oranges. Devine picked some and handed them down to members of the audience in the front row. A lady gave a sharp cry of delight as she discovered it was indeed real fruit.

Just one orange remained and the writhing, twisting leaves and branches became still. It must have been a device of intricate metalwork, wonderfully clever. Passing his hands over the tree once more, Devine directed our eyes to that single fruit which split open… to reveal a rolled handkerchief. He expertly shook it open by a corner: it was the same handkerchief of the lady in the audience, no doubt about it. Without a word he came forward and passed it to her.

It was impressive — a masterly series of tricks and illusions. The audience broke into loud applause, and Devine stepped back as the curtains closed in front of him. I looked round to Sabine. Her eyes were still staring at the curtains, a look of rapturous wonder in them. How easy it seemed for her to suspend disbelief.

The curtains reopened and Devine marched briskly to the centre of the stage again. The audience clapped.

"I would like my three subjects, please…"

At first no-one stirred.

"That is, if it does not discompose you…"

At these words, three men in respectable dark coats, stood up in different parts of the auditorium and then two of them made their way towards, and then onto, the stage. The third, somewhat older than the other two, merely stood at his seat. Was that clerical garb he was wearing? There was something in the manner of all three which wasn't quite natural.

Devine mumbled something to the two men on the stage and then snapped his fingers and it was as if they had come out of a trance. The two men now looked at each other with some surprise, as if for the first time recognising they were with the other that he knew. Indeed, they had such a similar appearance that they must have been brothers — tall, noble in their way, and both with brown, curly hair.

Devine began talking to them in low tones while a chorus of gongs and bells sounded, drowning out what was said. "So you will not be discomposed…" he said in a louder, more distinct voice, and the two resumed their trance-like state.

Over the next few minutes he made these two do some simple but rather ridiculous things which made the audience laugh until he waved his hands and the two gentlemen made their zombie-like ways to their seats again, where they not only remained standing but the third one stood up again. Devine snapped his fingers and the three of them now seemed to come back into the real world. Looking about them, a little confused, they sat down while the audience clapped vigorously.

I felt it was a little distasteful. Sabine looked at me, and was clearly about to ask a question. Before she had mouthed it I answered it for her: "Mesmerism," I said. I had read about it, but this was the first time I had seen it. And now certain things became absolutely clear to me.

The curtains closed again. The orchestra began playing its rather discordant music which it hoped would convince us was ancient Egyptian in origin, though I rather suspected the ancients liked a good tune as much as we do. A big scene change was obviously being undertaken.

When the curtains opened after an interval of five or six minutes, the scenery was of an Egyptian temple. Devine now entered, dressed as a High Priest — or some such — in a long robe. A jewelled turban covered what would have been his very twentieth-century haircut, and only the waxed points of his moustache seemed a little out of place.

"Mesdames et messieurs," he began, "some six years ago my company and I made a trip to Egypt, where the ancient history of gods and pharaohs adorns the walls of the great temple of Karnak." Here he gestured to one of the bulbous plaster columns which flanked either side of the stage, painted with hieroglyphs.

"And where by the light of the moon, on the edge of the desert, in the place where they buried their kings and princesses long, long ago, can sometimes be seen the remarkable sight of a princess rising from her tomb, throwing off her mummy bandages, and revealing once again her beauty which had enslaved the great Pharaoh Tutmosis. Once a year, on this very night, Princess Aya rises up…"

Through a trapdoor in the stage, a mummy in all its bandage-like wrappings appeared on top of a decorated sarcophagus, right behind Devine. He stepped back to be at its side and as he raised his arms, draped with the sleeves of his robe, the wrappings seemed to burst open and we were aware that the mummy was alive. As the bandages dropped away, folds of her diaphanous dress floated in a breeze that gave a startling effect.

"Mesdames et messieurs… the levitation of Princess Aya!" Devine announced, in his best New York French, "For the first time from the sands of Oriental Egypt to be seen here and now by the people of Europe!"

There were cries of disbelief as the figure slowly rose up into the air, defying all the laws of gravitation and with no visible means of support. At a height of perhaps a metre and three-quarters, the levitation ceased and the figure simply hung in the air. It was most extraordinary.

The Egyptian princess' face turned to us. A strange cry came from her pale lips. Was this the Hélène Johanson that Frickell's widow had told me about? — who had been The Great Orsini's lover in Prague? Yes, I think I could make out the same features as in those photographs taken on the Petrín Hill railway. Everything was becoming clearer.

Devine continued, "According to ancient ritual, and to prove to you the absence of all means of support known to mechanical science, I will pass this hoop over the floating body, not once, but twice." One of his assistants handed him a plain cane hoop.

I was straining my eyes, itching to get a glimpse of those tiny wires, each no thicker than sewing thread, which must be supporting the 'Princess Aya.' Devine passed the hoop over her two times, then threw the hoop back to his assistant. He stepped forward to the footlights and spoke to the audience in a quiet, matter-of-fact way:

"Tonight, on this first occasion of the levitation, I wish to convince you that the princess actually floats without any support and so I call upon any one of you to come on stage and look... a gentleman or a lady... someone perhaps interested in the occult or the mysterious... step forward down the aisle, please...."

I immediately felt Sabine rising; she was enraptured. I let her go. She could tell me about the wires! Sabine was indeed the first, and one or two others, who had started further back in the auditorium, melted back into their seats. Devine, the villain with no scruples, took Sabine by the hand and led her towards the floating figure. A spotlight suddenly came on, bathing Sabine in the limelight. She looked a little confused as Devine led her nearer the figure and whispered something to her. Sabine reached forward and touched the princess' hand. This done, Devine swiftly turned her round, the light went off, and he led her back to the edge of the stage.

Next Devine took up a flimsy cloth. "Princess Aya must return under her shroud," he intoned in his priestly voice.

He threw the cloth over the floating body, which seemed to stand erect for a moment then suddenly disappear, leaving only the shroud wavering in the breeze before it, too, fell to the stage floor. For a second there was an awestruck silence, then the applause rang out. Here was The Great Orsini's patent, stolen after all, reproduced and, so it seemed, very successful.

Sabine had returned to her seat. Over the applause I managed to ask her what she had seen.

"Nothing Madame. That bright light — it was in my eyes. I could hardly see anything..."

"The wires, Sabine? Weren't there dozens of wires... very thin wires?"

The poor girl was nearly in tears. "No, Madame. I really could see nothing."

A good trick, I thought. This whole thing was merely about fooling the audience. I supposed that Devine would make a lot of money out of it, but was it worth all that had gone before? My reflections were interrupted by Devine returning to the stage, this time dressed in his normal attire — with the same unspeakable waistcoat. Americans have the effrontery to call the garment a vest.

From the wings the princess — Hélène Johanson, without a shadow of a doubt now — stepped forward to take her bow with Devine. "And, of course, my three subjects..." Here he gestured towards the audience: "If I do not discompose you." At those words, the three stood up in their seats as if they had been dolls jerked upwards on invisible strings. The audience clapped loudly for them, Devine snapped his fingers and the three sat down, looking a little confused. Clearly mesmerism was potentially a very dangerous thing, if used by the wrong person. I even wondered if it could be used to subvert larger groups of people, whole nations, even... but that was obviously a quite ridiculous notion.

More bows by Devine and Johanson. A girl from the audience brought to them a large bouquet of flowers. The enthusiastic clapping continued as I kept my eyes on just one of the three subjects. Could he possibly be the priest for whom I was searching in Paris? Was this Father Antoine, lately of the Knights of Malta Church in Prague?

As the audience, after several more curtain calls, began to leave, I was determined to follow this priest. He was about to leave by an exit on the other side of the auditorium. I could, I thought, quickly get out to the foyer and then cross to where he was going. Luckily, his way was for the moment blocked by the press of other theatre-goers leaving the stalls. I managed to get to the foyer, and told Sabine to get my cloak, and, if she lost me, to go back to our hotel. I was determined not to lose him, but then I saw Philip Seymour — it had to be him, so obviously English, and looking around — for me.

Even if I barely spoke to him, I would, in the lost seconds, lose my quarry, so instead I tried to look pleased to see him.

"So you got my telegram. I am sorry it was at such short notice...."

"Yes. I looked for you, but couldn't see you. It was so damned dark in there. They allowed me to stand."

"I... well, I just had to see it..."

"All Paris will be talking about it tonight. The levitation was quite extraordinary. But you want a contact for the Archduchess of Tuscany, I understand? While you are getting your cloak, I shall be outside seeing if I can get a cab."

Sabine got me my cloak and soon we were in a fiacre.

"So where are we going?" I ventured to ask Philip.

"To St Sulpice. There's someone there who knows the Archduchess well, so I'm told."

"He's at the church?"

Philip Seymour laughed. "Oh, no. He lives in the street opposite. But he does call himself Abbé, although I understand he is no longer a functioning priest — some financial misunderstanding, they say, with the Jesuits. There was some princely family employing him as a tutor too."

I was surprised. Not the kind of company I would expect a Habsburg princess to keep. "And does the Archduchess know all this?"

"I have no idea. It's a mystery to me, too. However, I am assured he has the Archduchess' ear."

∾

The fiacre dropped Sabine off at our hotel, and we proceeded towards St Sulpice, only a few streets away. We came to where the rue Férou opens into the place St Sulpice. The church tower stood out against a yellow sky over which black clouds, like factory smoke, were racing, seeming to graze the chimneys, spires, and other towers that were visible in the distance.

I was hoping this wouldn't be a wild goose chase. The Johann Salvator connection to Rudolf was already something of a tangent, and then it had to be through his sister, and to that sister through some ex-priest. I really did find such enquiries exhausting. Quite exhausting. Especially on top of seeing that devil Devine... and who were the three gentlemen in the audience — and why did only two step up to the stage?

The building at the address which Philip Seymour had been given had clearly seen better days. The concierge admitted us and we found ourselves ringing at a dingy first-floor apartment. A plain and dour maid led us through a long hall into a sitting-room.

It was a vast, high-ceilinged room with a huge fireplace. Only a very meagre fire glowed ineffectually in the hearth. Four chairs were in the style of Louis XIII with tapestried covers needing repair. In front of the two windows were imitation Chinese vases mounted on stands and containing sickly palms. On the walls were religious pictures, without expression, and an ancient Russian icon in nielloed silver — these slightly relieved the plainness of the decoration. The rest of the furniture looked like that of a bourgeois household fixed up for Lent.

"Stinks of the sacristy, doesn't it?" Philip whispered as we huddled near the fire. It was a curious mixture, I was thinking. Yes, something of the sacristy, but other items more worldly than a priest. Perhaps he had come into some money once, though it looked like it had all been spent. The maid waited apprehensively, her eye on the clock. Nearly half an hour passed.

"Will he be long?" Philip eventually asked. "And where is he?"

"St Sulpice," she replied.

"Once a priest, always a..." I began.

"Didn't you notice the wine shop on the corner? I think that's the 'St Sulpice' she is referring to."

Suddenly we heard a door slam, and footsteps coming erratically down the hallway. Into the room staggered Alfred Saunière, who straightened himself up the moment he saw he was not alone. Philip looked at me. Clearly, the man was intoxicated.

He was thick-set, of middle height with the once well-fed aspect of a man of the Holy Church, and now rather gaunt-looking. No point in wasting time on too many formalities: "I am seeking some information on the Archduchess of Tuscany. I believe you know her. I want to talk to her about her brother, Johann Salvator Habsburg."

"The Archduchess… well!" he began dismissively, before glancing down at my card which his maid had passed to him. His attitude changed somewhat — a man clearly impressed by titles. "As Your Ladyship may know, I do enjoy a certain confidence with Her Highness."

I wondered how, but thought it best to let him tell me in his own good time.

"All I can say to you about Johann Salvator — who I suppose more correctly should be called Mr John Orth, after he had renounced his titles — is that Her Highness never speaks of him. Her desire is quite the reverse, you see… it is to speak *to* him."

I got the feeling that maybe he wouldn't have said this without the help of the wine shop. "No one knows what happened to him after his famous row with his distant cousin Franz-Josef — changing his name to that of a commoner and sailing off across the ocean has only fuelled the possibilities that he is still alive — and will return a much stronger figure than as he left."

"And Crown Prince Rudolf?"

"His secret, you mean? In Austria they believe that even if Rudolf passed his secret to Johann Salvator, it has died with him." He stopped himself again, clearly wondering if he were saying too much. "But the Archduchess is merely a poor distraught sister, like her mother before her — grasping at straws. Even at the séances…"

"Séances?"

"The spirit connection can sometimes be made. But it disturbs Her Highness… for if he has a roaming spirit, then it can only mean one thing…"

"That he is, indeed, dead?" Philip Seymour interjected.

"Yes — the very words taken from my lips. But my own brother, the Abbé Bérenger, he says two masses daily for Johann's life, not just for his soul."

"Here in Paris?"

"Oh, no. Far away. In the South. The Almighty can hear the prayers of the righteous wherever they are said."

"And it can choose, too, not to answer them from wherever they are said," said Philip. My brother Max hadn't mentioned his friend would be yet another sardonic Englishman, and probably a Protestant, too. I changed tack and got back to the priest:

"And these séances… is it you who organises them? For the Archduchess?"

"Oh, no. Emma Calvé does so. No one in Paris is more interested in the spirit world than Madame Calvé. The great Emma Calvé."

"And, Father, your role in all this?" I decided to ignore the fact that he might not at this moment warrant the title.

He was slightly taken by surprise at this question. "I really… well, I suppose you could say that I simply put the right people together…" and by the time he had said this, he was already ushering us to the door and the maid was advancing with our coats.

～∾

As we walked in the street to find a fiacre, I noticed the mean-looking wine shop squeezed into a corner opposite the porch of the church. At that moment St Sulpice's bell seemed to boom out with a special clarity and power. It sent a chill through me: hypnotism, levitation, and now séances. I wondered if Devine would be mixed up in this, too. But it would have been too easy to think that the public had been duped. Certainly, the levitation was no more than a very advanced conjuring trick — but hypnotism? It appeared to work, and how dangerous this could be in the wrong hands. What if the spirit connection was actually real? If I was to take this thing to its conclusion, I had to find out what was going on. As soon as I was back at my lodging I would send a telegram to Emma Destinnova. Amongst the great divas of the world — especially if they were called Emma! — there had to be, I felt sure, a certain camaraderie.

The next morning Sabine woke me with two telegrams: one from Emma Destinnova and the other from Emma Calvé herself. There was to be a séance on Saturday evening, and I was invited.

I really did not know what to expect as the fiacre came to a stop outside 124 Avenue de Wagram, in the fashionable Eighth Arrondissement — the product of all the swagger and confidence of the Third Republic. The imposing house was called Holyrood, according to the bronze plate — after the Scottish palace of that name, for it was the residence of Lady Caithness, who, my telegram from Calvé had informed me, was actually holding the séance.

No sooner had I been admitted by the servant than a graceful old lady, I supposed in her late sixties or early seventies, came across the hallway from the staircase to me. She introduced herself as Maria, and I detected what could have been a Spanish accent. She certainly wasn't Scottish, and she immediately picked up on the confusion. "Lord Caithness, God rest his soul," she explained, "was my second husband. Come… we are all waiting."

Her costume had strong Hindu influences which, had she not carried it off so perfectly, would have left her looking like a fairground fortune-teller. The vestibule was lit with oil-lamps.

"I hate gas!" Lady Caithness observed. I dared not say that in Prague, those who didn't like gas had already replaced it with the electric light.

As we climbed the stairs to the *piano nobile*, the arrangement of the florid drapes, the assault on one's nostrils of Oriental incense and the preponderance of mirrors in ever more exotic frames, the feeling of being in the realm of Indian mysticism, became overpowering. A short distance from the head of the stairs brought us to a pair of closed embroidered silk curtains. Lady Caithness parted them, rattling the beads and baubles dangling from them.

We entered a dark room with a large round table as its principal furnishing, around which were about ten people. The air of expectancy hit me immediately. There were three vacant places. Lady Caithness put me in one of these, and sat in another right beside me. She motioned towards the third unfilled one.

"That's for Claude, our absent friend. He is in London now," she said in a hushed voice.

"Claude?"

"Claude Debussy. I am sure you have heard of him..."

I nodded.

Her voice now was little more than a whisper: "On Madame Calvé's right, there, is Mallarmé, and to her left is Encausse, whom you might know as Papus. He gave that spiritual séance for Tsar Nicholas in St Petersburg."

At the mention of their names, Mallarmé and Papus each turned to me and nodded perfunctorily. And Calvé, of course, was famous throughout the world. Her so-called wild beauty was legendary. As she was entering middle age, I could see that it was merely a legend.

"And at the head of the table," Lady Caithness went on, "is the great Devine, tonight's master of the séance."

My heart seemed to freeze. Ira Devine. I was now face-to-face with him, in person this time. I pretended he meant nothing to me, and he — having gazed at me for a second, no doubt determining how gullible I was, or perhaps how susceptible I was to mesmerism — moved his dark, staring, beady eyes away. He was wearing yet another lurid waistcoat which would not have gained him admission to respectable salons in Vienna or Prague... but then this was Paris, where all such excess was blamed on Bohemians!

"So let us join hands. Let the power of the spirit world flow through us. We form a ring of energy..." Devine began. All those around the table raised their arms and linked their hands. What light there was in the room, and I couldn't see its source, suddenly dimmed. It was then that I suddenly remembered... my whole reason for being here: Where was the Archduchess of Tuscany?

I was about to whisper the question to Lady Caithness when suddenly, with our hands now all linked, everyone fell completely silent. There was a moment of absolute stillness... of excited expectation. I could not deny its thrill.

Then there was a faint knocking sound, three or four gentle taps only, then a silence, then the knocks repeated.

"Who is trying to communicate?" intoned Devine.

There were more knocks, this time clearer and a little louder.

"Is it he with whom we were in communication last month?"

Two knocks. I peered into the darkness. Devine's hands were still clasped with his neighbours.

"We are open to you…"

There was a discernible draught, as if a window had been opened. It rattled the baubles on the drapes and tinkled the crystal pendants of the chandelier.

At this moment a young woman whom I had not really noticed before, on Devine's left, began to speak… from her lips came the voice of a man… distant at first, then nearer:

"I live… I am dead, but I live… the dead live…"

It really was most disturbing.

"Who are you?" asked Devine.

"I… I…," and the voice seemed to choke in her throat.

"Are you John?"

Two knocks.

"O…"

Two knocks.

"R."

Two knocks.

"T."

Two knocks.

Before the last letter, H, was declared, Emma Calvé had already broken down, burbling incoherently. John Orth — Johann Salvator Habsburg's new name for himself.

Then there was silence, and the draught seemed to go back through the space, rattling and tinkling as before. Emma Calvé took control of herself. Our hands, still all joined, seemed to relax a second. Lady Caithness broke the chain first, bringing out a small bottle of smelling salts, and sprinkling them on a handkerchief.

I decided to test something. I contrived to knock the little bottle onto the floor. With a whispered "Oh, I am so sorry" to Lady Caithness, I bent down to retrieve it from the carpet. Despite the darkness, I could clearly make out Devine's legs — and onto his trousered left leg was attached some instrument, like a drumstick.

Suddenly the room was flooded with light as servants entered bearing oil lamps. "It is over," Devine was saying rather snappily, "I feel drained." And, as I rose into my seat again, placing the little bottle before Lady Caithness, I felt the glare of Devine's eyes.

"Countess Falklenburg, I believe," he addressed me icily. I knew what that meant. I had been marked.

Then I took more notice of the young lady next to him: could this be Hélène Johanson? She seemed different than the woman on the stage. But of course she would! A lot more things were becoming clear.

I was about to ask Lady Caithness about the Archduchess of Tuscany, John Orth's sister, but she beat me to it.

"What a terrible pity the princess wasn't here. It is all she lives for, to communicate with her brother, to hear him and speak to him again — to find out if he is alive or dead."

"But this was hardly conclusive. He is dead, but alive?"

"I do not know what it means. But finally we have made the spirit connection."

"And the princess?"

"She went yesterday to the South. There is a priest who says mass for her brother twice daily. Apparently they have also made the connection."

"And that would be the Abbé Bérenger?"

The various distinguished guests were bowing to her as they left, and it was a moment before she could come back to me.

"Yes. She has gone south, to the Aude, to Rennes-le-Château."

∞

I hurried out of Lady Caithness' home, hoping I wouldn't be waylaid by Devine or, worse still, find myself having to answer questions from the likes of Emma Calvé of how wonderful, stimulating, mysterious, or other such expressions of acclaim I found the so-called séance. It was a cleverly staged conjuring trick, no more, I decided. Was Devine after the alleged fortune that Johann Salvator, alias John Orth, left behind?

I looked across the Avenue Wagram to where the driver of the fiacre had said he would wait. I was slightly annoyed he hadn't already pulled over to the outside of the house — but I found then there was no fiacre waiting at all. And he hadn't been paid yet, either, always the greatest inducement for a cabman to wait!

Since I was reluctant to go back into the house to have them summon another fiacre, I decided to walk down to the big cross-roads — I had forgotten the name of which Place it was — where there would be a carriage rank. The afternoon had passed and already it was twilight. I had not gone more than a few metres when I had the distinct feeling I was being followed. There was a man in a black suit with frock coat hovering always about forty or fifty metres behind. It was unnerving. To return to Lady Caithness' now would mean approaching him, and that I would not do. The busy aspect of the Place de... whatever its name was... would mean I could lose him in the crowd. However, as I got to within one side street of the crossroads, the figure I was avoiding now seemed to be coming directly towards me!

I looked round. But he was still there, behind me. There had to be two of them. Heaven help me, was all I could think.

So I took the smaller cross street. I regretted it immediately; it was much narrower, for one thing, and sparsely occupied by pedestrians or traffic of the better kind. There was a peddler selling baskets from door-to-door, and a large cart was being unloaded of casks by a pair of swarthy types. I quickened my pace. I passed a Breton onion-seller, pushing his bicycle laden with heavy strings of his produce and calling up to householders.

Glancing back, as I had suspected the two had united — but luckily kept forty or so metres behind me until I got near to where this cross street emptied into another of the large boulevards. I hurriedly glanced back again; the two were now hurrying. I kept going. Then I could hear shouting, and looking back yet again, I saw that one of them had collided with the onion seller. There were spilt onions, a man shaking his fist, and loud recriminations. This gained me valuable seconds.

I crossed the other boulevard, now ablaze with its new electric lamps which suddenly came on, running recklessly through the surge of horse-drawn vehicles and motors to the other side. I realised how pleasant streets will be when there are only motors, for so many horses make a great deal of manure! I was about to go down another side street when I noticed, at the end of the avenue, the well-known shape — rising up like some great ship in a wild ocean — of the new Paris Opera.

Right by the Opera House I knew there were entrances to the underground Métropolitain railway. This I knew because there was considerable controversy that the design of these entries to the subterranean world were like bizarre flowers in the new *art nouveau* taste, clashing, so conservative correspondents to the newspapers said, with the solid neo-Renaissance style of the Opera. I looked back again, but for the moment I couldn't see those following me. Now it was my turn to nearly collide with a large man wearing a top hat and sporting a monocle. I knocked the cane he carried from his hand, and his glass was sent swinging on its cord.

"Madame!" he shouted to this hastily departing lady, replacing his eyeglass and hardly believing what he then saw. "Please watch your step."

Women of quality simply didn't rush… what need had they of it? Therefore our clothes were not designed for rushing about, and I recalled with horror how terrible I looked after chasing about Marienbad on the night the mystery was resolved. Indeed, good clothes aren't made for any kind of activity — it was servants who did all the bending and stretching. But I had to rush. I had no choice.

There, suddenly, was one of the controversial Métropolitain entrances, its large iron flowers, as if about to bloom, forming an arch and steps descending under the boulevard. As I rushed down those steps, trying not to trip on the hem of my skirt, I began to feel safe immediately. The sooty smell of the warmer air was welcomed by my nostrils. I would board the next train, in any direction, and be whisked away from danger. I should point out that this was to be my first ride on such a conveyance, or indeed on any powered by electricity. I would be whisked away as if by magic!

Having wasted valuable seconds in purchasing a ticket, I descended further to the platform. A number of people were waiting, so I assumed a train was expected. A whistle sounded from the tunnel in the northbound direction, and I could see the electric lamp of the train approaching. A guard on the platform was walking down its length to keep people back. I dutifully stepped away — but someone was right behind me. I looked round, I suppose to apologise for nearly pushing him or her… and somehow, on seeing the stern face, the black frock coat and the second figure right behind him — I knew who they were. And here I panicked.

I should, of course, have waited for — and boarded — the train. What could these would-be assailants have done, in a crowd? And perhaps I could have appealed for help? But here I did the worst possible thing: I turned and ran.

Up the steps to the platform… I didn't know where I was running to — perhaps up was the natural reaction… to the light. But then at the level of the ticket office I saw there was another line, another chance at escape. I hurtled down another tunnel for travellers to reach another part of the station, one lined with white tiles… a tube of perfectly white tiles. I passed some notices on a wooden board placed in the middle of the passageway, but I had no time to read them…

The tunnel ended in a further downward staircase. There were materials for building on the tunnel floor. The stairs were hardly usable and covered in sand. The electric light globes here were strung from loose wires. I looked round feverishly before I lost sight of the tunnel I had just run through: two figures, dressed in familiar black, were running towards me. And ahead of me was a builders' wooden partition across the staircase, with a closed and locked door. This part of the station clearly was still under construction. I was trapped.

I had read in a cheap novelette, when I was perhaps nineteen or twenty, before I was married and when I seemed to need wild fantasies — either of romance or danger or both — of such situations where the heroine is left with no way out. I had even experienced it at Marienbad last year on a very small balcony. It did not feel exciting, however. Now I felt like being sick.

As the two men descended the stairs towards me, I had a chance to look at them more carefully. They were far from being what one imagined as street thugs. They seemed perfectly well dressed and groomed, with intelligent faces, despite having their features distorted by grimaces indicating hideous intent. I had seen them, I suddenly remembered, at Devine's magic show only a few days before. Then I had thought how tall they were, almost noble: Devine's subjects.

They were advancing towards me. Their stares were fixed on me, grim menace in their eyes. And suddenly, less than five metres from me, they stopped. It was as if they were waiting for something... or someone.

Uneven, shuffling steps could be heard from the tunnel that led to the staircase, and then I could see the figure approaching down to us: a shorter figure, similarly dressed in black, and limping. His collar was that of a priest, and he had grey hair under his wider brimmed, ecclesiastical hat. The priest from Prague — the one whose footsteps I had followed through the snow... the elusive Father Antoine.

Although his expression was also grimly set, here — I hoped — was someone to whom, surely, as a man of the cloth, I could appeal to.

"Monsignor..." I began. But there was no reaction, and as he got closer I noticed he had one milky eye.

From inside his open frock coat he drew out a small leather pouch, and from this he pulled what, in other circumstances, would have been an innocuous shoemaker's awl with its lethal sharp point. Was this the very thing which had pierced and killed The Great Orsini that winter night? A train roared and clattered by in the nearby tunnel...

Chapter Eight

Deus ex Machina

In the terrible noise my body seemed to wonder if it should faint, or whether a last desperate moment of thought could possibly rescue me.

Then I understood. If only I could remember the words. I reached into my recollection of the performance in the theatre as the sound of the passing train died down... what were the words Devine had spoken?

"Gentlemen..." I tried, buying the smallest portion of a moment to catch the expression. "Gentlemen, I hope I do not discompose you?"

The effect was startling. It was the sole word "discompose" which did indeed seem to discompose them. The three were snapped out of their mesmeretic trance — at least that's what I thought it to be. They were suddenly transformed.

They looked around themselves, hardly believing they were there. Father Antoine stared down at the deadly little awl he was holding so aggressively pointed at me, and then he looked up at me. "Madame?" he said.

"The Countess Falklenburg. From Prague."

It was then I noticed a resemblance: these three were related?

Father Antoine read my mind. "We are three brothers. Our father was Loysel, Captain of the Guard to the former Empress Charlotte of Mexico."

The other two still seemed too shocked even to speak.

He went on: "And if you want to know why we are together like this, then it is a long story. But I don't understand... do you think we were intending to do you harm?"

"Look at that thing you have in your hand. You will eventually have to know what that device has already done, if it's the same one I think it is."

Father Antoine looked down at the plain-seeming awl which he flung down as if it had suddenly become white hot and scorching. It clattered to the floor.

At the same time he let out a cry as if the thing possessed hands, and they were around his throat — a strangulated howl of disgust. It was a terrible sound that I knew instantly I would find hard to forget.

I went on; I was shaken too. "This is not the place to discuss this. But you owe your predicament to Devine. Ira Devine. Thanks to him, the three of you have already become murderers."

The tallest one, with the curly brown hair, went white. Antoine put his arm round the other brother, who looked close to tears.

"What have we become?" this other brother sobbed.

"Monsters, Jean-Paul," replied the taller one.

Yet these were clearly all respectable men, now that their expressions of hatred had vanished. Perhaps they owned property or had high posts. It was all the more terrible that Devine should have perverted them like this. The question of whether or not they were guilty of murder or simply unwitting dupes was one to be decided in another place, whether on this Earth or beyond, I couldn't at that moment say.

"May God help you," I said gravely. I bent down and shook some sand from one of my shoes, then walked past them and began climbing the stairs.

Suddenly another feeling seized me. It was pity. They had been ill-used, shouldn't I take that into account? I glanced round. They were broken men; they would probably soon be able to recollect what they had done, now that the mesmerism was destroyed.

"I do not intend to report this to the police," I said on an impulse. Their punishment would be in having to live with the facts, as soon as they would inevitably find out how terrible were their crimes, for the rest of their lives. Besides, would any police officer believe any of this could be possible?

I turned back and walked on into the bustle of the Métro station. I just wished I were a man, and could stride into some bar — straight up to the barman — and without more ado, demand a large and restorative glass of Cognac. Instead I looked down; I had ruined a good pair of silk stockings. On the other hand, I was alive.

❧

A deep bath in the hotel assisted my recovery. I wished Sabine were here to soap me, but of course she was taking all the time off she could get. I felt quite sorry for her long-suffering French lover who so rarely saw her. Indeed, this was the first time since she had returned from London last year.

I had been thinking of the odd fact that I had now identified three of the men who were involved in Orsini's gruesome murder… but there must have been four. However, my dark thoughts had been interrupted by a distraction; it was the telephone.

The idea that one could have these instruments in bedrooms and bathrooms was quite new to me. In Prague our palace had but two of the things — one in the first-floor cabin, at the head of the stairs, and another in what my husband still thinks of as his Business Room. But now I could see these miracles of modern science could be installed in many other rooms. It would be good, for example, if Müller had an instrument, so that he did not have to stand on my floor bargaining with the local merchants or trying to secure the best seats in the theatres. Although, if one were to be installed in my bathroom, then I probably would never be off the thing.

"But Beatrice, this won't do," the excited voice of Philip Seymour was saying.

"Trixie, please."

"Very well, Trixie. I say again: Beatrice, this won't do. You simply cannot have these adventures by yourself like this. You must have a man with you, preferably with a gun."

"But I was going to a séance, Philip. How was I to know my life would be in jeopardy?"

"This whole business is dangerous. You're playing with fire. For example, that former priest we went to see is now dead."

I rose from my bath, my muscles still feeling stiff, gently putting the precious telephone receiver down and engulfed myself in the generous towelling robe provided by the hotel before I opened the doors to the little sitting room.

Philip Seymour still had the instrument to his ear, but spun round when he heard me. Now the conversation had to be in the flesh, so to speak. I advanced into the room.

"You mean Alfred Saunière is dead?"

"They said it was alcohol poisoning. He was taken ill at that wretched wine shop we passed."

"But the Archduchess is on her way to visit his brother, Abbé Bérenger, at Rennes-le-Château."

"Well, that drink killed him doesn't surprise me. But it makes you wonder, doesn't it, that it's a coincidence too many?"

He paused a second, taking me in. I wished I were dressed more appropriately for such a conversation — informal but not intimate. He pressed on. "You need a man, that's all I say…"

I could see there was that look in his eye. I was about to dismiss him (hoping he wouldn't be a nuisance) when Sabine, having knocked perfunctorily, came in. Seeing the pair of us, she seemed about to withdraw.

"It's is all right, Sabine, Mr Seymour is just leaving."

"The man you should have helping you, of course," he added — slightly put out at being put out — "is your husband. Does he know…?"

"He knows I am quite well, yes. I sent him a telegram. On the other hand, he never knew there was any reason for me not to be!"

He took his hat and gloves from the small side-table by the door to the corridor. "I am sure I am not the first to tell you, Trixie, but you are quite incorrigible."

That look had returned to his eyes again.

"Quite," I said, with an air of finality. He took the less-than-subtle hint, and departed.

Having closed the door, I looked round. Sabine was opening a package, and from it she held up the dress I had been wearing earlier. The hem was all torn and frayed.

"Madame, they say there is nothing they can do. They might be able to add a new piece, but they couldn't guarantee to find just the same colour…"

"No, that won't do at all. In fact I don't really want to see the thing again. This time I shall have no compunction in going to Worth's or Douçet's to buy a replacement. Mr Edward Palmer and his Royal and Imperial Dominion Bank will have to send funds from Vienna. For a woman of my station, I think it fair to say this is an emergency."

Oh, fiddlesticks… what the hell! I had been here several days and I hadn't even gone window-shopping along the Rue de la Paix, let alone set foot in the Place Vendôme. It's not as if I am going to spend willy-nilly at Cartier or Boucheron. I don't need jewels, I was thinking, just a good dress will do — on expenses. It wouldn't do to be seen with something from Au Printemps, for example. A lady really shouldn't be seen at a department store, let alone in any of its wares.

"So tell me, Sabine, how is your personal life? I hope it is more satisfactory than mine!"

"Oh, Madame," was all she would say.

༄

I managed, against my own prediction, to get a good night's sleep. Fear, as well as running for one's life, is exhausting and presumably my tired body and equally tired mind did not have the energy for nightmares.

Sabine had instructions not to wake me, but I had surfaced and could hear her at the door to our suite. Shortly after, she softly tapped my door. I told her to enter.

"This letter has just been delivered, Madame. I shall leave it here, on this book, beside the bed? Would Madame care for some coffee?"

"Very well, Sabine. Whether I like it or not, the day has obviously begun."

"And there was this package, as well." Sabine handed it to me directly, and as I opened it she plumped-up the pillows behind me.

Inside the normal wrapping was a small box tied with ribbon. My eye immediately caught the words printed on it: *Perfumier Guerlain.* My heart, for a moment, warmed. Had Karel made enquiries about what had happened? Had he telegraphed Guerlain's to send this round? Was he an angel, after all?

A card had dropped out. Unfortunately it read:

I N C O R R I G I B L E !!! — Philip

I was about to tell Sabine to have it sent back, when I found myself opening the box and then the bottle within. I dabbed my wrist. It was a beautifully fresh scent, with a hint of musk. Quite delightful.

"Sabine, should Mr Seymour telephone or try to make contact, please inform him I am indisposed."

I left the letter until I had a cup of strong coffee inside me. My instinct had been correct, I needed fortifying. The letter was from none other than Henri Loysel, the tallest of the three brothers. The book lying on my bedside credence was the "M" volume from the *Larousse Encyclopaedia*, kindly lent to me from the hotel's reading room. "M" for "Mexico." I needed to refresh my memory of certain facts, namely:

The late Emperor of Mexico had been Maximilian, Franz-Josef's younger brother — who had been keenly encouraged to take up the position by his brother. He sailed to Mexico in 1864 in high hopes with his wife, Princess Charlotte, daughter of King Leopold the First of Belgium. However, the welcome was less than the pair had been led to believe, and although they were duly installed as Emperor and Empress, by 1867 the Mexican insurgents (whom one might also call loyalists) had taken over the country and had Maximilian shot by firing squad.

The meat of the text of Henri Loysel's letter is as follows:

You told us yesterday evening that my brothers and I had been in the power of Devine. I realise now that this must indeed be true. We don't know what vile deeds that monster made us carry out for him, but discussing it together we realise that each of us has lapses in recollection over the past year. Indeed, we had thought that Devine was in fact working for us. The whole story goes back many years, to the time when our father, Loysel, and his companion, Almonte, travelled to Mexico as Guard Captains, first for the Empress and later for the Emperor. My father and Almonte were thus witnesses to the terrible betrayal of Maximilian which took place.

When the supporting French troops were withdrawn from the Emperor, Empress Charlotte came back to Europe to try to obtain help for her beleaguered husband. Those who refused included none other than the Emperor's own brother, Kaiser Franz-Josef. Other states took their lead from him, and the Emperor's fate was thus sealed. It used to be said that His Apostolic Majesty, the Emperor and King, Franz-Josef, can carry off anything with dignity — even the murder of his own brother!

Charlotte, ever since then, has been held a virtual prisoner of Kaiser Franz-Josef, and this confinement, compounded with her inability to help or even comfort her husband in his last days, has over the years driven the poor woman to madness. Her huge fortune has, it seems, disappeared. We would say it has been stolen by Franz-Josef.

As for our father, he met a terrible end in the service of the Emperor and we owe our lives to the fact that Empress Charlotte took us back to Europe as children. So we seek revenge not only for our father but also for the Empress, to whose service our father was dedicated.

I am the owner of a printing works, and some years ago my firm was to print the *Memoirs of Countess Larisch*, in which — since I had access to the text — I discovered that there was a second steel box containing a document which, it was said, would topple the Habsburgs. It was a secret so deadly that even talk of such a thing was dangerous. Kaiser Franz-Josef bought the entire edition after printing, and had the books burnt.

Countess Larisch had stated that the second box had been given to Johann Salvator on Rudolf's death, and it is presumed that today it is thus in the possession of the Archduchess of Tuscany. Our intention is, therefore, to gain possession of the box. That will avenge our family and Princess Charlotte.

Due to the investigation of this Saunière on the charge of simony — the selling of masses — my brother Antoine learnt that Johann Salvator had been at some time solicited by Saunière for money to restore his church at Rennes-le-Château. So we got Saunière to offer the Archduchess of Tuscany to say mass daily for the soul of her brother. Since in theory he should have been saying more than a hundred masses a day, Saunière was making sizeable amounts of money from this business. It was he who introduced us to Emma Calvé and her séance sect, and through her — may God help us — Ira Devine.

We made an arrangement with Devine to ensure that the Archduchess yielded up her secret box to us. This plan, which no longer involves Devine, has already been put into action. It does not involve any criminal activity.

However, from the events of yesterday, it seems that Devine has been using us. However terrible, we urge you to tell us what you know. We will have to deal with it, but it would be even worse trying to deal with something, the enormity of which we did not know — but about which we could only speculate.

And, importantly, if you wish to see Devine's farewell performance, then come to the World of Spirits show again tomorrow. You will not be disappointed.

I realised, as I put the letter down, that I had better get down to Rennes-le-Château quickly. But I didn't know that tomorrow would be Devine's last performance; this certainly wasn't announced. Something in the tone of the letter, and of course in the circumstances, drew me there. The day following I had a reserved seat on the train to Lyon. A local train, then probably the village donkey, would finally get me to Rennes-le-Château. I sent a telegram to the Abbé Bérenger Saunière to expect me, making no mention of the Archduchess — or anything else, for that matter.

To put the brothers out of their misery, and doubtless to create even more, I wrote briefly back to Henri Loysel outlining the gruesome details of the death of The Great Orsini on the Abt's Rack in Prague, and then — for I was sure it was they — the death of Wilajalba Frikell. What they had actually used to frighten the poor old man to death, I had no idea. Maybe in time I would learn. How they would reconcile this intelligence with their consciences, I also had no idea. That really had to be for them to work out.

༄

I attended the show alone. I had no wish to sit cramped too close to Philip Seymour, and Sabine had flatly refused to come — fearing, I supposed, that she would have to make a second appearance on the stage. As I sat in the Dress Circle, an empty seat beside me (a woman of quality would not go unescorted) waiting for the lights to dim, I noticed two things. Firstly was that where the brothers had sat before, there were now three empty seats. Secondly was that I noticed them, separated, elsewhere amongst the audience.

The show began and then proceeded very much as before. Devine was his usual slick, polished self — only once betraying any kind of surprise, and that was when he called upon two of the brothers… as before. But this time they didn't come. Peering out beyond the footlights he could, I presumed, see the empty seats. He quickly pasted over this crack in his performance and soon found other susceptible subjects from amongst the audience. I thought I noticed that two of the brothers had left their seats, but in the gloom of the interior I couldn't be sure. Then came the moment for the spectacle of the levitation.

The patter was the same: "*Mesdames et messieurs* — the levitation of Princess Aya! For the first time from the sands of Oriental Egypt to be seen here and now by the people of Europe!"

Hélène Johanson now obligingly appeared as the princess in her diaphanous robe, and soon she was gliding upwards — for all the world without any visible means of support. Devine stepped back, flourishing his arm in a gesture of satisfied presentation. Then something went wrong. Suddenly the princess seemed to slip to a strange oblique angle — whatever had been supporting her had obviously partly given way. Then, as she struggled to maintain balance and grasped some of the invisible wires, she seemed to get tangled and spiral upwards.

Devine rushed forward and made a grab for the wires himself. A light suddenly was illuminated and we could all see the web of wires quite clearly. The audience, thinking this to be a humorous sideshow to the main event, laughed. In fact they found it very funny indeed as they watched the antics of Devine struggling amongst the now very visible tungsten wires.

I glanced down into the stalls. The additional light enabled me to confirm that one of the brothers seemed to have moved. I saw a vacant seat where I thought he had been sitting.

Then the whole cradle of wires seemed to twist round. Devine was off the ground now as well, fighting against the vicious threads. They were thin, but they were strong... and sharp. At the sight of blood on one of his forearms, some of the audience gasped, but the vast majority, still thinking it a very clever joke, laughed all the more. The wires cut into Devine... like a cheese wire. Like the cheese wire which had beheaded The Great Orsini in Prague. Thus it was the perfect end for him. And all we could do, so it seemed, was watch. There is something both magical and forbidden about the stage — it is something you look at, but a world you do not enter, unless invited.

I could see Devine's mouth doing just that. The invitation, if we could have heard it, was his mouthing "Help!" Yet not only was the audience by now mostly quite helpless with laughter, but the band had kept playing, thinking they could smooth over this unfortunate episode with some rousing music. It was when the deadly wires started cutting across Devine's face that the audience was stilled, and the leader of the band — looking directly up at him — stopped the carnival music. There was a deathly silence as we watched the end of Devine.

I had raised my opera glasses. Seeing the scene in terrifying detail but through the artifice of the glass lenses increased my sense of detachment, which enabled me to watch rather than act. I could clearly see Devine's eyes. No longer had they that cold stare which had sentenced several people to their deaths. Now they possessed an entirely different look, one familiar in some way. It took only a moment to remember why. It was precisely the look of terror fixed in the eyes of the late Wilajalba Frikell, when I had encountered him dead in his chair. It seemed justice had turned full circle.

Concentrating as we were on Devine, we had quite forgotten about Hélène Johanson, who had disappeared up into the darkness of the void above the stage. There was a scream as she came thudding down, having finally lost her grip somewhere up there in the flies. Snagged in the cutting wires she fell directly on Devine, and both of them fell a good three or four metres onto the boards of the stage itself. There was a full second of deathly stillness as neither bloody wreck moved. It was all over.

A moment later stagehands and other theatre staff rushed onto the stage, and a moment after that the band struck up again and the safety curtain hastily descended. If there was indeed a world of the spirits, Devine was now there. Or more likely he was roasting in the fires of Hell.

❧

The Worth seamstresses had worked their famed magic and completed in record time the dress I had ordered. I have to confess to having looked in at Lucille's the dressmakers first, where I'd bumped into Princess Isenburg ordering a mass of things, but I'd gone on to Worth's: the best and most fashionable — the doyen of *la haute couture Parisienne*. A dress such as I had ordered would weigh considerably less than one of Karel's guns, yet its effect would be far more explosive. Maybe heads wouldn't exactly turn by my wearing such a confection, but it would empower me — certainly giving me the confidence to meet an Archduchess on, shall we say, more equitable terms!

Naturally, there was no question of payment being necessary to receive the handsome box when it arrived at the hotel; the word of a countess — even from the distant Austrian Empire — was considered wholly reliable enough. I had telegraphed Herr Palmer for funds, and he had responded in a very timely fashion, giving me the details of the correspondent bank in Paris where I could draw what I needed. The morning following the Devine tragedy, trying hard to dispel the ghastly images my mind retained of the magician's very public finale, I had time to collect the money, to pay Worth, and to meet Sabine at the Gare de Lyon, all in good time for the midday express south.

I had glanced at Herr Palmer's telegram only long enough to read the bank's address. As I entered the premises, all seemed to be in a very sombre mood. I cannot tell you how a not-so-sombre bank should feel, but I could recognise one in the reverse state. The doorman, in frogged tailcoat, wore, I noticed, a black armband.

Soon I was standing before the reception desk: "I have come to see the director," and here I consulted the telegram I had had crumpled in my handbag, "a… a Monsieur Jean-Paul Loysel, please." But of course I recognised the name as soon as it was on my lips. Good heavens, it could only be him! What a coincidence.

"I regret to have to inform you, Madame," came the reply from the bank officer who was wearing a black tie, "but Monsieur Loysel took his own life last night. As you can imagine, we are all in a state of shock. Unless it was on private business, I can pass you to his deputy, who will attend to your requirements, I am sure."

"I am so very sorry," I said. Tears were already rolling down my cheeks. I was taken to a private room and given a glass of Vichy water. I refused a Cognac. It must have been my letter which had tipped the balance. I was therefore responsible. On the other hand, should I have done differently?

"Do you have a telephone I could use, please?"

"Of course, Your Ladyship. If you would come with me." By now a more senior employee had appeared, aware of who I was.

I was shown into a very superior office furnished in the Louis XVI style. On a highly polished table stood a telephone. I had the terrible feeling that this room was probably the late Jean-Paul's. This thought made matters only worse.

The number I gave was procured for me.

"Oh, Philip…" I found myself wailing as soon as the connection was made. Who else was there? Even Sabine was on her way to the station, and Karel…? Where on Earth could I have started with him? It would have sounded to my husband like some delusion fuelled either by the opium pipe or by the onset of madness. "Come and get me, please."

In the fiacre with Philip, I blubbed like a child. All the cool and reserve — and bravery — of the last days burst like a summer thunderstorm. I couldn't help thinking of what he had said two evenings ago: I needed a man for these adventures. Better still, I needed to be a man! And what had men got that I hadn't, for Heaven's sakes, apart from an inconvenient appendage?

"So you are wearing the perfume I sent," he observed, suddenly edging rather close to my neck.

Yes, that was what men had! A total lack of human feeling: blow compassion, to hell with sympathy! He was after one thing only — and ironically that was the one thing (unless he was homosexual, of course) he had to come to a woman for!

I was glad to shake him off at the station, but in a strange way he had empowered me. As for needing a man, I decided that the next time I would set out on some adventure from Prague, I would take Müller with me. What he did with his appendage was beyond the scope of our relationship.

When I caught up with Sabine, she was leafing through a pile of newspapers. "There is still all kind of speculation about the death of Ira Devine, Madame," she said. "Did it seem to you it was just the failure of the machinery?"

Should I have explained it all to her? As far as the brothers were concerned, better to let sleeping dogs lie.

"I know the dining cars on French express trains are excellent, but let's fortify ourselves for the journey, shall we?"

Sabine smiled, and soon we had taken the mirrored lift up to the restaurant, which overlooked the platforms, just as had that of the Gare de Nord, except that last year it had been quite dark.

As I sat first savouring, then enjoying, a simple *omelette aux fines herbes* (I liked the way the French make even simple food so delectable), I found myself looking over Sabine's shoulders.

"Madame, the last time, it was I looking over your shoulder," she said. She'd exactly caught what I was thinking; how clever of her. Yet suddenly I felt the briefest chill, as if someone had trodden on my grave, as they say. But there was no Jenks, or no Brodsky lookalike out there this time. Of course not; it had been just a stupid fancy of some kind.

"If Madame does not mind my saying…Madame should eat her omelette while it is still fresh."

I smiled at her, ever watchful for my comfort. "Of course," I replied.

In the train, as we began to move off and the suburbs of Paris edged by the windows — and finally fields and villages and the slender spires of ancient churches began to pass briskly by — so the drama of the brothers seemed to pass out of my consciousness, and as for Devine, he was already out of it. Death had concluded my worries about him.

I pictured my meeting with Inspector Schneider, whenever that would be — my explaining to him how the whole case of the headless magician had been solved — and that natural justice had overtaken the perpetrators. I supposed he would have to go to Paris himself to complete his enquiries, to make the final notes in his file, but I would not be involved by then. I would do my best to shield the identity of the brothers, unknown subjects mesmerised by Devine and now impossible to find as they had moved on to a different life. Perhaps that would be sufficient?

I made a mental note to send Schneider a telegram either from Lyon Station, or perhaps from my hotel in Carcassonne, where we would be spending the night.

I reached into my handbag and drew out a rather tattered bundle of cards. Here were all the clues, or so I had once thought. But nothing could have led me to work out the identity of the three murderers, for so these three respectable men in late middle age, automatons of the hideous Devine, had become. I riffled through them, stopping at the card headed "Wilajalba Frikell." On it I had also written "Frightened to death. But how?"

Did it matter now? Clearly, it didn't.

And then there were all the clues about the photograph taken on Abt's Rack. It had been Devine's ploy to construct an entirely different motive for Orsini's murder when all along he had simply been anxious to steal the secret of levitation. I squared-up the pile of cards and retied the ribbon around them.

"Sabine, could you throw these old cards away? And get me a table in the dining car as soon as possible. In my writing case, I think you will find some new cards I cut up last week. I will need those."

"*Oui, Madame.*"

Soon I had a table on which to start my new cards. How odd that the Devine affair so neatly dovetailed into this other matter — except I did begin to wonder if my following clues to the whereabouts of Johann Salvator's steel box, and the great secret he was supposed to have been given by Crown Prince Rudolf, was not a wild goose chase. On the other hand, I seemed to have precious little else to go on about what could have been on Rudolf's mind in 1888.

I made out cards for every detail of the deaths at Mayerling. Several of them seemed to point to the importance of the time which had undoubtedly elapsed between the shot which must have killed Mary Vetsera and that second shot which blew a large part of Rudolf's head away. And I still didn't know where the incident had occurred six months before — the shot which had only just missed Kaiser Franz-Josef. I made out a blank card for this, simply headed "Where?" For that matter, I wasn't even certain of the date either, so I then added "When?"

But I was confident that the Archduchess would be able to tell me a great deal. She must have spent the last fifteen or so years pondering over the death of Rudolf and its repercussions, for it was this which propelled her brother to row with his cousin Franz-Josef, and to disappear. However, to feel it necessary for her to go down to the Styx to meet this second-rate parish priest, accused of simony, might be thought of as clutching at straws. I had now no idea of what was lying ahead.

Luckily, as we progressed southward, the low wintry sun bathed the landscape in golden hues, lifting my spirits. As we steamed into Lyon, a most curious edifice was visible on an eminence.

"What is that, Sabine?"

"Why that's Notre Dame de Fourvière," she exclaimed, quite excited. "It's quite new!"

It was indeed a most extraordinary exercise in various flamboyant styles, what one might call a mishmash. If Lyon was the gateway to the South of France, then this sight would prepare me — or maybe forewarn me — of what I might expect. I just hoped that, this far south, the food wouldn't be as bizarre. Something inside me, just at that second, yearned for a Bohemian potato soup with dumplings.

"And will Madame be sending a telegram from here?"

"No, Sabine. From Carcassonne will have to do." I was tired; relaxing on a train is indeed tiring. And in the south, I understood, nothing needs to be done in a hurry.

From Lyon we travelled down through Nîmes to Montpelier, where finally we could glimpse the deep blue of the Mediterranean, then along the coast with its high mountains, sub-tropical vegetation, luxuriant gardens, and beaches for sea bathing — very reminiscent of that golden stretch of coast by Abbazia on our own Austrian Riviera, on the Adriatic.

At Narbonne we struck inland on a connecting train. As we were changing trains, I caught sight of another passenger from First Class also making his way to the other platform. It was only a brief glimpse, but I felt I knew the man from somewhere — yet I couldn't quite place him. Wasn't he connected with the events of last year? At Marienbad, or was it Prague? It was as if a cloud had suddenly darkened the sky. I'd felt this way at the Gare de Lyon.

Next I knew, I felt Sabine's hand clutching my elbow.

"Is Madame quite well? Should we sit down?"

That brought me back to my senses: "No, Sabine, it was nothing."

Maybe I had been mistaken, which was all too probable, and before I could look at him again, he had been swallowed up in the crowd. It was late evening before we glimpsed the almost magical towers, turrets and city walls of the Carcassonne *Cité* rising like something out of a children's storybook over the more mundane modern town below it. Sabine would remain here at a hotel while I travelled on.

✦

At midday the next day I was being jolted in a pony and trap up the lonely road to the remote hilltop village of Rennes-le-Château. From a distance, for it was visible from the flat, dry, and almost treeless landscape for quite a while, the place seemed to have nothing of interest to distinguish it. As we got nearer, and before the unpaved road started to climb more steeply, there was still nothing to excite the eye — except a curious gothic tower, which appeared to be new.

I asked the driver what it was.

"That's Abbé Saunière's," the rough-looking fellow replied gruffly.

"Oh, yes."

"He calls it the Tour Magdala. Funny kind of place, if you ask me."

I shouldn't suppose that I had much in common with this man, but in this we were in agreement. As the poor pony hauled us up into the village proper, which seemed deserted since it was lunch-time, we passed the parish church — a simple enough building, and then ahead of us was what was probably the priest's house, behind which was this Tour Magdala. Coming towards us was a very smart carriage in dark purple with two greys in its traces. As it passed, close to us, I could see a grand-looking lady inside.

"And who's that, driver?"

"Archduchess, they say. The coach is Emma Calvé's — she sent it down from her castle near Toulouse for the lady to use. Smart, isn't it?"

"I dare say…" But I was nonplussed.

Was this the very person I had come to try to meet, going in the opposite direction? However, I could hardly turn about and give chase. In any event, I was pulled by a pony with its ribs showing, and the Archduchess by two strong horses! I shouldn't have thought of the expense, and I hired a proper carriage in Carcassonne. I was in a panic, and suddenly found myself asking: "And is there a hotel here?"

"Hotel?!" — and here the driver laughed.

I supposed there was nothing for it but to continue with my interview with Abbé Saunière, and I made arrangements for the trap to wait for me.

The door to the priest's house was answered by a sour-faced housekeeper, who took me to the Tour Magdala, the solid, square structure like some ancient gothic castle. Attached to it was a circular, battlemented turret, affording, I had no doubt, an even better view than the already broad vista which I could see for myself as I waited at the huge iron-bound door while the housekeeper announced me. Eventually, as if the person I was about to see was some grand seignior and not a mere parish priest, I was admitted.

Saunière was a short man in his fifties, I supposed, as he advanced to shake my hand. He had piercing, shrewish eyes, although one of them did not move, which was slightly unnerving, as his gaze was shifty, questioning. It must have been glass. His standard priestly garb seemed at odds with the magnificence of the interior of his tower: here and there were high-backed seigniorial chairs, thrones, and stools. Against the walls were sideboards used as book-presses for ancient vellum-bound tomes and on whose carved panels were bas-reliefs representing the Annunciation and the Adoration of the Magi. On top of the sideboards, upon lace runners, stood painted and gilded statues of female saints. There was a large coffer in the centre of the room fastened by great metal clasps and overlaid with leather, near which was the elaborately carved chair in which Saunière evidently sat. The curtains beside the great gothic windows were embroidered with armorials and the vaulted ceiling was sprinkled with stars. Saunière motioned me to one of the high-backed chairs with a tasselled cushion.

He sat with his hands in his lap, twining his two thumbs round each other. He had strangely large hands, freckled with blotches and terminating in milk-white nails, cut to the quick. His attitude was one which demanded I stated my business.

"Did I catch a glimpse of the Archduchess of Tuscany just leaving?" I began.

It was the perfect opener. Saunière flushed with pride, although I detected a slight shiver of surprise too. "Her Serene Highness is a frequent visitor. On this occasion I had the honour to show her the new Shrine to Our Lady of Lourdes."

"I understand that her brother had been a benefactor to the church here…"

Now he looked distinctly shifty. He thought for a second. "And, Your Ladyship, your interest in these matters…?"

"Oh, I am merely a family friend. I am distantly related… in fact, I would dearly like to have spoken to the Archduchess. Have I missed her?"

He relaxed a little, but was still on his guard. "Indeed, you may well have done. How unfortunate."

"And might I ask where she was staying?"

"She was staying in Carcassonne…"

"Oh, where?"

He thought for a moment, clearly deciding whether or not to tell, or perhaps to lie. "She was the guest of the Bishop."

I decided to change the subject slightly. "In the family they say that Prince Johann Salvator of Tuscany's donations helped the restoration of the church here."

"That is so. When you will have taken coffee, I shall show you."

"That is very kind. And have you heard the sad news?"

He merely furrowed his brow.

"It is very fresh in Paris," I went on. "Ira Devine, the stage illusionist, is dead."

He went white. His expression was fixed — his good eye emulating the dead stare of the glass one, trying not to betray the importance of this event to him. Then a thought obviously crossed his mind — something to excuse his sudden shock.

"You must understand my shock… coming hard on the heels, as it does, of news of the death of my dear brother. But did you know Mr Devine?"

"I ran into him at one of Emma Calvé's séances, at Lady Caithness'."

I was watching him more carefully now. I didn't even know what I wanted from this man, but I knew he was up to something and he could not hide his feelings completely.

"Ira Devine... dead? And how did it happen?"

"One of his stage illusions failed. There was a ghastly accident. He did not suffer for very long."

Saunière stood up abruptly. "Then we should look at the church."

As he guided me to the door, we were met by the sour-faced housekeeper carrying a tray with the coffee. Saunière simply ignored her. I was shown, in an otherwise plain, although undeniably antique, church building, several rather clumsy additions made by Saunière in recent years with rather grotesque carvings. He seemed in a hurry, and I was soon shown to the street gate of the churchyard. Walking to where I had arranged to take the trap back, I glanced behind me. Saunière was running through the graveyard towards his house — hardly the reaction to such news I had anticipated.

The pony had been hitched so that it could take advantage of the shade of one of the espaliered trees in the little square; the driver was in the *café-tabac*.

On my way back to Carcassonne, I had a moment to reflect on my meeting. Saunière had been careful to tell me nothing — and certainly nothing about the Salvators. And he hadn't even asked me what I had wanted. The whole thing did not quite add up: the Tour Magdala was evidence enough of some wealth — wealth beyond a priest in a dead-end place like Rennes-le-Château, and how had the likes of Archduke Johann Salvator been interested in helping the rather vulgar restoration of such a church? And if it were all financed on the proceeds of simony, then Saunière must have committed himself to saying literally hundreds of masses daily. And why was he running? What did he need to do so urgently after having heard of Devine's death?

As soon as I arrived at the hotel in Carcassonne, I asked Sabine to get out the Worth dress. At a shop I had passed on the way from the station I had seen just the parasol which would complement the dress's quite gorgeous daffodil satin. Since it was on Herr Palmer's expenses, I would wear it for the next stage of my investigations… in about forty-five minutes!

"At quarter past I intend to go round to the Bishop's Palace, Sabine. That means we have to work fast."

"And when will Madame be having something to eat?"

"I simply haven't thought. Anyway, I find it hard to digest when I am excited… or anxious. Now, is the bath run?"

"*Oui, Madame.* And I think the lace camiknickers will be more comfortable in this warmth. Shall I put them out? And the length of the gloves… we have wrist- and opera-length in cream? I'm afraid I didn't pack any of the mid-length."

"I don't know what I would do without you, Sabine. You are so thoughtful."

"But this is my own country, Madame, and I come from the south."

"And, any lovers here you should visit?"

Sabine blushed. "*Mais, non, Madame.* I left for Paris when I was fifteen. Here, in the villages, there was nothing."

Thinking of Rennes-le-Château, I could only agree with her.

❧

The Bishop's Palace, close to the cathedral church of Saint-Nazaire and to my hotel on the Place de l'Eglise, was exactly what I had come to expect of such buildings — dowdy magnificence. Being an eighteenth-century building, it now seemed rather out of place in the city which, originally under the great French architect Viollet le Duc, was being returned to its gothic splendours. Work on restoring the medieval fortifications had ended some years ago and now the city resembled once more one of those almost fantastical images from *Les Très Riches Heures du Duc de Berry.*

A servant admitted me and took my card up. In a minute or two a nun came down and told me the Archduchess would be pleased to see me. So she was still here! Had I believed Saunière, I would not be here at all.

The Archduchess of Tuscany was truly a *grande dame* of the old school. She must have been in her late fifties or early sixties, and yet somehow she could still carry off pale satin and pearls. Her grey-blue eyes, although tired and showing a deep underlying sadness, were kindly. She had the air of someone who is so tired of battling with the world that she might as well fight it with kindness. She immediately motioned me to sit down beside her.

"My dear," she began, "I think I know your mother. She's a von Morštejn, is she not?"

"Yes, she is. I am sure she would wish to be remembered to you had she known of my visit."

"And so, what brings you to Carcassonne?"

"Well, I went to see the Abbé Saunière at Rennes-le-Château."

"And, for whatever reason, you are trying to find out if he is a charlatan?"

Her adroitness rather took me by surprise. "I suppose you could say that, yes."

"Then who has put you up to this? Surely the affairs of the Aude are normally of no concern to you in Prague?"

This was awful. I had not expected the Archduchess to be... like this.

"Please, Your Serene Highness, I beg you not to enquire further. I have very good reason to be here and to be asking these questions — it comes from the highest authority. But it is a strictly confidential matter."

"And you have told no one about your mission? No one at all?"

"I may not, and I have not."

"I don't believe you."

"All right, I admit the only person in whom I have confided is my mother. That is only natural." There was also Henry von Taaffe, of course, but I wasn't obliged to tell her everything!

"Oh, very well then," replied the Archduchess, somewhat more relaxed. "I will ask your mother round for coffee next time we are both in Vienna."

So much for confidentiality!

"I attended a séance at Lady Caithness'. Mr Devine was the master..."

I was trying to find out if she knew about Devine's demise.

"…they said Your Serene Highness had been there. That Your Serene Highness wished to contact your brother."

"Enough of the 'Serene Highness,' please. When we were the royal family of Tuscany, that was in order. Now I am just an inconvenience in Austria. The loss of Tuscany was, as I am sure you know, due to the Emperor's meddling in military matters."

"And might I ask if you read newspapers? I think there was something about Mr Devine in the Paris papers recently…?"

"Newspapers!" she exclaimed, "I've already read enough of them in my life not to need any more, thank you. They are all the same: politicians of almost equal ideas — or lack of them — jockeying for position, some small wars somewhere on the globe — a mighty power against lightly armed natives who happen to sit on land rich in something the said mighty power needs — and as for the Social Register… huh! Now the only things my eye is drawn to are the Death Notices. I fear that if I read any more of them, one of those announcements that I shall be reading will turn out to be my own! No, newspapers, I do not read. Monsignor Beuvain de Beauséjour, the bishop, has already told me all the gossip."

"And what of the Act that is going through to separate Church and State, then… isn't this important?"

"It will be catastrophe for the Church, that's all I know. Poor rural parishes will be greatly hit."

"Like Rennes, for instance?"

"Well, the Abbé is very industrious, as I'm sure you know. I make no secret of the fact that I am drawn to his offer to put me into communication with my brother. The fact that he is doing this without making one of his customary 'restoration' charges is perhaps evidence that he may have something. Emma Calvé and that whole séance set in Paris give me hope. But I am just a desperate sister, clutching at straws…"

"It is quite right that you should…"

"You must think me a fool, and there's no fool like an old fool, I know. But I must not ignore any chance that presents itself. I live for the moment when my brother will speak to me. And at this moment, do you realise that I do not know for certain if he is alive or dead?"

"Marie Larisch claims he was seen in Tibet!"

"Given a choice of believing either Marie Larisch or the Abbé Bérenger, then I would select the latter."

"And when is this communication going to take place?"

"Now that's the strange thing. It was to have been in four days' time. But this afternoon I received an urgent telegram from the Abbé informing me that now it will take place tomorrow evening."

So that was it! For some reason, Saunière was clearly afraid of the story of Devine's death catching him out. Maybe he was thinking that the newspapers had caught on to Devine's rather prosaic way of summoning the supernatural — that, after all, he was merely a mechanical illusionist, nothing more.

The Archduchess continued: "The Abbé warned me that the communication he is proposing — I shall actually see my brother — is very difficult. 'Extreme measures' will have to be used, he said. But since you are here Beatrice — if I may call you that? — then I see no harm in you accompanying me… in fact it would be a positive benefit if you were to be at my side. Would you do that for me?"

Things couldn't have worked out better.

❧

In Calvé's well-appointed coach, the Archduchess and I made our way back to Rennes-le-Château the following afternoon. The Archduchess was in a much more amiable mood — so I took a chance, saying, "I've been trying to understand the events of 1889. Your brother and Crown Prince Rudolf were friends?"

"Of course. They were the two bright hopes of the Empire — the glittering future … intelligent, more liberal, sensitive to all the changes that the second half of the last century was making in society."

"And not long after the Crown Prince's tragic end, your brother had a terrible row with the Emperor?"

"It was well reported, yes. It was that which made him leave."

"And what was said? Do you know?"

"I have had many years to puzzle over it. I just don't know. It is one of the things I would like to ask him."

"And what of the Crown Prince's relations with his father?"

"I don't think they could have been worse. Each had lost the respect of the other. Do you know what the Emperor said of his son, when told of his death? 'He died like a *Schneider*.' You couldn't get much worse than that… could you?"

I was about to ask what she — or, for that matter, Franz-Josef — meant. The word means *tailor*, perhaps the occupation of my Prague inspector's forbears. But why on Earth should he call his son that? However, before I could ask, the carriage began to jolt as it climbed up to Rennes-le-Château, and a moment later, even before we had got to the dusty village square, a horseman rode up to us and spoke to the coachman.

The Archduchess leant out of the window. "What did the man want?" she called up to the box.

"Ma'am, he says we are to follow him. The event is not in the church itself," replied the coachman.

"Very well," she called back, and then addressed me. "These people are quite strange. But I still have my hopes."

It must have been a good three kilometres beyond the village, over a rough field track, when we came to a stand of pine trees by an outcrop of some of the pale limestone of the area. There were horses tethered beneath them, and a man who was clearly a lookout ran off as he saw us. The sun was low now, the shadows long and the onset of twilight was discernible. As the carriage came to a stop, the Archduchess lifted her veil and peered out. It seemed an odd place… yet I couldn't have said what would have been a more appropriate one.

Saunière appeared in a black frock coat of square, boxlike cut, looking more like an undertaker than a priest. It was he who opened the door.

"Your Serene Highness. This is our chapel."

He bowed as the Archduchess stepped down. Then he straightened up and looked at me suspiciously with his one watchful eye. I could see my presence didn't amuse him one bit.

In only a few steps it was possible to see that the limestone outcrop was, on one side, a sheer cliff — and in that cliff-face was a big square entrance. Behind some bushes I could see some old rails and other industrial detritus. This place had been one of those underground quarries that are common in the region. I knew this because in my guidebook to Carcassonne, which I had been reading only this morning, such quarries were mentioned as sources for the stone for the extensive restoration works of recent years.

A rough-looking character appeared with a lantern to light the way inside and I followed the Archduchess and Saunière down a long flight of worn stone steps. Suddenly we found ourselves in a space of cathedral-like proportions. What we could see of its walls and roof were of natural, unhewn stone, the bedrock. The scent of incense caught my nostrils. It really was quite dark, and, on a limestone block which served as a rude altar, candles guttered. As my eyes grew accustomed to the semi-darkness, I was suddenly aware that this "chapel" was full of people. The suppressed sound of them even being still and quiet echoed round the natural vault above us. Those few who were speaking were doing so in tones that were hushed and grave, which ceased abruptly as they caught sight of the Archduchess.

We were shown to simple rush-seated chairs in the front row. From this perspective I could see a dark shape between us and the altar. The Archduchess was looking at the candles. She leaned towards me. "My dear, have you seen them? They are black."

She was right. The candles were indeed made of black wax. But before one could think of what this meant, an altar boy came out with a taper and lit another row of candles some way behind the altar. To our horror, what was illuminated was a large crucifix against the back wall — but it was hanging upside down.

I gasped. The Archduchess gripped my arm: "I suppose this is what the Abbé means by extreme measures."

The gathering now hushed completely so that there was not a single sound. The canon who would celebrate this mass, if that was what this was to be, entered preceded by two more altar boys. The canon wore a scarlet bonnet from which what looked like two buffalo horns of red cloth protruded. In front of the altar, he turned to his congregation. To my horror I saw that he was wearing nothing beneath his priestly vestment. His black socks and his flesh bulging over the garters, attached high up on his legs, were plainly visible.

He made his genuflexions before the altar, then his voice rang out in a strange, high-pitched tone: "Master of darkness, administrator of sumptuous sins and great vices, Satan, thee we adore, reasonable God, just God!"

This was too much for me. I was about to rise, to leave, when I noticed that the Archduchess was gripped.

"We are gathered here together to witness, oh Divine Power of Darkness, your taking of a fleeting soul to bring that spirit to us here and now…"

This mockery of a priest now moved forward, as did the two altar boys who moved with him until they were each one side of the dark object between us and the altar. They lifted a cloth from it and we found ourselves looking at a plain table, on which stood a glass box. An almost unseen figure raised the wicks of the oil-lamps which surrounded the table, bathing it in slightly better light.

Inside the box — although rather dimly lit — was a human head.

"Who are you?" the weird priestly voice intoned.

It was amazing. The head moved, as if to look up at who was calling it. Then the lips moved. "I am now known as John Orth."

The Archduchess was peering forward, into the infuriating half-darkness. Certainly the features — or was it just the set of the face? — resembled the Johann Salvator I had seen in the photograph in the Archduchess' salon in Carcassonne. She gripped my arm again. "My dear brother," she said to the head.

"Is that my sister, Maria?"

"My dear brother... where are you?"

"Beyond all earthly powers."

"My little Ludwig..."

The head paused, just enough for the batting of an eyelid. Then he began to carry on. "Maria—"

The head was interrupted. "And what do you want? Why have you been sent to us?" the Archduchess cut in.

"My steel box. It must be given to those who need it — those who would use it for good..."

So I could clearly see where this was leading, just as Henri Loysel had indicated. Indeed, a dark figure I could just make out in the second row, could well have been him. But more importantly I noticed something: it was something under the table. It seemed to be something floating in the air. My mind wandered over scenes it had witnessed in the past... what was it? Then I was there, at the premises of Mr Moses Reach, looking at that ghastly cabinet of the Great Orsini. And suddenly the head in the glass case also had a jarring familiarity.

What was floating under the table this time was slightly different. It was the impression that a hand would make on a glass surface. At Mr Reach's, it had been a bloodstain. I suddenly recalled that passenger I had seen on the Express to Narbonne, and I remembered...

For the second time in my life I found myself saying, also rather loudly, "Nice try, Mr Grübbe."

Suddenly the head froze. Its eyes swivelled to find the voice, and I found myself, once the artificial pose of his features had relaxed and all pretension had suddenly been withdrawn — staring into the eyes of the actor Hans Grübbe. The last time had been at Marienbad. He was nothing if not versatile, and quite convincing too.

Abruptly he stood up, lifting the glass box off his head as if discarding a helmet. He had been crouched behind the deceptive mirrors that created the illusion of clear space under the table. I had to admit it had been a brilliant piece of acting. Grübbe was mouthing curses, I think aimed at me, but in the general confusion and uproar I was fortunate in not being able to hear them. Then he bellowed, now in his own deeply theatrical voice, which immediately stilled the disorder:

"'Twas an ill wind which blew me forth from Prague!"

He was somewhat mixing his metaphors, of course, and in this he was in appropriate company; wasn't it the great Shakespeare himself who had referred to "the shores of Bohemia"?

Then he abruptly lapsed into the rough street-German of Prague with its distinct whiffs of Yiddish together with the softer consonants of Czech. "If only Devine 'ad been 'ere. Things wouldn't 'ave gone wrong!" And he stormed off, trying, as he did so, to wipe off the pallid grease-paint from his face with his sleeve.

I was immediately worried about the Archduchess. Would this sudden disappointment crush her? I turned to her. Her eyes were filled with tears — and yet she was laughing.

"What a fool I have been to be taken in by any of this nonsense for one moment. Come Beatrice."

Then as we were approaching the carriage, now turned about, its lamps glistening in the darkness and with the coachman already on the box, she squeezed my arm and leant close to me. Almost whispering, she said , "And, by the way, I never called him Ludwig — he was my other brother!"

༄

I continued to accompany the Archduchess on the train back to Paris. Now she was in black silk, and although in a subdued mood, it seemed somehow as if a great weight had been lifted from her.

"It takes something like this," she said, "to make me realise that my dear brother is long dead. I cannot resurrect him. I will never hear his voice again — just as he will never hear mine. It has taken nearly fifteen years for me to come to terms with this. I have to recognise it, and now I do."

"But the stories…?"

"Yes, he had a very strong craft and a crew of more than thirty on the *Santa Margareta*, but the waters of Cape Horn are the most treacherous in the world. It is true he wanted to start a new life, and may well have thought of doing so as an ordinary citizen somewhere, quite incognito. But there are two facts against his surviving the journey: one is that even if he had done this, he would somehow have sent a message to his mother and me — just to set our minds at rest. He was not cruel, and would not have dreamt of torturing his dear mother and sister. Two, is that he was a quite exceptional and extraordinary person. Even if he had started again on some simple ranch, or travelling the cities of some South American country selling knick-knacks or whatever — his innate special qualities as a man of distinction would have been recognised, and soon news of such a man would have leaked out. No, that he is alive is just wishful or plain fanciful thinking. I can see that now all too clearly."

She fell silent for a minute or so. The view outside the window was gradually changing from the luxuriant south to less temperate areas, where the same grey skies would no doubt greet us on our arrival in Paris.

She spoke again, but continuing to look out at the view this time:

"Some said he was still alive because sums of money continued to be withdrawn from his bank account. It turned out that these were payments taken out — under some arrangement before my brother left in 1890 — by the Abbé Saunière or that brother of his. When mother contacted the Abbé, he explained that he was paid to say mass for her son, and — seeing a mother and a sister in their grief — he decided to take advantage of us. The final result was what happened yesterday evening."

"They say Saunière made a lot of money…"

"Maybe to the uneducated folk in that village it seemed like it, but what does it amount to? A church with some rather ugly carvings, and that tower of his — one big room filled with unusual things he has picked up in the flea markets of Carcassonne. It certainly doesn't add up to the fabulous fortune his so-called 'housekeeper' says he found, thanks to secret scrolls that were discovered under the floor of the church or in some such unlikely place. No, what with this separation of Church and State, and the fact that I shall see he doesn't get another sou from my family, I should think the high days of the Abbé Saunière are well and truly over."

"But you were keen to believe in the séances?"

"Well, I had the evidence of my own eyes and ears... the undeniable energy present at those gatherings at Lady Caithness', the mysterious rappings on the table — and the plain fact that Devine could indeed command the power of levitation."

I held back from explaining how most of this was good old-fashioned stage illusionism created by very Earth-bound wood and wires.

"And the steel box... what is that?" I feigned ignorance.

"Ugh! That wretched steel box. Yes, it had been purposely left for my mother, with a note stating that it had been entrusted to my brother, the late Prince Rudolf. It was an elaborate gothic piece, but when I inherited it, I found it quite unsuited to the decoration of my apartments..."

She turned to me, gauging my reaction. She saw on my countenance that I thought this a rather feeble excuse to what she would no doubt say next. Then she looked out of the window again. A peasant girl was chasing geese across a field... we glimpsed the scene only briefly.

She went on: "And perhaps, too, because it had been owned by the ill-fated Rudolf, I wanted to be rid of it. Maybe it was the cause of all the bad luck we had had since Rudolf died. Did you know that five days before Rudolf was born, the great chandelier in the Hall of Ceremonies at Schönbrunn Palace suddenly fell to the floor and smashed to pieces? Everyone at Court thought it a very bad omen. So in the end, I sent the box to Count Wilczek. He collects things like that. He immediately sent me a letter thanking me for it, as indeed it was just up his street. I sincerely hope it didn't bring him any bad luck."

She seemed distracted by the village we were passing through. A rural station flashed by... eager faces on the platform, chickens in crates, a railwayman smoking a pipe in the signal box.

"And — if I recall correctly — he even sent me a second note. But I was travelling. I can't remember now if I replied to it, but he was certainly as glad to have the thing as I was not to."

The old Archduchess turned back to me; the view could continue to whisk by without her attention to it. Now I seized my chance and said, "And you sent it to him with whatever was inside?"

"My dear, it was empty. I had the key. I opened it. There was nothing inside it at all. I really don't know what all the fuss was about with that wretched box. Marie Larisch started the thing with her memoirs. I hope that last night will have been the last time I shall ever hear of it."

I decided that now was the time to go and see that Sabine was all right; besides, I needed to powder my nose. It was inappropriate that Sabine should sit with us, so I had banished her to Second Class. I simply couldn't send her to Third, the normal domain of the domestic. Doubtless there would be others of the higher servant class she could talk to, if she were so minded, and the Second Class dining car on a French train, of course, was more than adequate.

Passing down the corridor I found myself casually looking into those compartments which did not have their blinds drawn. Suddenly my eye was drawn to a man stretched out in one otherwise empty compartment. It was Henri Loysel. I assumed it was he whom I had spotted at the black mass.

I was too surprised at seeing him to then go and speak to him. Maybe I would do it on the way back from seeing Sabine. The next carriage was the beginning of Second Class, and I was further surprised to see Hans Grübbe in another compartment. The fact that he was at Rennes-le-Château meant that whatever his punishment had been resulting from his impersonation of Kaiser Wilhelm at Marienbad last year, it clearly hadn't been a long stretch in gaol! In my quick glance at him I could see he looked tired, and possibly fed-up. He probably hadn't been paid. I hurried on; if he was fed-up, then it most probably would have been with me, first and foremost.

In fact the train seemed to be full of people trying to put as much distance as they could from Rennes-le-Château, a place they hoped they would never see again! Only the Abbé Saunière seemed to be left in that dead-end spot, which would now return to its moribund self — its only extravagance being that ridiculous tower, gazed at by those grotesque new carvings installed in the old church.

Soon I found Sabine, and dealt with arrangements for when we would arrive back in Paris, and I informed her that the following day we would be returning to Prague.

"That will mean we will have one more night in Paris, Sabine. You shall be off-duty."

"Oh, Madame. You are so thoughtful."

We could have gone directly to Prague via Munich or across to Vienna first, but I wanted time to think if there was anything more I needed to accomplish in Paris before leaving it. Now it was time to confront Henri Loysel. Having got to the door of his compartment, I drew a deep breath and knocked. Luckily, he was alone inside. We greeted each other in the usual way, and he invited me to sit opposite him. Then the conversation proper could begin.

"I thought I saw you in the 'chapel' at Rennes," I began.

"Yes, I was there. Long ago it was planned that Jean-Paul and Antoine would have been with me."

"And what of Antoine?"

"He has returned directly to Prague."

"Directly?" This seemed odd.

Loysel hesitated, then collected his thoughts: "Yes... I mean directly from Paris... of course."

Which, I felt, was precisely what he didn't mean. But I couldn't guess what he was hiding, or why.

"And he will soon enter an order of extreme penitence," he carried on more confidently. "The last time the three of us met, it was shortly after the accident which killed Devine."

"Accident?"

Henri Loysel did not answer. Then he seemed to decide to tell me something and he began thus: "We went through our diaries and found there were certain dates which appeared to be blank in them, common to all three of us. These must have been the times when we were obeying Devine's ghastly orders. Mesmerism is such a deadly power."

"As The Great Orsini and Wilajalba Frikell found out — all too deadly. But it is unfair of me to dwell on this; the perpetrators were not you and your brothers. You were then... *other* beings."

"Monsters," he said, gravely. He hung his head, and again there was a pause while he considered what to say next. "And it looks like we will never find out what is in the steel box — we will never avenge our father. For that, Countess, I do not thank you."

"The game was up before I unmasked Hans Grübbe. Johann Salvator never answered to the name Ludwig. That was a little trick of the Archduchess. She's no fool. But who devised this whole idea… the illusion, the actor…? Or can I guess?"

"You are right. Devine. You see, we thought he was working for us, embracing our cause. But all the time it was something different."

Yes, he had been motivated only by greed — to fleece the brothers and steal either a hidden fortune or a very usable deadly secret.

Then, with an air of finality, he asked, "And the box…?"

"I asked the Archduchess about it. It was empty. All along there was nothing to the story. Marie Larisch must have made the whole thing up."

"So there's nothing left. We failed."

"I don't think so. If your goal was to see Franz-Josef humiliated or punished, then history has done that very severely: his son and heir a murderer and then a suicide. Sissy, his beloved wife, first of all unfaithful, and then herself murdered. And the Empire? First, the Italian possessions all lost, then total humiliation at the hands of the Prussians, with all of Bohemia conquered. I can't see that any of you could have done more to the old man."

"You are right. We were taken over by devils other than those supplied by Devine. Vengeance gave all three of us something to live for, but ultimately it eats you up from the inside."

He turned to the window. It seemed almost impossible that this man, who, with his brothers, had managed to do well, despite having their lives almost ruined by the death of their father, had not only been one of the murderers of Orsini — and perhaps perpetrated other horrors of which I was not aware — but might also have been responsible for my own murder, too.

Then I thought to ask him about the fourth man who must have helped them on the Abt.

"According to our diaries," he answered, "before the blank days, we each had notes of a telephone call or a message from this Hélène Johanson. In Antoine's diary there is a note of a meeting. I have been thinking about this too. She must have known who it was?"

"But too late, now."

On the other hand, it gave me an idea. Perhaps it was Johanson herself. I remembered at the very beginning Inspector Schneider had said there'd been some confusion about the height of the passenger going down the Abt... to the point that Schneider had wondered whether this was including or excluding the head! If it was Johanson, then that would explain it, and yet I couldn't imagine anyone able to act so callously to someone they knew, let alone a woman. However, Devine had the power to put her within his total control. Thank heavens he no longer had it.

I left Henri Loysel staring out at the landscape slipping by, with the almost mesmeric effect of the telegraph wires swelling up and down between their posts like brisk ocean waves as the train passed them at speed. I recalled, when I was eight or nine, being on the express between Brunn and Vienna with Max, staring out at the telegraph posts, and Max using a single word: *hypnotic.*

About half an hour later, seated with the Archduchess, we were suddenly jolted from our places by the train stopping sharply, its wheels screeching on the metal rails as we ground to a halt. There was no station at this point. We were on an embankment, not long after we had passed over a high bridge across a river valley.

Soon the conductor was knocking on the compartment doors. "*Mesdames, messieurs* — there is nothing to worry about. We will be starting again shortly. *S'il vous plaît*, keep to your seats."

Instinctively, I knew what was up. I left the compartment and caught the conductor a little way down the corridor, and asked him what the problem was.

"Carriage Four, *Madame*. A passenger jumped from the train. We will be able to start again in a moment. There is nothing we can do. The body must be down in the valley. Another passenger saw what happened. It must have been a case of *le suicide*."

"I may have more information I can give the authorities if the person who jumped is who I think it is."

"We will be stopping at the next station, *Madame*, and an agent of the Railway Police will board the train. I am sure your assistance will be most welcome."

Chapter Nine

The Deadly Thaw

I wish I could say that I felt uplifted at seeing the spires and domes of Prague again as the train crossed the bridge over the Moldau before disappearing into the tunnel that brought it into FJ1 Station, but I felt weary. I didn't think I could cope with any more deaths. Perhaps I wasn't cut out to be a detective, after all. Men are used to seeing corpses piled high on battlefields. For a woman, each death is some mother's son, a heartbreak, a futile waste of all that love and nurturing. For a man, a corpse has no more worth than the value of its boots.

Sabine and I had left Paris quickly, as on the journey from the south I had realised I had nothing more to do there. I had given a detailed statement in the same building which contains La Sainte Chapelle to the Deputy Prefect of Police about Henri Loysel, but stating only that I had found him depressed — without saying I knew why. In Prague I would probably have to tell the whole truth to Inspector Schneider in order to close the file on the murder of Orsini. So far I had sent him a letter which I had had time to compose in Carcassonne, setting out the bare bones. For the moment, however, I didn't want to think of that. In Prague, first I would rest — in my own, wonderfully comfortable bed.

Sabine came into the compartment. "Was everything Madame wanted here?"

"Sabine, indeed it was. While they serve the breakfasts, you can pin up my hair."

But we had no sooner entered the station when Sabine pointed through the window: "Ee's 'ere, Madame!" she exclaimed.

"There's no need for such excitement, Sabine. I had telegraphed Müller from Paris." I had wanted to see a familiar face on arrival, who better than Müller?

"But... but..." she began.

But it was Karel at the door of the compartment. He entered, as was his right, without knocking. He held in his hand a bouquet of hot-house flowers.

"My dearest," he said, shaking my hand, and thrusting the flowers forward. I just wished he knew about passion. Daringly, I offered him my cheek, which he brushed affectionately with his lips. "Your exploits are the talk of Prague."

It was then that I noticed under his arm a sheaf of newspapers. He spread them out on the banquette. *Mystery of the Headless Body Solved, Magician's Death in Paris Ends Prague Murder Mystery, Mesmerism Fiends in Death Plot* were some of the headlines. I quickly scanned the articles to see if the Loysel brothers were mentioned. Indeed, they were, but Father Antoine was not named personally and it was not stated that he actually lived in Prague. But it would only be a matter of time before some eager member of the press put two and two together.

I felt it my duty to go and see him. What I could do for him,

I had no idea — warn him, console him, convince him of his true innocence... I just didn't know.

"Dearest, have you the carriage here?"

"Naturally."

"Then, please, a detour on our way home. To Malá Strana first. I can explain *en route*."

It was just after seven-thirty when we set out from the station. I could sense in the air, in the weak sunshine, in the singing of the first returning birds that the long winter had finally ended in Prague. Everywhere water was dripping from what had been ice and snow. It would soon be time, I mused, for 'gold collectors' to return to the streets of the city — pushing their little box-carts to collect the horse manure. Snow and ice were their enemies!

As if to mock my silly, optimistic thoughts, in the streets, blackened mounds of old snow lay like the corpses left on the battlefield of Solferino. As our carriage arrived at the end of the Charles Bridge, on the Malá Strana side, we had to dismount as a large coal wagon was blocking the way to Maltézské Square. As Karel and I began walking, I noticed the appearance again of the cobblestones, hidden since the beginning of winter, gleaming fresh under the merest cover of clear ice like shellfish at the fishmonger's. This ice, I might point out, was absolutely treacherous for good shoes. For certain, winter was on the run and spring was coming.

I could see ladders on the roofs and men roped to chimneys calling down as they detached huge rafts of snow so they wouldn't simply fall on passersby.

"But we had extremely bad weather these last two weeks," Karel said. "Intense cold and heavy, blustery snow. We thought the dratted winter would never end."

A band of gypsies was employed clearing the street beyond the coal wagon, colourful women and shirking men, and they seemed to be having only a faint impact with shovelling away the slush and old grit left after the final melt. Now I could see the residence of the Maltese Knights, next to the church where I had seen the footprints in the snow in what seemed another lifetime.

There were men on the roof dislodging the snow. One was calling down: "Mind there below, stand back…. mind there below, stand back."

Karel and I stepped across to the other side of the street. A huge cascade of snow fell… and in that second I noticed the wicket in the big central doorway of the residence opening, and an old man stepping out. The man on the roof saw him, but the snow was already falling… "Back, back…" he shouted. But the old man, in priest's clothes, took no heed. The snow — perhaps a ton of it — landed with a terrifying thud.

Others who saw it ran to the scene. But there was nothing they could do. After digging, the frail, twisted body was hauled out. The old man — Father Antoine — was dead, his face crushed by the weight and impact of the snow. He was almost unrecognisable — except for one chilling item. Under his cassock, his bare legs were showing, sprawled out as the body was on the pavement. I had seen those sock-suspenders before, with the bulging white flesh just showing above. Now I knew why the late Henri Loysel had said that his brother had travelled directly to Prague… but not from Paris. There had clearly been more to Father Antoine than I would ever find out.

The man who had been the watcher and warner on the roof was now down on the street. "He must have heard me," he was saying. "Anyway, the street gate had a rope across it. He must have known we were working…"

But I knew that was precisely why the late Father Antoine had unlocked the door, and stepped boldly over the rope and out… to his death.

"Please, Karel, there can't be any more deaths, can there?" I sobbed.

He cannot have known what I was talking about, but he took me in his arms and kissed me. "Take me out of here," I beseeched him.

"Home — and plenty of rest, as you were saying," he said somewhat reassuringly, "and there you can tell me all about it."

This last remark was said somewhat in the manner of a father to a spoilt child. Where on Earth could I start? And I certainly couldn't tell him anything about the Emperor's special task, so as usual I didn't say anything. He would put it down to having a temperamental wife. Since he always preferred "spirited" mounts (as he called his horses, and for all I knew, his women), then he thus imagined me as a "spirited" wife.

I had been looking forward to seeing Müller again. A stalwart butler is the bedrock upon which a properly functioning household is founded — and that rat Philip Seymour had been right, I needed a man on my adventures. But apart from Müller's greeting and then seeing him instructing the young footman to unload the luggage, I saw little of him for the next three days since I took to my bed. I needed to think, to reflect, and simply to rest. Around noon on the first day, he appeared briefly with a tray on which was a silver soup tureen, a china bowl, three pieces of cold toast, and a glass of mineral water.

"Try this meat tea, Milady. It is perfect for invalids."

I turned him away; "I am not an invalid," I said rather briskly. I hated anything connected with invalids, crutches, and wheelchairs.

The second day Müller arrived again with the same tray. "You need this hearty beef broth, Milady. It will restore your strength."

"I am not lacking in strength, as far as I know," I replied. But this time he left the tray. However, I didn't touch it.

On the third day, Müller again brought the same concoction, but the toast had been replaced by fresh rolls and there was a rose. "Sabine has suggested this *boeuf bouillon*, Milady…"

"Very well, Müller, you may leave it, but I don't guarantee to drink it."

And this time he left the lid off the tureen, and the smell wafted across to me. My resolve to be some kind of martyr soon weakened, and since I had had nothing since I had returned, I devoured it all. However, I still kept to my bed.

Müller clearly tried another tack, and later that day he knocked, stood in my boudoir, next to my bedroom, and coughed. Without waiting for a reply, he announced a visitor in his stuffiest voice, as if addressing an entire Hofburg Ball:

"The Countess von Morštejn, Your Ladyship's mother."

"Yes, I am fully aware who my mother is, thank you Müller," I managed to croak back, as into my room sailed Mamma, Sabine following rather sheepishly behind.

"Müller informed me that you weren't well, my dear," Mother began at once, with no greeting. "But once you are up, I am convinced you will feel a lot better. Now here's Sabine to get you dressed. Come on now!"

"But what about Karel?" I protested. She should have asked him first.

"He said you were resting. People don't rest for three days in a row, so I called again, and thank heavens, Müller picked up the instrument. I did get some sense from him."

I decided to change the subject entirely. "Your hat, Mother — it looks as if a dead cat were lying on it."

She huffed. "The hat, by the way, is the very latest thing in London, having been worn first by Queen Alexandra. But now I know you must be on the mend, Beatrice. It was the same when you were a child. The colour would come back to your cheeks after an illness, and with it the cheek."

৬০

Dressed and correct, I had tea with Mother in the drawing-room. Although I didn't want to admit it, I was glad that things were nearly back to normal. I was home. Home was safe. Cucumber sandwiches, made with her approval and with the correct amount of salt and pepper (a pinch and a light sprinkle respectively), were safe. Smoked China tea was safe (Lapsang Sooshong but mixed half-and-half with the best Ceylon). Our dear palace was safe. I was safe.

Best was simply to tell her everything. If I didn't, she'd have winkled out parts of the story from me and perhaps not made sense of any of it.

"How ghastly!" was her final commentary as I finished my narrative,."It verges on the incredible."

"Ghastly, Mamma? It was terrible…"

"Yes, terrible that a daughter of mine should get mixed up in all this."

"*A* daughter of yours? I'm the *only* one you've got!"

"Then more's the pity! And this other thing you are doing, what a pity it is that you are simply employed to look into the K&K's dirty linen basket. Why couldn't you have been selected for... for... I mean to be, for instance, the companion of the All Highest in..." she really was quite worked up, "...in ...in lawn croquet?"

"Mamma, I'm not cut out to play croquet. It's far too violent. You have to be so calculating and vicious."

"Vicious? Why, last year I found myself playing it with two bishops and the mayor of Pardubitz..."

"Exactly, Mamma. You have proved my point! Anyway, I think the Emperor's question needs skill and patience. It's difficult work."

"I don't doubt — the most difficult of all. Who cares if magicians try to steal each other's ideas? What more could one expect from illusionists? Nothing concrete, that's for sure."

"But, Mamma, the murders were only too concrete."

"I know. They must have been most upsetting for you."

"Particularly upsetting for those involved," I pointed out.

"Now don't twist my words, Beatrice. It was terrible for you, threatened by those fiends. But on the other matter, I hope you realise the Archduchess has inadvertently marked your card. Count Wilczek is a very special character, a striking personality, surrounded by a halo of romance. He is immensely rich, and they say he's as distinguished on battlefields as he is on the waxed floors of aristocratic mansions. The Wilczeks own most of the coal mines around Ostrava and that part of Silesia. When Sissy was trying to get her secret memoirs printed, it is said that Wilczek collected the manuscript from Sissy's window, three floors up, and then jumped back to his house which backed on to the Hofburg Annexe in order to frustrate the guards. He is gallant, an adventurer, and I am sure he will shed new light on that time when Rudolf and his father were at loggerheads. As soon as I am back at Morštejn, I shall write to him and suggest he receive you at the earliest opportunity."

"Another slice of *Sacher dort*, Mamma?"

∽

After Mamma had finally been packed off to the Hohenlohes', I could relax somewhat — well, after just one more task. She really was such a snob. For example, she always used everyone's full name, however ridiculous a handle it was. On leaving she had said: "Prince Chlodwig Hohenlohe-Waldenburg-Schillingsfürst is a quite charming host, my dear Beatrice. And I believe the Duc and Duchesse Doudeauville will be staying. And if the Mensdorff-Pouillys join us from Boskovice Castle, it will be quite a party!"

Quite — and quite a mouthful it would be. But my mind was already on my next appointment: Inspector Schneider's visit. This, I sincerely hoped, would put an end to the whole business which had begun that snowy night on the Abt's Rack. When that was over, I could really relax a little. I could organise a small dinner here — it had seemed ages since I had done so. I summoned Müller to go and ask my husband if he would be free one evening the following week. I could invite the Brezina-Kraselovskys, just because when she heard about it, Mamma would be apoplectic. She thought they were fakes — along with their heraldry. But in the end, I knew I wouldn't; I couldn't stand to. The wife was just too insipid.

When Müller returned, it was also to announce Schneider, already taken up to the drawing-room.

The inspector seemed both a little nervous and the set of his face was now a little more serious than I had remembered it. I supposed that age and experience were now bringing him into the darker realities of the world, where the sun is not always shining — especially in the criminal world.

"Countess," he said, rising and shaking my hand. A peck on the cheek, as I thought I had taught him last year, would have been more cordial. "I am so dreadfully sorry…"

"Sorry?"

"For the press reports. They were premature. I wanted to wait until we had had this meeting, and I had heard the full story."

"But you had my letter? And I can tell you that since then, there have been two more casualties in this affair."

"Yes, I had your letter — then it was seen, or rather taken, by the Police Commissioner. He then called Paris, and I know he had a long conversation on the telephone with Inspector Bourgoine of the First Arrondissement. He's their murder specialist, and was investigating the death of the magician Devine. From what he knew, and from your letter, we pieced most of it together. But, as I said, it should not have been printed — but you know what journalists are…"

"I do know, but I can hardly repeat it."

"However, I do have one question." He waited.

"Then ask it, please."

"I can't imagine how you managed to come up with the notion that the murderers were under the influence of mesmerism."

"My dear Inspector, when your back is up against the wall — and I can tell you that at the moment I came to the conclusion, my back was, quite literally — then one's brain spins through all the possible alternatives, which range from one's own death right through to the solution of the problem. Luckily, my brain had just enough time to get to the latter."

"I am sure that this will go down in the annals of great detection, Countess."

"Please, put it down to chance, to luck, to the sheer accident of being there. However, I do not recommend this as a technique."

"You are far too modest, Countess."

I felt we had finished our business once I had told him everything that had transpired in Paris and in the south, and sensed he was ready to leave. Then I thought of something. "Inspector," I said, "one more thing. I want my butler, Müller, to have and to be able to use a revolver. Would you be able to assist in this? I will need to procure a weapon, and Müller will have to have some practice."

"It will be my pleasure. And, if I may be permitted to say, it's a very wise move."

He was just leaving, when he suddenly turned back to me. "But I've forgotten the most important news!"

"Yes?"

"Maybe you don't know, but Devine's assistant, this Hélène Johanson, survived. She's in hospital, in a pretty bad state, and I am going to Paris to interview her. I have no doubt she will be charged in connection with the murder of Orsini. Then, when she is well enough to travel, she will find herself coming back to Prague."

"So justice will be seen to have been done, after all."

"I hope so. Good-day, Countess."

I walked over to the French windows leading to the balcony and watched the tall, almost elegant Schneider as he crossed the street, twirling his hat on his finger. I felt I should tell him that if he were to do that in Paris, especially on the Rue de St Denis, he would be signalling to women of very unsavoury character.

What an extraordinary turn of events! That night I had an entirely normal night's sleep. Remarkably, there were no nightmares, so hopefully I would fully recover from my ordeal. What a resilient creature the human being is.

After breakfast Müller hurried in to tell me my mother was on the telephone.

"I am finally back home. Morštejn seems to have survived the winter with only two leaks so far. A little water is running down Great Grandfather's face... the big equestrian portrait in the stair-hall. It always leaks there, as well you know. And there's a new leak above the music room."

I was relieved that Mamma didn't tell me yet again how neither the best architect from Prague, nor the building contractor who works for the Archbishop had been able to cure that leak which hits Great-Grandfather around this time every year. The matter had been solved when Mamma had finally condescended to ask Mr Černík from the village (who had known the castle man and boy) for his opinion. He had come, taken off his cap and scratched his head: "Why sure," he had said, "that leak was there before the castle was built." Based on that gem of folk wisdom, the leak was simply left!

"Your boys have been magnificent in clearing the roofs," Mamma went on.

"I hope you haven't been feeding them too much."

Mamma chose to ignore this, which meant she was guilty. I hoped she wasn't spoiling my charming urchins. She changed subject. "Count Wilczek replied to my letter by telegram. I couldn't wait until I was back home, so I wrote from the Hohenlohes. He'd be delighted to see you."

"In Vienna? He lives there?"

"Oh no, my dear. He lives about an hour away from the capital, on the way to Znaim — in Kreuzenstein Castle. An extraordinary edifice. You are very honoured to get an invitation. He's become quite reclusive in recent years. He says he looks forward to meeting you on Friday."

"Friday?"

"That's what he says. Good luck!"

Chapter Ten

A Castle Beyond Imagination

Müller knocked on the compartment door with his usual discretion.

"Yes, I am quite decent — you may come in now."

He stepped in, and I handed him a bundle of clothes which he proceeded to pack into his small travelling valise. "You can put the blinds back up as well," I told him.

"I think the ruse worked well, Milady. The photographers are probably still waiting for their countess detective!"

And I had almost forgotten how simply liberating my urchin costume was. I had mingled with the crowd, all looking expectantly up to my balcony, as one of them. It seemed a shame that I couldn't share my secret — that they were all wasting their time!

One journalist had gained an interview. He was from one of the Czech daily papers. It must have been in a moment of weakness that I'd allowed it. After fielding most of his questions, on the way back down the stairs (I had chosen to meet in the drawing room, when it should have been in Karel's Business Room), the rather desperate young man had looked up at my portrait and asked if he could send a man round to take a photograph of it. I was on the point of agreeing to this when he stated that he found the wretched picture "beguiling" — at which point I declined the request, as I had also declined to be photographed in person.

Coming back upstairs I stopped a moment, drawn by that portrait. I never noticed it these days. It had been ordered on my honeymoon in Venice from the popular artist Vittorio Corcos. He drew the preparatory sketches in his studio and his assistant had taken a photograph. Six months later, the painting had arrived in Prague. What expectant eyes I'd had then — hoping that by marrying Karel the Earth would indeed move and we would conquer the world — or, at least, Austrian Society. Such hopeful eyes — the Italian artist, who clearly knew women well — had captured me exactly as I was then, even to the point of painting something doleful behind my allure. He had foretold the disillusion that I would soon experience. And he'd suggested the green velvet dress, copied from out of an antique portrait of one of the Medicis.

I had married too early. Mother had been anxious to get this rather rebellious mixed-race creature into any dratted marriage, fearing none would transpire. The problem was that I seemed more than willing at the time…

I wondered how Signor Corcos would portray me now. I had lost the rather foolish optimism of youth, certainly, but what has replaced it? I hoped I still had spirit, though world-weariness had no doubt made its mark. The experiences of the last weeks must surely have taken their toll.

Müller sat facing the engine, sinking back into the cushions. "The last time I travelled First was when I was going to be interviewed by Prince Schwarzenberg. A fine gentleman, if I may say so. Very generous to his staff. But I didn't get the job, as in those days

I lacked experience with royalty. He said he would bear me in mind for a future position, but then I got work quick enough back in Prague."

"You are a most valuable asset to any household, Müller. I had a terrible row with His Lordship to let you accompany me. I hope you didn't let on about the revolver."

"As Milady requested, His Lordship has no idea about it. However, I would feel more comfortable if I'd had time to practice with it. Inspector Schneider simply placed it in my hand and said 'With the compliments of the Police Commissioner,' two days ago, and that was it."

"And you have our itinerary?"

"Naturally, Milady. In Vienna we simply change platforms, and there should be a wait of only a quarter of an hour for the train to Stockerau. But we descend two stations before, at Leobendorf. The castle informed me they will have a carriage waiting for us at the station. We should be there by about three-thirty."

"In time for tea. Mamma… I mean the Countess of Morštejn… brought me up in the English tradition, Müller, which in her view is the only civilized way to exist on the planet. But then she's English, of course!"

❧

The carriage took us first through a small village, then beyond it the road — or more accurately, the driveway — climbed into a dark forest. The way snaked ever upwards and the spring sun slanted between the straight, dark pine trunks, sometimes catching in its rays rising mist from the damp woodland floor. And suddenly, in this magical setting, we could see it, towering above us: the most fantastic castle, everything one had ever dreamt of in fairy stories, beyond one's wildest imaginings.

"My God!" Müller exclaimed loudly, then looked round at me, a little embarrassed. "I'm sorry, Milady."

Then it disappeared as the drive wound round again, gaining more height. Through a gap in the tall trees at the next bend we could see the otherwise flat landscape far below us, dotted with farms and villages, and then a final sweep round and the trees cleared and Kreuzenstein Castle was before us in all its bizarre splendour.

It was as if the knights, ladies, lords, foot-soldiers, and kitchen boys of the fifteenth century had stepped away for a moment, leaving their perfect fortress for us to inspect. The Count's coachman turned round from the box, saying, "Of course, it's all new. His Lordship has a passion for history, you understand."

The poor fellow sounded almost apologetic. But why? This was the most wonderful confection, without doubt the most romantic castle I had ever seen. Müller was almost open-mouthed as he looked up at the profusion of towers, spires, turrets, and battlements as our carriage rattled over a very practical-looking drawbridge, and then along a defensive defile between the outer and inner walls of the fortress to a second gateway and drawbridge. I also looked up. There was a huge stone balcony between carved columns, and I thought I glimpsed a tall, robed figure surveying us.

"Are there many staying at present?" I asked the coachman.

"No, ma'am. The Count is alone. Only he and us servants."

We had to wait at the second gate while it was hauled open for us. Within was a mighty bastion fully prepared for a medieval siege, and beyond that, two low gothic-style buildings housed the stables and the servants' quarters. The carriage stopped here briefly for Müller to get down. Then we passed under an enormous archway, shrouded in wooden scaffolding, through which we entered the inner courtyard. Stepping out of a small doorway was the tall figure I had seen earlier.

The robe was in fact a shooting cloak, which was now over Count Wilczek's arm. He wore a loose country suit in tweed, and was at once a noticeably very tranquil character. He must have been in his late sixties. His hair was almost white and he wore a neat beard and moustache, but what I was drawn to were his piercing blue eyes. They were magnetic, and I couldn't imagine that many women hadn't instantly fallen for them — and their charming owner. I remembered Mamma's words: "striking... surrounded by a halo of romance." Yes.

"Welcome to Kreuzenstein, Countess," he said as he advanced with a hand thrust forward. "I am sorry we are still doing building work — that's the famous Kaschau gallery I'm installing there, above the great arch. It originally supported the organ in the cathedral of Kaschau, but I found the bishop was going to remove it and break it up. It is the best example of pure Slovakian gothic that exists. I shall give it a good home!"

"Your coachman said it was all new."

"The walls up to a certain level are all original, but the castle was virtually destroyed in the Thirty Years' War. So I have had to find almost everything to make it glorious again. But everything I have imported is original... hands that held swords in the name of Maximilian the First have touched these stones, the skirts of medieval ladies have brushed these ancient tiles, and all my treasures have been seen centuries ago by the eyes of kings and princes from Burgundy to Bohemia. Come, I work up in the Northwest Tower..."

He pointed to a tall tower which had a gabled room high up, right under the peak of its fish-scale tiled roof.

"I hope you don't mind a few stairs," he said calmly, without giving me the chance to reply.

It was quite dark inside, and once my coat was taken from me, I followed Count Wilczek, who walked quickly and with long strides, through the most extraordinary ensemble of rooms: an armoury complete with all the weapons an entire medieval army would need, a staircase with curious carvings, an enormous hall with a huge old ceramic stove and hung with tapestries. Then, after more twisting passageways and steps, we entered a spectacular chapel with soaring stone vaults, yet we were on a gallery looking down on it. Late afternoon sun blazed through the stained-glass windows, dappling the pale stone columns with many colours. Through a small gothic door, which opened with a satisfying clunk, was a spiral staircase which twisted up and up until we arrived at a room lined with antique books and containing the only comfortable chair I had seen in the entire castle.

"My study. Do sit down, Countess. I hope you will be warm enough."

In fact, unlike the other rooms which were freezing, it was hot in here, thanks to a wood stove which hissed in the corner.

"I shall ring for some coffee." So saying he tugged at an old velvet-covered rope in a corner of the room. The bell it sounded must have been an extremely long way away, deep in the subterranean bowels of the place. More daunting was the thought of the coffee having to pass through all those freezing passages and to come up the staircase we had just climbed.

The Count sat down on a simple, but extremely old and worn wooden chair. I could only think of all those medieval hands which had polished parts of it so smooth over the centuries. "I knew your late great-uncle very well," he began. "We were both at the battle of Könniggrätz in 1866. That was quite enough to dispel any thoughts of the glories of war. My interest in the Middle Ages is strictly romantic."

"Uncle Berty used to speak of it. He blamed the military authorities for not supplying the correct rifles."

"Military authorities, Countess? You meant the All Highest, and he alone. And your uncle was quite correct. But what brings you to see me? These days I don't get many social callers. I grant you this is not your normal Vienna drawing-room."

I went straight to it. "Archduchess Maria of Tuscany said she had once sent you an old steel box. I am interested in it."

The Count stood up and went over to a book-press, on top of which was an array of elaborate iron caskets. He reached up and took one down. "You mean this one?"

He moved nearer the window, where the light would be better, and turned it over, examining it carefully. "It's a copy — sixty or seventy years old, I should think, and in the style of the fifteenth-century Nuremberg workshops. It's a beautiful piece. Since it had been sent to me by the Archduchess, I wondered if the elaborate locks had been made by Archduke Johann's brother Ludwig. You know he became a well-known locksmith?"

"I don't know," I replied, "as it came originally from Crown Prince Rudolf."

"Rudolf, eh?" and he continued to look at its fine gothic detail.

"Tell me, was it empty?"

"I don't know what your interest is, but that's an odd story."

"The Archduchess said there was nothing in it."

"Well, a couple of weeks after I first got it, I sat down with the thing one afternoon. The original boxes usually had secret compartments. After a few minutes, I managed to find this rivet here…" and he pointed it out, a plain flattened rivet which seemed to look just like the others, "and I could see that it didn't seem to be forged to the frame of the box. I could prise it out a bit with this knife, and then, turning it… see…? A little drawer on a spring comes out."

As he said, a shallow drawer emerged.

"And in that there was an envelope. From the paper, I could tell it was quite modern — that is, within the last sixty or seventy years. It was sealed with gum, and no wax, and bore no names, words, or marks of any kind. I should think it must have contained three or four sheets of ordinary letter paper."

He stopped.

"And…?" I was desperate to hear more.

"I wrote at once to the Archduchess, saying that I had found the envelope, and would she like me to send it to her. I told her not to bother with a reply if she was busy and didn't want the thing — and that if I hadn't heard from her within a month, I would simply burn it, and I thanked her again for the box, which I greatly liked. I never received a reply."

It all added up.

"Do you know what the box is?" I asked, and didn't wait for his answer. "It's Crown Prince Rudolf's famous Steel Box. Or, rather, it's the duplicate copy of the original, which he let fall into the Emperor's hands after his death."

He stared at the box as if for the first time. "Well, I never! The famous Steel Box. I could never have guessed."

"I thought that maybe Marie Larisch had made up the whole story— about there being a second box. But I see now she was right. So, I wonder if what she said about its contents was correct too."

"Which was?"

"That Rudolf had discovered a secret that would destroy the Habsburg monarchy if it came out..."

"You mean, he thought — perhaps hoped — it would destroy his father!"

"Yes, that was probably it." I feigned laughter. "And he entrusted the second box to Larisch to give to Johann Salvator, which she did."

"So, I had better tell you straight away that I did not open the envelope. I believe in the confidentiality of letters, and I did exactly as I had written to the Archduchess. A little after a month following my letter to her, I opened that stove there, and dropped it in."

He looked at me to gauge my reaction. My jaw must have dropped.

"I consigned it to oblivion!" he added with a flourish.

We looked at each other. And we both laughed out loud this time.

At that moment, a bell boomed out from the spire beside the keep tower.

"Ah, that's our coffee. We have to go down for it."

We went back down to the gallery over the chapel, and from there went a different direction to his library, a big chamber with carved red marble columns, twisted like barleysugar. I was tempted to ask him where they'd come from, but I had work to do. We sat on either side of a large open fire. On a table was coffee and cake. He seemed to like to keep his servants out of sight, perhaps because to his eyes they would appear in the costume of the wrong century.

"I've been thinking of that terrible secret," he said. "It can't ever have worked. What if it was that F-J is, in fact, a goat? Or, probably nearer the truth, that he is a bastard, and that his brother, Maximilian, was the only true Habsburg of the two of them — but he didn't have any heirs anyway? What could it possibly have been that would have made the slightest difference? No, FJ is KandK, and that's it. Nothing will shift him, but God or a frightened horse!"

He held out a small pewter plate on which was a slice of *dort*. Yes, King and Kaiser — and he would stay so.

"So why do you want to know all this?" he said with sudden seriousness.

I used the moments it took for me to cut my cake with the side of my fork, and to consume the first piece, to decide whether I should tell the Count about my real task or not. So far, I had only told two people — my mother and Henry von Taaffe. Count Wilczek's attitude already appeared to be quite outspoken on the Emperor — and there was no doubt he knew a lot. It was worth the risk, as I had drawn a blank so far.

So I told him everything. The light was fading, and the main illumination in the library was now coming from the fire. The

Count didn't say anything after I had finished, but got up and walked over to the table, on which stood a pair of big wooden candlesticks. He struck a match and lit the candles.

"I can help you. I just wish you'd seen me earlier. You'd better stay the night. I'll tell them to put your manservant in a room in the South Wing. You'll be on the floor above in the Oriental Rooms. My housekeeper will find you nightclothes and anything else you might need."

It struck me that he seemed very used to ladies arriving without luggage, something quality hotels do not permit.

"You are very thoughtful." I smiled.

"There will be some supper later, too. The incident you refer to, the shooting accident, took place a full year before the tragedy at Mayerling. I have often thought about it. I wasn't there, but I was told of it in great detail by someone who was, Count Hoyos. Can you imagine if F-J had been shot dead? It was foolhardy in the extreme, if Rudolf had meant to kill him. Could he really have taken up the reins of power, if he'd just been responsible for his father's death — even if it had been explained away as an accident? In the Middle Ages, maybe, but not in the nineteenth century. There would have been an international outcry."

At this point, presumably having been summoned by another bell discreetly pulled, the housekeeper appeared, and was given instructions regarding my stay.

The Count continued. "It took place on January 3rd, 1888, on the Emperor's Mürzsteg hunting estate, at a place called Höll-graben. Tomorrow morning I'm going to telephone Mürzsteg myself and get them to get hold of Martin Veitschegger, who has recently retired from the estate. He was the poor fellow who took Rudolf's ball in the arm. He will be able to show you exactly where it happened, and how it happened. You will have to come to your own conclusions. But there's a lot more you must know. What do you also know about that dreadful night at Mayerling?"

"I've been through the secret files. I can't tell you how I managed it, but I can see clearly that there are two hours unaccounted for, maybe longer, between Mary Vetsera's death and that of Rudolf. The fact that there seems to be so much covered up about this makes me think that it must be very significant..."

Should I tell him?

"...in fact, I had the coffin of Rudolf opened and a doctor looked at his remains."

"My God, Countess... Beatrice isn't it?"

"Trixie."

"You are brave." His eyes sparkled.

"The results were somewhat inconclusive. But there seems to have been more to his death than his one shot to the head."

"Go on..."

"He could also have been bludgeoned. The official version of events ended up being quite terrible, when one thinks about it — Rudolf not only a suicide but also a *de facto* murderer. Why on Earth should the Court have allowed that to be let out?"

The Count thought for a moment, then asked, "Because the truth was even worse?"

"That's the second time I have heard this said."

"And," he began with a lowered voice, "I can introduce you to someone who was there that night at Mayerling, and who will unlock for you the whole mystery. Then you will be able to answer the All Highest's question."

శ

My room was pleasant enough, and contrasted with the somewhat spartan quarters of the Count. The walls were decorated with hand-painted Chinese wallpaper in golden hues; there was even electric light. With a bathroom, it would have been quite comfortable. However, I did feel as if I could hardly move, as the room was stuffed with Oriental curiosities. The Count's unimaginable income from his coal mines meant that he had virtually unlimited buying-power for things which attracted him. I had just been reading the new novel by the German author Thomas Mann, in which he stated: "Life's décor is so rich, so varied, and so overwrought that it leaves no room for life itself."

I felt almost suffocated by everything around me, and really couldn't sleep, so I decided to get some air. It was April, so not yet warm, and I wished I had my coat, which was down near the main entrance somewhere, having been taken by the servant. There was an Indian shawl draped over the sofa and that I took and wrapped round me, then stepped out onto the small balcony.

An almost-full moon hung serenely in the heavens, and I looked out over the nocturnal landscape. I wondered how many other young women had stood here, their thoughts on the extraordinary Count, maybe dreaming of his strong, manly hands, his wonderful mind, his wicked blue eyes… maybe hoping he would visit, emerging from some secret door of his own creation. *But don't be mad*, I said to myself. He's far too old… and yet was he? He had experienced so much of the world; that showed on his beautiful face. His Arctic explorations were legendary (according to Mamma); his relationship with Sissy rumoured about...

At first everything in the view before me was completely quiet except for the sound of a distant dog-fox in the dark forests which surrounded the castle. Then, almost imperceptibly at first, I was aware of a faint droning sound. As the sound began to be properly audible, I could see a hazy cloud of dust, caught in the moonlight, rising from the trees as whatever was making this sound zigzagged up the long, snaking driveway.

I was able to see where the drive broke the cover of the trees and passed over some open ground, where patches of melting snow glowed luminescent, just in front of the castle. A motorcycle emerged from the forest darkness, heading for the first drawbridge — then it was lost to my sight until it passed directly below me, in the defile between the inner and outer walls of this fortress. Peering down, I could see I was not the only one interested by this visitor. Below me was the big balcony on which I had first spied the Count. And I could see him there again, this time holding a lantern. He turned and made to go to the courtyard, and I had to go into my room and cross it to get a better view from the other side.

The motorcycle, now making a lot of noise within the echoing walls of the castle courts, passed under the big arch with the Kaschau gallery, and stopped directly before the main doorway. The Count, his steps lit by his lantern, crossed the gravel of the courtyard to meet the rider. The newcomer was somewhat shorter than the Count and wore a long coat, and his face, which I would not have been able to make out clearly from where I stood anyway, was obscured by goggles. He disappeared with the Count into the dark building, and I could see the yellowy lamplight proceeding through the succession of leaded windows up and up to the top of the tower which housed the Count's study. From the spire of the chapel the clock struck one.

The next morning I was awoken by the familiar knock and entry of Müller, bearing a tray with all the things I like for breakfast, arranged just as I like them. He drew the heavy curtains and the morning sun flooded in. It seemed hard to realise I was in the same dark, gothic castle of yesterday.

"What time is it?"

"Eight-thirty, Milady. His Lordship has given me the timetable of the trains that will take us from Vienna through to Mürzsteg, and he has given me the name Herr Veitschegger, who, it has been arranged, will meet us at the Mürzsteg Estate Office at eight tomorrow morning. We are to be taken to the station at nine-thirty. I am sorry that is so soon, but the Count was adamant we had to catch the nine-fifty-five train to make our connections. He himself sends his apologies, but he has business to attend to and has already left the castle."

I was still half asleep. "You mean he's said good-bye?" *Oh...!*

"I believe so, Milady. And he wishes me to convey to you that he will send you a telegram about the person you are to meet after your trip to the mountains."

❧

Eventually, it was a very small train which took us from Mürzuschlag up into the Alps. Here the snow lay in patches on the meadows and the distant peaks were snow-covered. We were to leave the train at Neuberg an der Mürz, where we were assured of finding a hotel, and early tomorrow we would continue our journey to Mürzsteg, a further two stations up the line. Indeed, we found a charming old inn and hotel, the only one in the small town, where I was extremely well looked-after. The innkeeper, a

Herr Holzer, didn't have special rooms for servants, so I simply asked for as good a room as mine for Müller — but separated by as much distance within the premises as possible. I didn't want people to gossip… especially for no reason!

After dinner, which I took alone in the private room behind the public restaurant, Herr Holzer engaged me in conversation.

"I suppose Your Ladyship has come to see the beauties of our abbey?" he said.

I thought of replying absolutely truthfully with the single word "no," but on the other hand I was alone, a little bored, and maybe I could learn a thing or two.

"Not really," I replied. "I've come to see Mürzsteg, the Royal Hunting Preserves. I'm… I'm a writer. I'm writing about His Majesty and his love of hunting."

"And to see the Jagdschloss? The hunting castle is all shut-up these days. His Majesty hasn't come in years now. Not like the old days. In fact that's why the railway was built. Two or three times a year the place was so busy that the whole valley benefited. Now there's talk that the railway might close. But perhaps they'll keep it open to Neuberg, as today plenty of people come just to look at the abbey."

"And the Abbey is special?"

"We're very proud of it. It was Cistercian, founded in 1327 by Duke Otto the Cheerful. But Emperor Josef closed it in 1786, and since then the town here has looked after it. We saved it from being turned into a farm or some unpleasant factory. My grandfather Hubert was determined it would not go to ruin. Now the old abbey church is our parish church."

"A very noble thing to have done. I hope I can find time to visit it," I said, fully aware that I doubtless wouldn't have such a moment spare. But now it was time for facts: "I have been given the name of Herr Veitschegger. I believe he knows the mountains and forests of the estate. I understand he used to accompany His Majesty."

"Oh, yes. He's the right man to show you the area. He was His Majesty's loader, but… that wasn't all… perhaps I shouldn't say…"

"Oh, do! I don't have to write about it."

He thought for a second, then said, "Well, he was probably the best shot in Austria — before the accident, this is. Not only did he load, but he stood directly behind His Majesty. So when His Majesty missed a shot, then old Veitschegger would fire so quickly that hardly anyone would be able to hear there was a second report. And he never missed!"

"And the accident?"

"In '88 it was. That's when the Crown Prince was here hunting with His Majesty. His last time. Well, the Crown Prince did break the elementary laws of shooting and turned back to fire again at his quarry as it passed. Missed His Majesty by a hair's breadth, but hit poor old Veitschegger in the arm. He was never quite the same after, and for all his pains, he was given fifty guilders."

"Which, is surely, a paltry sum. Especially if you're a Habsburg!"

"It's their way. If any one of them shoots a beater, or one of the guests, or insults anyone — or for that matter, gives some lady a venereal disease, then he behaves as though the victim has been honoured! So you will find old Martin Veitschegger feeling rather less than honoured, although he did eventually become estate superintendent, so I suppose that was something."

"And who was the Crown Prince's loader?"

"He was from the estate too. Karel Platone's his name. But he was just a loader. The Prince had no need of a marksman; he was a crack shot. That's why the accident was so strange. They said, at the Prince's death, that in his twenty years of shooting, he had killed over forty-three thousand wild animals."

"Platone is an unusual name in these parts, I would assume?" I was simply trying to coax more information about the fellow. As for his name, I admit I didn't care an iota.

"Yes. His father was from Pola, on the Adriatic, so I understand; married a local girl from Krampen."

"And is this Karel Platone still here?"

"I think so. I haven't heard about him for a while, but his cottage is by the road in the hamlet of Lanau, that's between Krampen and Mürzsteg. You'll be going by it tomorrow."

"Well, we were going to go on the railway. But, Herr Holzer, would you be able to arrange a horse and trap tomorrow, if I get my manservant to see you early in the morning?"

"Of course, Your Ladyship. That will be no trouble."

I should point out that in his current role, it was better for me to allude to Müller as my manservant, as Count Wilczek had done. Butler has undertones of silver trays and carafes of port. On my last adventure, the poor man seemed to spend most of the time rescuing me from high places by means of a ladder. Now he was armed.

"That must be it, Milady…"

Müller was pointing to a small, lonely, stone and plastered-wood cottage which lay end-on to the roadway.

"Yes, it fits Herr Holzer's description, except it doesn't look very used, does it?"

"True. One would expect smoke from the chimney at least."

"I shall get down and inspect," I said.

The cottage was deserted. There were weeds under the door, a broken window, and absolutely no signs of life.

"Do you want to go in, Milady?"

"Well…"

Müller took that as a "yes." The door was clearly locked, but he simply wrenched it open, so feeble was the simple and rusty old lock. Inside the one-room dwelling were plain rustic furnishings, and over the table, the dusty outline of where a picture had hung for many years. Behind the only cupboard, I found a framed photograph which fitted the outlined space perfectly. It was a photograph of Prince Rudolf, in hunting costume. The mountain peaks behind the posing figure could be those visible from here. On the back of the frame was stuck a note, which I took to be in the hand of the Prince, warmly thanking Herr Platone. But apart from this there was a marked absence of personal possessions.

"I'll have to ask Herr Veitschegger about this man."

"It could be that he's passed on," Müller commented.

It did seem odd, if he had died, that Holzer did not know of it. "Let's hope we will be offered coffee in Mürzsteg," was all I said.

Up to the moment of finding Platone's cottage I had been thinking how fresh and charming was this little mountain valley, with its rushing brooks tumbling down into the Mürz. Based on my comforting reception by the innkeeper and his wife in the picture-book town of Neuberg, I had been speculating on the charms of an existence in such a quiet and peaceful place, and that perhaps I was wasting away in the more decadent world of Society hostesses and blatant insincerity. But this unexplained empty cottage was the first jarring note in this little slice of heaven. It was not to be my last.

The road continued to rise steeply, and the mountains ahead seemed to close in around us with a sense of foreboding. According to Müller's map, they were the Schneealpe, the Snow Alps, and against the sun, they now presented a dark and jagged outline, like the teeth of a rabid dog. The village of Mürzsteg consisted of very few buildings, mainly clustered outside the prominent gates and gatepiers of the Royal Hunting Castle. A picturesque structure beside the gates bore the sign "Estate Office," and so we stopped.

An upright man in his late sixties or early seventies strode purposefully up to us and announced himself as Martin Veitschegger, recently retired as estate superintendent. He was a portly man with a heavy white moustache and side-whiskers and wearing a smart huntsman's green outfit.

"I had a message from Count Wilczek, and I'm aware what you want to see. If I may jump on the back, we can start out for Höllgraben, where it happened. We'll have to go on foot a fair distance, but for the first kilometre or so, we can use your trap."

Müller interjected: "Her Ladyship would welcome a cup of coffee in the office first, if that would be possible."

"I've coffee and rolls in my pack enough for us all," Veitschegger replied somewhat gruffly. "I'm afraid I don't see eye-to-eye with the new superintendent."

Müller looked at me. What choice did we have? "Very well," I said, "let us proceed."

When we were safely out of the village I asked Veitschegger what had caused this rift.

"I started on the estate when I was fourteen. I've given the place over fifty years' loyal service. I've never spoken of any of the things I've seen and heard here; and His Majesty could always rely on my discretion. And yet when I come up for my retirement, I get visited by this gentlemen who's come all the way down from Vienna to see me. He tells me in no uncertain terms that if I say anything to anyone about all my years in Royal service, then my pension's at stake. I ask who he thinks he is, and he shows me some badge he keeps in his waistcoat pocket as an agent of the Imperial Royal State Police. 'What do you think I am?' I say to him, 'some kind of criminal?' 'You don't talk to me like that,' he replies. And I walk out. The next day I'm told my retirement has already begun, and my pension's been cut by a third. No leaving celebration. No medal. Nothing. That was all the thanks I got…"

He seemed about to stop his rant when he suddenly had another thought. "Oh, but I forgot. I did get fifty guilders in 1888 — and that was supposed to pay for the fact that I could no longer shoot as a marksman. Some compensation!"

What could I tell him? I was beginning to realise what a gang of ruthless rogues the Habsburgs were. Perhaps all monarchs are — and that's precisely how they stay as monarchs!

"So you don't mind showing us what happened in 1888?" I asked.

"Not a bit of it," he replied bluntly, staring ahead of him at those mountain slopes where he had spent so much of his life.

In half an hour or so we arrived at a small hut by the side of the road, opposite a little Calvary where a rusting iron Jesus waited out the centuries, arms outstretched.

"We'll be going on foot from here," said Veitschegger as he helped me down.

Then he helped Müller put the horse in the paddock by the hut, from which he took some hay.

"Well, you look the part, Milady, if you don't mind me saying," Müller remarked, eyeing me from head to toe. He was a consummate professional.

I had been kitted out by the innkeeper's wife in a hunting costume jacket, a thick skirt, and stout Alpine boots. I had despaired, until meeting Count Wilczek, that is, of ever getting properly to the bottom of this mystery. Had I known, of course, Sabine could have packed something appropriate. At least I had Müller's seal of approval, so all was not lost!

We started up a narrow path that led up towards the forests which cloaked the lower slopes of the jagged peaks. The air was fresh and bracing and tiny yellow flowers had started to appear amongst the grass which had been recently liberated from the burden of the winter's snow. In all the hollows and areas shaded by the shores of the woods, the snow was still lying in heavy, seemingly indestructible drifts.

After about seven or eight hundred metres of this upward hike,

Veitschegger paused to allow us all to catch our breath. He looked out at the view.

"That's the Göller over there, and the Windberg's just behind it." He spoke of the mountains like old friends, which I supposed, in a way, they were — certainly more friendly than his erstwhile employers.

"And where's Höllgraben, exactly?" asked Müller, hoping to pinpoint it on the map he held.

"That was where we left the trap. That's the last printed name on the map. We mountain folk have our own names for all the folds and crags and ridges, of course. And that ridge ahead, the one we call The Hog's Back, that's where we'll stop for our coffee. Then we'll be only half a kilometre from the place."

"So we're in the wilds," observed Müller, somewhat ruefully.

After another brisk hike, we stopped where Veitschegger had indicated, for hot coffee from his flask with bread rolls and salami. The ridge, which had seemed quite close when pointed out at our first stop, had seemed to get further away the more we walked towards it. Even Müller was puffing when we finally gained the small outcrop of rock where Veitschegger was unpacking our refreshment. My calves itched terribly — it was those woollen socks from Frau Holzer. She'd made me take my silk stockings off, as if the idea to wear them underneath those socks was both unheard of and a venal sin. I could hardly explain that even dressed as a common urchin, as I had been only two days before, I always wore them!

Now a hidden valley revealed itself between us and the main slopes of the mountain. Veitschegger pointed down at it and explained that that was where the accident had happened seventeen years before.

"The beaters were driving a herd of young deer up through the trees, and then when they emerged into the open, they faced the guns. We'll go down and see the stands of the Emperor, the Prince, and also of Count Hoyos, who was with them. He shared his stand with Baron Giesl."

"So the deer were trapped in the valley?" I asked.

"Precisely. But there's more to it, which I'll show you when we are down there."

We started out for the narrow valley, directly below the ridge on which we stood. On the way down I wanted to clear something up. "I thought, Superintendent Veitschegger, that deer were hunted by carefully following them. My husband certainly says he spends days, sometimes, following an animal."

"That's stalking," he replied. "This is shooting."

Once you have a word for something in the Austrian Empire, then that defines it, legitimizes it, and means you can start a register for it. So this is *shooting*.

Finally we were down on the edge of the valley which was little more than a narrow ravine into which the deer had been driven. He stopped by some bushes. "This is where the Emperor's stand was," he said, "We were aiming down there — at where the trees stop — the open ground where the deer broke out. His Majesty was standing just where I am now, and I was right behind him."

He pointed to his left. "Count Hoyos was almost at the head of the valley, over there." And finally, pointing to the opposite side of the valley, he said, "That's where the Prince had his stand."

I was trying to picture the scene, with the deer being driven into the trap, when Veitschegger suggested we go over to see the scene from the Prince's stand. "Herr Müller, if you would, stand here — where His Majesty stood. I will be able to show Her Ladyship the relative positions."

We scrambled over to the other side, and suddenly Veitschegger halted in his tracks. "Well, that's odd," he said. In the rough grass of the steep hillside was a small cairn of stones, and nestled in the topmost ones a bunch of fresh alpine flowers.

Veitschegger was looking down at them, quite surprised. "This is where the Prince was standing. I wonder who can have done this?"

"When was the last time you were here?" I asked.

"Not for three or four years, I suppose. It's strange."

"So tell me what happened."

"Well, the first herd of young deer was driven out of the woods and they were shot — all four guns bearing down on them as they tried to climb up. One or two even contemplated going back towards the beaters, and while they hesitated, they were shot, too."

I was quite shocked. "It was slaughter."

"That's the sport, Your Ladyship."

"Sport? It's no better than those shooting booths at the Nusle Fair. In fact, far worse. Those were living creatures."

"But there's more," Veitschegger went on. "When the young deer had gone down, by chance, the beaters had disturbed another herd, which they hadn't seen. They came from over there, that defile between the trees and the bowl of the valley here. This smaller herd was led by a great stag, a twelve-pointer he was, a magnificent beast. His Majesty took a shot first, but he did not go down. Then the Prince yelled out 'He's mine,' and opened fire. But the beast moved up towards us. There was another shot from the Prince, and then the Prince — determined to get him — leapt forward from his stand here to fire again…."

"But that would be almost directly across the valley, surely?"

"Exactly, Your Ladyship. Right across to where Herr Müller is standing now. His Majesty, at that moment fortunately, turned to me to get the next loaded gun — and the Prince's ball missed his head by a hair's breadth, catching me in the sleeve as I was about to hand him the gun."

Veitschegger stopped suddenly, and looked more closely at the stones. "In fact, the stones are not where the Prince's stand was — but where he had leapt forward… where he had taken that shot. The stand was behind these bushes."

"What happened then?"

"Well, His Majesty was red with anger, but tried to make light of it — or that's what I thought. He banned Rudolf from the shoot the following day for breaking the rules, and we all returned to Mürzsteg. But His Majesty never addressed the Prince again for the rest of the hunt — in the end, the next day was cancelled, too."

So whoever put these stones here had erected a monument to the place where the whole course of European history could so easily have changed, or were they put just there by someone close to Rudolf? That gave me an idea.

"So, tell me, Superintendent, what has happened to Karel Platone?"

Veitschegger was clearly taken aback. "You are well informed," he said. He began climbing back towards where Müller was still standing. Then he decided to level with me, although clearly the thought had crossed his mind that I was some kind of Imperial spy.

"It's odd, that's what I say. Platone took the whole thing very badly — as if in some way he was to blame for it. The Prince's death the following year made matters worse. In recent years it's affected him more and more. It can only have been him who put those stones down there."

"And where is he now?"

"No one really knows. He left his cottage about three years ago, it must have been, and they say in the village that he's taken to living out on the mountain, using the huts that provide storm shelter. Sometimes, but very rarely, he's seen about the place. He had a little nest-egg from the Prince's will, and there's his small pension — so sometimes he goes down to the post office. They say he looks quite wild now. I can't understand it. He was once such a carefree fellow."

"You think his mind is gone?"

"Maybe. Yes, maybe it's that."

We rejoined Müller, and I pointed out to him the main points of the story.

Veitschegger was looking up towards the peaks. "Well, we'd better start back. I don't like that sky one bit."

Indeed, it had suddenly got dark, and down in the bottom of the narrow valley there appeared to be wisps of mist. Veitschegger noticed me looking. "There's a little brook down there, if you're wondering about that bit of mist. But much worse is the mist that rolls down the mountain. If we don't hurry, we may get caught. It's the time of year."

Hardly speaking to each other, we made our way across the broad, desolate slopes towards the downward path to the hut at Höllgraben, where we would find our trap. Veitschegger, despite his years, was striding ahead of us — also, he just knew the ground. I found myself stumbling on loose stones.

"Stay very near, Müller, will you?"

"I'm right behind you. Don't worry, Milady."

It was as if Veitschegger was slowly disappearing, and I realized he was being swallowed up in the enveloping mist. I called out to him, but he still couldn't be seen.

"Can you see him?" I said, turning to Müller.

"I'm afraid I was thinking the same, Milady. We've lost him."

The mist was now swirling all around us. It reminded me of standing next to the bonfire of leaves the gardeners of Morštejn used to set in the autumn. For a while I could lose myself in the smoke. Mamma used to make me wash my hair afterwards, saying that I smelt like Joan of Arc. For some reason, that wasn't good.

"What do we do now?" I said, after we had continued on for a few minutes, although "continued" seems to imply that we were following some kind of route, which, however much we fooled ourselves, we weren't.

"Well, I suppose if we keep walking downwards, that will help. And, although I don't want to say it, we are lost. I just wish we'd got as far as that first track. We could have followed that."

Then, from far off, it seemed, was a distant flash followed swiftly by the sound from the gun whose fire we had witnessed.

"Are they trying to find us, do you think?" I shouted to Müller. But in my heart-of-hearts I knew that was not it.

"I think we'd better keep our voices down," he replied. And I noticed that he had taken out the revolver. "Keep very still," he urged.

I froze. We waited. A second or two seemed an hour.

Suddenly, there was another flash and the bang, but the two events were much closer to one another. That could only mean the firer of the gun was nearer. Müller reached out to me and gently but firmly guided me down with his hand. My heart was pounding as I lay down on the ground. He picked up a rock and threw it. It landed with a thud somewhere out there in the mist. Another shot rang out, and we could hear the ball pinging on stone.

Müller was being brave and was still standing. He was peering out into the white world of the swirling mist, straining all his senses. He picked up another rock and sent it flying in the same direction as the first, but this time his eyes were glued elsewhere. There was another flash, and a split second afterwards, Müller fired towards it. There was nothing. He fired again — and this time there was a cry. I wanted to congratulate him.

"I don't want to leave you, Milady." He was helping me to my feet. "Follow me at as great a distance as possible, but don't, for heaven's sake, lose me."

A moan came from the direction of the cry. But Müller was the first to realize that this could be a trap. He held the revolver in front of him, ready to fire again. We advanced like this about fifty or so metres, and the moaning got louder. Then Müller almost fell over a man lying on the ground, clutching his shoulder. His shotgun was lying discarded a metre or two away from him. This was no trap.

I rushed forward. "Herr Platone," I said. The wild appearance of the man was obvious enough. In some ways he resembled a picture from an edition of *Robinson Crusoe* that my brother Max had been given for a birthday present. Here was, indeed, a modern-day Crusoe, now lit up by Müller's electric torch.

"You won't get me," he moaned.

"I don't understand," I said.

Müller was loosening the man's jacket around the wound. Platone was, from what I could see of him, a smallish man with dark hair, taking the looks of his Italian father from Pola, no doubt. I took Müller's pack, in which I knew was some water, from off his back.

"I suppose you want to take me," Platone went on. "I saw you looking at my stones."

"I think I understand more than you realize," I replied. I wondered if he might die, for there seemed to be blood coming from his clothes lower down. Maybe it was now or never.

"We have not come to take you. Now tell me about the shot. The Prince was a marksman — and he missed that stag... the twelve-pointer?"

"The stag..." he mumbled, "but it was a *Schneider*."

"A *Schneider*? What does that mean?"

"A beast that can't face up to the guns — a coward. Instead of having the courage to try to escape, it just stands there, paralysed with fright, detaching itself from the rest of the herd in its fear. So, it actually ends up presenting itself as a sitting target, so to speak, and yet it is hardly sport."

So that's what the All Highest meant when he referred to his son as dying like a *Schneider*: dying like a coward. "So what happened?"

"I was very experienced. I had a loaded gun in my hand. I aimed at the stag's hind-quarters and clipped him there — this had the desired effect of making the beast leap forward. I shouldn't have done that, of course — but then the Emperor had his loader ready to fire, too. That was when Prince Rudolf seemed to lose control, and leaping out from the stand, he swung round to fire at it as it ran past, and..."

"And he hit Herr Veitschegger. But what had he meant to do?"

"I've had many years to think about it. He knew the rules, all right. He had never done anything like that before. He must have known what he was doing..."

"And, yet, conveniently it would look like an accident — a foolish accident, I grant you — a rash act... but an accident nonetheless."

"Yes. That's the only conclusion I have come to. A man driven to try and change the Empire, to modernise it. And he missed by a whisker."

"You might say by the prodigious whiskers of his father!"

"Quiet a moment, please," said Müller insistently.

In the distance we could hear voices calling. There was also the sound of metal being beaten, as beaters do, with tin trays. It could only be Veitschegger with some of the gamekeepers. Müller shouted back, "Over here! Over here!"

The calling back and forth continued, and Müller waved his torch about. Soon, through the mist, we could discern a line of lights, lanterns swinging this way and that, as a line of men was approaching. Gradually the welcome lights came nearer and nearer and the sound died down as they could make out Müller's torch. Eventually the lanterns revealed the shapes of legs and feet advancing with Veitschegger's stout calves in the lead.

"Thank God!" I cried as he came up.

Veitschegger ordered four men to go back and get a stretcher for Platone, who was still alive. Another two were to wait here for them, beside Platone. The rest of us made our way back down to the hut. The agonised features of the Redeemer were still looking down on us from the little wayside shrine by the entranceway. Half of the refuge was a hay-barn and the other half a quite well-equipped room with a stove that had been lit, and soon the schnapps came out.

"You were quite magnificent, Müller — and such a good shot."

"Beginner's luck, I fear, Milady. I may not be able to replicate the feat."

"But how did you know about firing into the adversary's gun like that? It was very impressive."

"I was reading a book recently by one of the staff officers of the Dutch General Krueger, about his experiences in the recent Boer War in South Africa. At a place called Spion Kop, the Boers occupied trenches, and this was the trick they adopted to shoot back at the British snipers who were waiting for them if they so much as raised their heads."

There was obviously more to Müller than I had previously imagined. But then I thought that every time.

᧓

Despite the horror of the previous day, I found myself waking in my comfortable bed at the Holzer the next morning at a quite respectable hour. I couldn't even remember stumbling into the place at whatever hour it was, especially, as at Mürzsteg, every-thing had had to be written into some kind of Estate Diary, which had taken an age. What was not written was that I had finally solved the mystery I had been engaged to solve. But before I could report to the Emperor, there was one more meeting I should have. Then I might know what to report.

Without my asking, Müller had arranged for me to have break-fast in bed, and again the tray was set out just as I liked it. And my favourite — braised grapefruit! He was a gem! Propped beside the coffeepot was a telegram. From Vienna. I ripped open the envelope:

MEET MY CONTACT 1900 TONIGHT ABBEY
CHURCH NEUBERG STOP WILCZEK

How remarkable, and I would have the day to rest and recuper-ate. If only Sabine were here to run me my bath and dress me properly — and do my hair, which must by now look an absolute fright, but one cannot have everything.

Müller was still hovering, which meant he wanted to say something.

"Yes, Müller?"

"I hope you don't mind, Milady, but I took the liberty of also having breakfast served in my room this morning. I am quite willing to pay for the extra expense, of course…"

"Müller," I said, "that is my treat — and I trust you had everything you wanted."

"Oh, yes, Milady. The salami selection was most excellent with local alpine cheeses, and the eggs were timed to perfection. But best of all was that it was I who was being served."

Müller's normally poker face actually broke out into a beaming smile. It was all most gratifying. But what on Earth was I going to find out at my rendezvous in the early evening?

Chapter Eleven

The Bitter Truths

Herr Holzer — Hubert, like his grandfather — had arranged for me to visit the old monastery at six-thirty. He assured me that the abbey church would be open in any event; it was never locked. So shortly after six-thirty, at six-forty, to be precise (to be punctual is rather bourgeois; to be early is utterly unforgivable — what happens if your host or hostess is not quite ready? — and to be terribly late is just plain bad manners), I knocked on the ancient door. Ten minutes after the announced hour is thus, in my opinion, the correct time to arrive.

As I have said, the correct hour to arrive is only my opinion. To Mamma it is a hard and fast rule. My father once tried setting all the clocks at Morštejn forward by ten minutes to cope with my mother's obsession (which he called English madness), but it didn't last. He got caught out in the end, since he hadn't been able to alter all of Mamma's watches.

Deputy Mayor Herr Stoller welcomed me. "And would Your Ladyship like me to give you a guided tour?"

"Herr Stoller, your offer is most generous, but I would prefer simply to walk at will, to soak up the atmosphere of the ancient place, if you don't mind."

He acceded to my wish, and I was free to roam. There was the wonderful cloister, from which, as a woman, I would have been forbidden when it was still a working monastery. The chapter house was a great, still space where the debates of the white-robed monks had once been heard. It was hard not to be taken over by the romance of such buildings, although I was not really sure exactly what that romance was. Perhaps it was simply the peace and tranquillity of a monastic enclave, away from the treadmill of the outside world.

Today it was sunny, the complete obverse of the day before. The sun streamed in through the gothic tracery of the various windows, throwing networks of shadows over old flagstones, decorated tiles, marble steps. My footfalls echoed in the gothic silence. It was soon only a few minutes before seven, so I entered the abbey church through the old monks' entry, from the cloister.

I noticed a shadowy figure lurking near a pillar. Good — Müller was here. Just as a precaution, he would observe the proceedings.

The evening light was flooding through the west window, bathing the interior in a warm glow. The gilding of the enormous Baroque altarpiece, which must have been ten or fifteen metres tall, seemed to shine. I took a seat in one of the old oak pews, and waited. Indeed, I would use the time to say a prayer, except that when I came to say it (under my breath, that is) I found I couldn't. *For what* was I praying, I thought? That I would make that damned Habsburg Emperor happy? That I would lie successfully to save my neck? That the dark events of the past were, like this church, shrouded in golden sunlight after all?

Minutes passed, but they were tranquil, peaceful minutes and I didn't mind. I looked at my watch. It was ten past seven, and then I began to hear it.

First it was that almost imperceptible drone, gradually getting louder — and I smiled. Ten minutes late, but not late. I sat just where I was, staring at that altar, until I could hear the sound getting much nearer, and I turned. The west doors of the church stood open, and coming down the straight, tree-lined avenue to it was that motorcycle. It had to be that same one.

The rider dismounted just in front of the doors and strode into the church. I turned back to the altar as I listened to the boots of the stranger gradually getting closer. Whoever it was found a seat a few rows directly behind me. I waited.

"Countess," the stranger said, "please continue to look forward, then I can take these damned goggles off. For a variety of reasons, I don't want to identify myself. Our mutual friend, Count Wilczek, has told me about your need for information. That I can supply."

I couldn't quite place the voice in the social hierarchy. Educated but not aristocratic, so probably a member of Vienna's bourgeoisie. Jewish? Not impossible.

"In those days I worked directly for Baron Gorup, the Commissioner of Police attached to the Hofburg. Gorup reported directly to the President of the Imperial Royal State Police, Baron Krauss, and Krauss only to the All Highest. How I got into this work, I will not trouble you with, but it was not something I had intended, and it was not something I liked, either. I have the qualifications to be a teacher at a university, but then the pay would not be as good. Dirty work is expensive, because it was not only my time that was being paid for, but my conscience, as I have found — and one's conscience not only works day and night, but continues to work long after an assignment is finished. In this case, sixteen years and still nagging. Shall I begin my story?"

"Yes, please go on."

"All Prince Rudolf's movements were watched, under the direct orders of the All Highest. Every day a report landed on his desk with the previous day's movements of the Crown Prince, and his contacts — and conquests — duly set out. There were between twenty and thirty full-time agents involved in this work, and in addition, certain coachmen, porters at buildings, newspaper sellers on street corners had all been roped-in as informers. Some of these had been coerced in the normal way: blackmail, threats, withholding of certain privileges. It was an elaborate network. The Crown Prince couldn't pick his teeth without it being reported.

"So, naturally, the All Highest knew about Mary Vetsera the moment she had first visited her lover. Mizzi Kaspar, his preferred mistress, had been under our surveillance for some years. My colleague, Dr Florian Meissner, kept watch over her house in Heumühlgasse on the Wieden.

"1888 saw an increase in our activity. ER — which was our code for the Crown Prince — had an even larger number of contacts whom the All Highest disliked, especially the Jewish ones — Moriz Szeps, the liberal journalist, and Baron Hirsch, the banker, to whom ER owed large sums of money. Other contacts were more unsavoury. They were all observed, noted, and reported to the All Highest. ER was thought to have been plotting something with the Hungarians, and then his relationship with his cousin Archduke Johann Salvator was also under scrutiny. The All Highest was suspicious of everyone, which gave us a guarantee of employment for what we thought would be many years.

"But by the end of 1888, we'd had several reports that ER had discussed committing suicide with various individuals. In December, Mizzi Kaspar went to see Baron Krauss personally to report that she thought ER was intending to kill himself. She told him that ER had asked her to go to the Hussars' Temple in Mödling with him — and there to die together. It seems Krauss hesitated to take any action. What if Rudolf did not commit suicide and in due course became Emperor? Then this alarm would have spoilt his chances. On the other hand, perhaps Krauss had discussed it directly with the All Highest and together they'd decided that no interventionist action should be taken. For once in his life, ER would be given freedom of action!"

"Yes, I can see the irony in that."

"The intelligence coming in from the Vetsera surveillance, including the watch on Countess Marie Larisch and her contacts in January 1889, brought the department to the conclusion that ER had planned to end his life on the 29th. On the 28th, ER spent most of the night with Mizzi Kaspar, the full details of which — mostly gained from the 'friendly' house porter — were submitted in the morning report of the 29th. On that morning I was summoned to Baron Gorup's office, unaware of the information already gathered on ER's intentions. I found myself being interviewed by Gorup personally, and he asked me to affirm my loyalty to the Empire and to the Emperor, saying that a very special mission, approved by 'the Highest Authorities,' had been selected for me. It went without saying that it was also secret.

"It was then explained to me that ER was intending to commit suicide at Mayerling that evening, along with his lover Mary Vetsera. Since it was a free country, then that was his prerogative. He had had an unfortunate life, and ER now realised that he had wasted it. A catalogue of ER's misfortunes was related to me, which, when placed end to end like that, did paint a pretty bleak picture. It was stated to me that ER was actively conspiring with the Hungarians to destabilise and destroy the monarchy as we knew it. The hunting 'accident' of the year before was not mentioned, however. Then came the instructions:

"I was to proceed to Mayerling. I would wait in the wood-shed, and I was to be provided with a set of keys to ER's private rooms. At two in the morning, I would gain entry to ER's rooms and assess the situation. In short, if necessary, I was to 'give every assistance' to ER to kill himself, if he had not already done so. If he was already dead, then I was to collect any letters that may have been left and get away as quickly as possible. I was not to raise the alarm, which would be left to the normal course of events. Nothing was said about what I should do with regard to Mary Vetsera — for example, what if she were alive, but ER was dead? That option was not discussed. Depending on what I had to do, I would be rewarded for my work. If I did good work, and the task was accomplished, then I would be retired immediately from the service and given a State pension.

"I asked only one question, and it was: 'By 'Highest Authorities,' did he mean one man? Golup had nodded. So I knew that ER's own father had sanctioned this, which in the context of the work I had to do, was in fact an advantage. So I got to Mayerling by a means which had maintained my invisibility, and, as instructed, waited the hour or so that I had in hand before two o'clock. At that hour the whole castle was quiet, ER's guests having gone to bed, and at the appointed time, I admitted myself to ER's rooms.

"Loschek, ER's butler, had a room almost next to ER's bedroom, separated only by a kind-of dressing room, which I had entered. The door to ER's bedroom was ajar. I was horrified by what I saw. Mary Vetsera's naked body, with a terrible wound to the head, was lying on the bed. ER was lying beside her, sobbing. His revolver lay on a side-table. He was clothed.

"I had two ways to play this situation. One, was simply to work out if ER did intend to kill himself, and if he did — but just could not manage it — to do it for him, so to speak. He would not see me; there would be no awkward conversation. Or, two, was to introduce myself as an agent of the police, then convince him that in view of the fact that he must have murdered Vetsera, however willing she was to die, then his only way out was the suicide he had intended all along. Then, I hoped, he would do the deed. But ER was well-known for being a physical coward. There was that bear hunt in Transylvania, which I'd heard about, where he had literally run away. The tens of thousands of animals he had slaughtered in his life — yes, tens of thousands — had needed no bravery in their despatch, although that carnage had inured him to the physical presence of death, which, I suppose, was why he could be so relatively calm beside Vetsera's corpse.

"I chose the second option. Taking my courage in my hands, I stepped without knocking into the bedroom. Despite his condition, he looked at me angrily, and it obviously crossed his mind to call for assistance, but then matters would have quickly spiralled out of control. He was cornered, so I did not even need the pretext of being from the police. I could use that later if I needed to. I told him in no uncertain terms that his only option now was to end it all. What then followed was the worst couple of hours of my life.

"The time was filled by his pathetic appeals, the pleading, the tears, the self-justification and the attempt to persuade me, who was a nothing in his world, of the value of his life. It was heart-rending, but it was all based on weakness, as far as I was concerned. He even said we could try to make it look as if Vetsera had committed suicide, except that she was not left-handed!

I couldn't help looking over at Vetsera's body. There were what seemed to be other blood stains on the coverlet, as if the body had been moved… but I began to think I was simply going mad. I just wished all this would come to an end.

"The first streaks of dawn were already colouring the sky out-side by this time and I was getting fairly desperate. ER was straightening himself up a bit and told me he needed to go and instruct the servants. Had he not come back, or had he given the game away, I would then have used my police powers — for, although any Habsburg Prince was above the authority of the Law, he was answerable to the All Highest, whose name, rightly or wrongly, I would invoke. But he did come back, and it was remarkable how he'd been able to become a completely differ-ent person. I supposed it was his 'public persona.' I hoped the servants would have no idea what had been happening over the last hours — and what would soon happen. But I had to think of something, and quickly.

"It was then that I found his Achilles' heel. I had on me a little notebook which I had obtained from the floor of his fiacre shortly after he had vacated it a few days before. It was his 'Register of Conquests.' I shall leave it on this seat when I leave. Please do look at it, as it provides such a valuable insight into the way ER's mind worked. When you have done with it, give it to Johann Wilczek to return to me or simply burn the thing. I showed it to ER and explained to him why I had found it so interesting. Despite his apparent liberal attitude, his reforming zeal and his devil-may-care ways in matters of love, he had inherited the same petty bureaucrat mentality of his father. He was not big enough, despite his exalted position, to depart from an arbitrarily imposed standard or regulation. In the book, every conquest was neatly listed, numbered, and categorised. There was no mention of feelings. In short, he was his father's son.

"This is what finally tipped him. He looked into the mirror — and in that reflection he saw everything he hated about his father. Killing himself would rid the world of another Franz-Josef. He grabbed his gun and, had I not intervened, he would have shot that reflection in the mirror, which would have ruined everything. So now he was determined, but still his physical cowardice held him back. I got him to hold the gun to his head, but instead of pulling the trigger, he began to lower the thing. 'I can't do it,' he was wailing, 'I just can't do it.' He was trembling so much that he would probably miss, even if he did pull the trigger. My patience was exhausted, I grabbed the nearest object to hand — which happened to be a an empty Champagne bottle — and struck him with it. Hard. It shattered against his temple. As he fell on the bed, the weapon discharged. That was a piece of luck. I hardly needed to check that he was dead; indeed half the top of his head had been blown off. There was the mess of his once-great brain everywhere. I made sure his fingers were nicely clenched round the trigger, and made my exit through the other door, as instructed, having locked the bedroom door behind me. Since I had almost forgotten to do this — the keys had to be left in the lock, according to my instructions — I had had to cross the room again. It was as if my mind took a mental photograph of the scene: the naked body of his lover, a girl of only seventeen, who still should have had everything to live for, lying so innocently, such a willing victim, on that bed but her head so horribly damaged. Yet still visible on her lips was a faint, triumphant smile. Strewn around the room were her clothes, a hat with a veil, her shoes carelessly discarded, her underthings. Slumped over on the other side of the bed was him. In death, just another corpse. A large pool of blood was forming around what remained of his head. I tried not to think of that brain which had been destined to rule half of Europe, and which was now spattered over the wall, but I did know I was looking at a scene that would be the scandal of the century — and which would haunt me forever.

"I also forgot to take the letters lying on the writing table, but I understand these were retrieved successfully later in the morning and quickly delivered onto the All Highest's desk. You now know why the All Highest, on reading my report, stated that his son had died 'like a *Schneider.*'

"I took myself back home and wondered if I had dreamt the whole thing, or if whatever powers there were in the universe would ever forgive me. The only thing that later saved me from total personal disintegration was finding a place on the Payer-Weyprecht Arctic Expedition which Count Johann Wilczek largely paid for. In fact I had to bring back a pack of Eskimo dogs for the Count. As a member of the expedition to those stupendous white wastes, we were allowed to comment on the suggestions for naming various features. I was in full agreement for the naming of The Wilczek Isles, but objected, in vain, however, to the naming of 'Franz-Josef Land.'"

Here he paused, then said, "That's my story."

"My God," was all I could say, with "Thank you for telling me."

"I thank you for listening, but before saying anything more, please think about it a moment. You need a little time to let these things settle in your mind."

I did as he asked, and sat — still staring at that altar — thinking of that night. The morality of it all was unfathomable.

"And why have you told me this?" I asked.

There was no answer. I waited some moments, then I turned round — but he had gone. The sun had almost set now, and again I heard that drone... gradually fading away into the distance. Müller stepped forward from the shadows.

"I know it is probably inappropriate in the House of God, Milady, but I have a small flask of schnapps. Would Milady like a little?"

I wondered whether bringing a gun into the house of God was also a sin. It had certainly made me feel safe. Suddenly, I remembered the book which... I didn't know his name!.. which he had left on the pew. I was just about to stand up to go and get it, when Müller produced it.

"I took the liberty of retrieving it for Your Ladyship," he said with his usual calm dignity, and he handed me the small purple Morocco-bound volume, on which, under an archducal crown, was stamped, in gold, E. R. — *Erzherzog Rudolf* — Archduke Rudolf.

I put it in my handbag and we went back to the hotel. We would be taking the first train in the morning back to Mürzuschlag, and then on to Vienna.

Back in my room, I decided to examine the book. As I opened it, I saw a little slip of paper. It was a note, presumably by the motorcyclist (as I was forced to call him). It was typewritten:

The ladies listed are all his conquests — and once consigned into this book, as far as he was concerned, they would pass out of his mind, and the matter was disposed of by his sending each one an identical silver cigarette case. The cases differed only in the engraving — a key to which is to be found in the front flap, in his own hand, and the same letters are also used to denote the five classes of ladies in the actual list.

I then flipped through the pages… a lot of pages with lists of women's names, hundreds of them. Fortunately, they did not reach the forty-three thousand of his hunting kills. The form was name, date, class. I was jolted to see some names I recognized — and plenty of family names I knew, at times reading like an extract from the *Almanac de Gotha*.

The writing was neat and clerk-like, and the categories carefully described on the front flyleaf:

> (a) Ladies belonging to princely family of equal birth — box with engraved facsimile signature.

(b) Ladies of high nobility but not of equal birth —
box with inscription 'EH. Rudolf GM'.

(c) Ladies from ancient / noble families but not
admissible at Court (i.e., great-grandmother a
commoner etc) — box inscribed 'R' under archducal
crown.

(d) Ladies of less ancient nobility — box with archducal
crown only.

(e) Ladies of lesser aristocracy and commoners — box
engraved with standard archducal coat-of-arms.

The motorcyclist was right. It somehow said a lot about Rudolf, and certainly made one doubt that he would be the radical reformer that everyone hoped he might have been.

Perhaps this was also the great secret that could topple the Habsburgs? Rudolf had very probably infected many of these high-born ladies with syphilis. Would this thus weaken the aristocracy of the Dual Monarchy? In England the problem of a degenerated nobility had been neatly solved by taxation. Taxes had made many a duke or baron a little impoverished, and rich American heiresses had been the answer: strapping young women, only a generation or two away from frontier adventurers, rich in cash and from families desiring European respectability — this had brought in much-needed new blood. Those peers who didn't need to bring in New World money had simply married Gaiety girls — comely dancers from the chorus at London's Gaiety Theatre. It was surprising how well some of these quickly seemed as if they had been "to the manner born." If that was the famous secret, that is, Rudolf's affliction, then it had better be forgotten. I certainly couldn't relate something like this to the All Highest.

Mamma told me that in 1885 the British Parliament passed an act which was aimed to ban homosexuality. She had told me this last year when we were finally discussing the sordid affair that poor Uncle Berty had been involved in. She told me that Prime Minister Gladstone had had the unenviable task of describing the nature of the legislation to Queen Victoria, for her to sign the assent. Gladstone was asked afterwards why this Act had not mentioned lesbians. According to someone Mamma knew, Gladstone had said "I had difficulty enough explaining homosexuality to Her Majesty. I wasn't going to torment myself further with what women do. I just couldn't." So to the K&K, the All Highest, on the topic of his son's sexual activities, I would keep mum.

So now all that was left in this mystery was to go and see the Emperor, but as Mamma had pointed out, what would I tell him in answer to the actual question he had entrusted me with answering? It would seem that Rudolf did mean to do away with him. The Prince was simply too good a shot, and a most experienced huntsman, to make an error like that. I supposed I could hardly give an answer which wavered maybe yes, maybe no. I had been engaged to come up with a conclusive answer, so that is what I had to do. If only Mamma were here, she might advise me again. On the other hand, I couldn't risk all this new information circulating around Vienna or Prague as gossip. The only other alternative I could think of was to have two answers ready, and see which way the wind would blow during the audience.

I would invite Müller to dine with me in the restaurant, in order to have a last dose of the Holzers' hospitality and go to bed early, having written my telegram to Herr Palmer. I went to the window to have a final look at the abbey — the huge red-tiled roof of which was just visible from it. The moon was clouded, so only the dark shape of the building was to be seen, but my eye was caught by the figure of a man in one of those nondescript outfits that scream out as deliberately nondescript, loitering by a lamppost on the opposite side of the square. As if sensing his being seen from my window, he briskly moved on. Oddly enough, I could have sworn this man, or one very like him, had been walking by the Estate Office in Mürzsteg. I stepped back, attempted to shake off my ridiculous suspicions, and pulled the curtains tight.

॰ஒ॰

To get to my Hofburg appointment, I had to pass the outrageous Neueburg, or New Castle, which was still under construction. It was monstrous both in size and in the grossness of its ornament, and represented what must be the final flowering of Kaiser Franz-Josef's dreams of Imperial glory. It was ironic, of course, since the Empire was shrinking — and all of the losses could be laid at his door.

I hoped my Worth dress would get the notice it deserved, since Sabine had had to travel to Vienna with it — but the old courtiers in the Emperor's office would probably not bat an eyelid, and nor would the All Highest, either. But I felt good in it — that was important. In fact, I felt quite confident that I had taken up the Kaiser's challenge, and I had succeeded.

As I entered the main courtyard of the Alteburg I noticed, coming towards me, a familiar figure — but I couldn't quite place him. Only after he had passed did I think I knew him; he could easily have been that man loitering outside my hotel window two days ago. But wasn't Vienna full of people looking like that?

The ritual of getting into the Hofburg now seemed quite normal to me. I was an old hand (well, this was my second visit), and at the appointed time, 11.25 a.m., I entered the Kaiser's office, steered as ever by Prince Rudolf von Liechtenstein, who closed the doors behind me.

The Emperor stood up on seeing me.

"Good. We normally have a little lunch at eleven-thirty, and we would like you to join us. We can talk then."

He came to me and took my arm. As we walked to the double doors near to his desk I noticed one bulky file in particular amongst the neat piles awaiting the Emperor's attention, or maybe already finished with. The bulky file bore the initials 'Gräfin B. v. F.' — my initials. What on Earth could it contain about me?

We entered a small dining room. Small, that is, not in the size of the room, but in the size of the dining table — just big enough for two. I was honoured, but nervous about that file. I wondered if the All Highest liked to fatten up his victims first!

The Emperor seated me before taking his place, and liveried servants appeared. Once seated, he lifted his table knife and examined his reflection in the highly polished blade, fingering and smoothing his beard as if to give himself an air of dignity. Then he looked me in the eye. It was against protocol for me to initiate the conversation, so I smiled back instead.

"We normally have just soup and bread. It's a simple lunch."

The servant brought a large silver tureen and served the Emperor first, then me. Another approached with bread in a silver bowl. Their white gloves were very tight-fitting, I noticed.

The gloves would suit my staff; there must be some royal K&K outfitters in the streets around the palace, I was thinking as I waited for him to take the first sip, then followed suit. A single Salzburg liver dumpling floated in the almost clear broth. I was petrified that if the dumpling didn't get soggy enough to cut with the edge of my spoon, I wouldn't be able to eat it in a suitably ladylike manner… Oh, help!

"We were right, weren't we?" he suddenly asked.

Now I was in a real panic. This wasn't the question I'd been asked to solve, surely? Was this a trick...? Oh, help again!

"Yes, Your Majesty." I said. I wasn't expecting I'd be saying this, but on the other hand he was probably right, given all the circumstances that I now knew — and certainly that must be what he wanted most to hear.

"Do you think we were cruel?"

Well, that's extremely relative — isn't it just? Again, words came out: "Your Majesty has myriad tasks to perform and I'm sure some of them must involve — from time to time — unpleasant decisions."

"Quite so, quite so. When we meet our Divine Maker... we just want to be able to say, in all sincerity and humility, 'We did our duty.'"

I couldn't think what to say in addition, so again I smiled. I realised that men don't have such an option. Men smiling sweetly all the time would be considered rather funny in the head. And if they were wearing Worth dresses they'd be considered even funnier!

He paused, soup spoon in mid-air, as a thought struck him: "We make no secret of the fact that we are extremely pleased with the way you have conducted your mission," and then he looked at me very intently — it made me uncomfortable. "No secret at all," he repeated slowly, emphasising each word.

The Emperor then returned to draining his soup, and I could feel that this rather awkward conversation would soon come to an end.

"Herr Palmer should be in the Outer Office by now. We want to make sure you are content with the financial arrangements.

Your expenses were quite modest, especially when one considers the distances you travelled. But we are glad you didn't visit that Larisch woman. We are sure she must have invited you to Munich. A troublesome, meddlesome creature."

He stood up abruptly and the servant pulled back his chair. I stood too. In his office again I curtseyed, kissed the Imperial and Royal hand, and backed to the door.

᧖

I only understood the full meaning of the Emperor's words when I was sitting in the train on my way back to Prague. 'No secret at all,' he had said. So that was it, was it? Had he been just using me all along, knowing that sooner or later I'd come face-to-face with that hoary old chestnut — the dreaded secret that could topple the dynasty? And as far as it was possible to do so, I had found it had been destroyed — that's if it had even existed in the first place, or unless it had been that Rudolf had singled-handedly degenerated half the aristocratic womanhood of the Empire. His agents had followed me (and done a lot more snooping, besides, no doubt) to people whom they didn't realise knew things, and to places where they didn't have the kind of access I had gained. Yes, I had been used! On the other hand, was he what he had first represented himself to be — a contrite old man worried about meeting his Maker? I have to say I rather favoured my first notion, unless, in the way that nothing — especially in Austria — is ever simple, and it was a mixture of both. One set of expenses, and two questions answered! Bravo, Trixie! I felt quite drained by it all.

Ach, the so-called *Belle Epoque*, with its damn peculiar mélange of public chastity and private transgression, as some now forbidden left-wing journalist had once written. A Jew. But one mustn't complain. At least hypocrisy looks as if things are all right — a lot better than seeing the bald truth.

At FJ1 Railway Station I found there was a welcoming committee awaiting me. Mamma had come up from Morštejn with the four now rather smartly dressed urchins, who had learned to salute very smartly. And there was Karel!

"I understand congratulations are in order, my dear," he said, deigning to kiss me drily on the lips. "And I hope you've had no more deaths?"

"No, Müller and I were shot at this time. But as you can see, we both survived."

Poor Karel, I suppose he felt out of it. In trying to make further conversation, he only made matters worse: "By the way," he said, "how is the bridge coming along?"

"Bridge?"

"Yes, we were looking at those plans you received, you remember? The blueprints?"

"Oh, those," I replied, trying to think of something to say. "It's fine," I lied. Would I have to tell him everything that had happened, I wondered? How tiresome.

Müller was helping Sabine with the baggage, and finally a porter began to take it to the carriage entrance, heaped on a trolley. Assisted by a generous envelope from Herr Palmer, I'd been shopping in the Kohlmarkt, such a fashionable street. And so wickedly expensive! I'd peeked into Rodek Brothers, the Court jewellers, but I'd been good.

The remembrance of this, even though only yesterday, made me perk up. To Hell with glooming about the wretched Empire!

I found myself walking with Mamma.

"And how was the old fox?" she asked.

"Eating soup, mostly… but also studying a file with absolutely all my movements since I first started out on his damnable question. Herr Palmer showed it to me. I feel I've been used, Mamma — just like a stalking horse."

"That wouldn't be the first time someone felt that way in the Hofburg. No, not by a long chalk. My dear, it is best to live in the country and not muck with the Habsburgs!"

I noted she'd been over the moon when I'd first received the Emperor's invitation. This was just typical of her!

"But then for whom would one be dressing, Mamma? Pigs and chickens? What would be the point?"

"And what makes you think they're any different in Vienna or Prague, my dear?"

Acknowledgments

I would like to thank
Derek Banham, my old friend and mentor,
for his comments and advice;
Siegrun and Hubert Holzer
of The Gasthof Holzer,
for making my visit to Neuberg an der Murz
and the Imperial Hunting Reserve
both comfortable and memorable;
Miloslav Černik, for local advice and help;
Leonhard Colloredo-Mansfeld, for essential time;
Sylvio Spohr for sustenance;
Tana Kindlova for encouragement and support
on the last lap of this work
in Prague.

Author's Note

As in all of The Countess of Prague's stories, I hope I have brought to life many real characters.

Again Trixie has rubbed shoulders with the great and the good of the Austro-Hungarian Empire in the halcyon days of the *belle époque* — but here we see the darker side of Emperor Franz-Josef, a benign-looking but ruthless ruler whose only son and heir had committed suicide sixteen years before — or had he?

The séances in Paris took place. There was indeed a stage magician by the name of Wilajalba Frikell as there was a celebrated pawnbroker in the Prague Ghetto by the name of Moses Reach, and I believe Trixie was quite right in finding the Abbé Saunier at his church in Rennes-le-Château a complete fraud (although many have been taken in by his nonsense — even though he was defrocked by his bishop for the fraud of Simony). Count Wilczek was a wonderful personality, and I hope I have depicted him and his fabulous castle with special care as he is an underrated character and many modern day visitors to Kreuzenstein Castle probably don't quite understand his reconstruction of it. It's certainly worth a visit.

I visited the Royal Hunting Grounds at Mürzsteg in the foothills of the Alps, in Trixie's footsteps, where still the memory lingers of Crown Prince Rudolf's pot-shot at his father in 1888. Had he been successful, then there would have been no Great War, no Second World War with its holocaust...

I believe that Trixie came to the only logical conclusion about the events at Mayerling in 1889 — but the man on the motorcycle is a fictional character. Rudolf's 'black book' is real, however, and its contents accurately stated.

Stephen Weeks
Prague, 2017

To see more Poisoned Pen Press titles:

Visit our website: poisonedpenpress.com/
Request a digital catalog: info@poisonedpenpress.com